# The Inn at Lavender Bay

## The Lavender Bay Chronicles Book 1

## Michele Brouder

# PART ONE

## NADINE

# CHAPTER ONE

## NADINE

Nadine Eberhardt stood at the stove and stirred a pot of coq au vin, humming to herself. She'd seen the recipe on a food show and figured, how hard could it be? It looked a bit dry, so she added more Pinot Noir. The heady aroma rose and floated toward her; she closed her eyes and sighed. Satisfied, she poured some wine into her glass and sipped it.

Dinner was in less than an hour. She began taking plates and silverware out and laying them on the table, reflecting on her day. She'd spent the morning with her daughter, Emma, buying things she'd need for her dorm room. Her only child was leaving for college soon, hundreds of miles away, and it was strange to imagine their home without Emma in it. Nadine would soon be setting places for two instead of three, alone with her husband again after all these years. It was going to be a brand-new phase for their marriage.

That, at least, was something to look forward to, especially after the wonderful tropical vacation she and Richard had just enjoyed in Hawaii. She smiled to herself. It had been a week in paradise, almost like a second honeymoon.

Her musings were interrupted by the ringing of the doorbell.

Their dog, Herman, a rangy Irish wolfhound mix, came tearing in from the other room, looked at her, and tore off for the front door.

"Oh, Herman," Nadine muttered as she set the plates down and made her way to the front of the house. "It's not like you can open it." *And God help us if he ever learns how.*

"Coming!" she called out.

Herman sat waiting for her at the double door, peering up at her through his unruly hair no amount of product could ever fix, his tail thumping against the floor. Herman loved company: visitors, the mailman, delivery men, and especially those Girl Scouts who sold cookies.

Assuming it was Richard at the door, Nadine opened it and said, "Did you forget your keys again?"

Two things happened simultaneously. First, Nadine realized it wasn't Richard standing there on the porch but a pair of strangers, a woman with a young boy who looked to be about four or five. Second, Herman tried to lunge outside to greet the unknown visitors, confident they would like to be jumped on and covered in sloppy kisses. Reflexively, Nadine closed the door partway and put her knee in front of the narrow opening. Not to be deterred, Herman stuck his snout over Nadine's leg and whined, his tail wagging happily behind him. These were new people that he did not know and must win over.

"Stop it," Nadine said, grabbing hold of his collar and trying to pull him back. He whined some more. Through the gap in the door, she said, "I'm sorry about him. He gets a little excited with visitors. Can I help you?"

The woman, petite with neat sandy-blond hair, seemed to hesitate. Her green eyes were clear and bright, and she had enviable skin. But Nadine reminded herself that she had at least ten years on the woman. In another decade, she would have similar lines to the ones Nadine now sported. It was inevitable.

"I'm looking for Richard Eberhardt," the woman started. She kept her gaze locked on Nadine. The boy, holding his mother's hand, appeared more interested in Herman than Nadine.

"I'm sorry, he's not here."

The woman appeared unsure.

"I'm Nadine, his wife. Can I help you with something?" she asked. Her gaze was drawn toward the dark-haired young boy, thinking she'd seen him somewhere before. He had his mother's bright green eyes and a splash of freckles across the bridge of his nose. He looked awfully familiar. For a moment, she wondered if they were the people who'd recently moved into the house three doors down.

The woman turned her head to look one way down the street and then the other.

"Is everything all right?" Nadine asked, thinking she was acting strangely.

"I'm a friend of Richard's," the woman offered.

"He went for a run, but he should be back soon." Gripping Herman's collar tightly, Nadine held him back as she opened the door wider. "You're welcome to come in and wait, if you'd like."

The woman bit her bottom lip, then nodded.

"My name is Julie," she said, stepping inside, "and this is my son, Sam." She blew out a breath and her wispy bangs lifted off her forehead.

Nadine led them down the wide hallway, the recently refinished parquet floor glimmering in the late-afternoon sun shining through the beveled glass windows of the front door. Julie looked around her with interest, taking in the ornate sideboard flanked by two antique Chinese floor vases filled with artificial flowers that had been so expensive they looked real.

Nadine ushered the guests into the living room, which was all white with navy blue accessories, like the blue-and-white striped throw pillows on the plush sofa that had cost an arm and a leg. The twelve-foot-high ceilings made the room appear expansive, and the floor-to-ceiling windows brightened the place with natural light. It was one of Nadine's favorite rooms.

Herman pushed past them, wanting to get into the room first. He was always first. But he turned around and walked backwards into the room. It was a Herman thing.

The woman scowled and the little boy laughed. Nadine laughed, too. "He struggled in obedience school," she said, "but we love him anyway."

Nadine held her arm out toward the sofa, indicating the visitors should take a seat. Herman immediately sat down near Sam's legs, leaning against the sofa, looking up at the boy, who giggled and leaned against his mother. This made Herman put his paw on the boy's leg and whine.

"Don't worry, he doesn't bite," Nadine said with a laugh. "He can be overly friendly. Would you like something to drink?"

"If it's not too much trouble," Julie said.

"Lemonade all right? Or I have wine if you'd prefer that."

Julie frowned. "Wine in the afternoon?"

"Lemonade it is then," Nadine said. "Come on, Herman." But the dog ignored her and continued to stare at Sam.

Giving up, she headed to the kitchen, walking quickly. Hurriedly, she emptied the half-full wine glass that sat next to the stove and loaded it into the dishwasher. She set out a tray with three glasses, two tall and one small. She'd gotten rid of all the child-friendly plastic cups years ago. But she did have a package of Oreos, Emma's favorite cookie, and she arranged a pile on a plate.

Sam had warmed up to Herman and was tentatively touching the top of his head. Smiling, she set the tray on the coffee table between the neat stack of *Architectural Digest* magazines and a coffee table book on the works of Mary Cassatt.

Nadine handed out glasses of lemonade and offered Sam the plate of cookies, but he buried his head in his mother's side and shook his head.

"Are you sure?" Nadine asked.

"No thank you," Julie said tartly. "It will spoil his dinner."

Nadine nodded, set the plate down, and took the single chair across from them.

"You said you were a friend of Richard's," Nadine said by way of an opening. Since their arrival, she'd been wondering where this woman fit in his life.

"I'm an events planner," Julie answered. "I orchestrate the company's Christmas parties and Fourth of July barbecues."

Nadine smiled. "You're responsible for all that? We love the Christmas parties, they're amazing. Of all the places Richard has worked over the years, these company parties are the best."

"Thank you," Julie said. Despite her youth, there was a no-nonsense way about her, and Nadine could easily see this other woman organizing those spectacular gatherings. The fireworks show for the Fourth of July celebrations drew not only company employees but people from the surrounding towns.

Nadine was about to ask another question when Julie said, "How was Hawaii?"

Nadine's lips parted and she felt her frown lines deepen along her forehead. How did Richard's company event planner know that they'd gone to Hawaii? Maybe he had mentioned it in passing at the water cooler?

Before she could answer, she heard Richard in the hallway, sneakers squeaking along the floor.

"Nadine?"

"In here," she called out.

He appeared. "I turned the stove off, the dinner is starting to burn—" He pulled up short, spotting Julie and Sam.

Richard, late forties, looked great for his age. He had a pleasant face with cropped gray hair. He glistened with perspiration from his run, which highlighted his Hawaiian tan, and his T-shirt clung to his toned abdomen. He was, in Nadine's estimation, a very good-looking man.

"Julie!" he said. Beneath his tan, he'd gone ashen, as if he'd had a shock.

Julie stood and crossed her arms over her chest.

"Daddy!" Sam cried, and he went sailing into Richard's arms. Herman stood and barked.

Nadine blinked several times, her mouth hanging open as her gaze bounced from Richard to Sam to Julie and then back to Richard.

"What?" she said out loud, wishing the floor would open up so she could fall into it.

# Chapter Two

It took Nadine a minute to recover as shock raced through her body and took up residence in every nook and cranny of her being. Slowly, she stood, her legs shaky.

"What is going on here?" she asked. Her voice came out in a squeak.

Julie pressed a finger against Richard's arm and muttered through gritted teeth, "You promised you would tell her when you were in Hawaii."

Nadine almost asked what he wanted to tell her, but she realized that *this* was what he was supposed to tell her: that there was another woman, and a child. He had a son. *No, that can't be right.*

"It didn't come up," Richard said.

"How would it come up," Julie asked, "if you didn't bring it up?"

Sam was comfortable with Richard. Richard had picked him up, and Sam's little arms were wrapped around Richard's neck. *He knows him,* Nadine observed. *Richard spends time with this boy.* But when?

*Richard's son.*

Her eyes opened wide in amazement. Sam was the spitting image of Richard at that age. That's why he'd looked familiar. Her gaze traveled to the bookcase, to the framed photos that stood amongst the books. There was an old, faded color photo of Richard at a similar age, standing in front of a yellow school bus, one foot on the stair, waving to his mother as he went forward boldly to his first day of kindergarten. But that was Richard: bold and fearless.

Nadine studied Julie. The other woman saw only Richard, her expression open and soft, and Nadine realized sadly that this young woman with the clear complexion and the toned body was in love with her husband. She couldn't hide it. Nadine knew because she, too, had looked at her husband like that at one time. In the beginning. As time wore on, that had been tempered and buffered and their love had grown deeper, or that's what she'd thought. Had their marriage been only one-sided?

Even though the obvious truth stared her right in the face, it made no sense, and Nadine caught a sharp breath as she tried to process it. Her stomach roiled around inside of her, anxious to rid itself of its contents.

"Richard?" she said.

Her husband of twenty years gave her a pitying look, which made her angry.

"I w-w-wanted to tell you, Nadine," he started. "But there never seemed a right time."

"I don't believe this!" The words, on their own and out of her control, burst forth from her.

Richard set down Sam, and Julie took the child's hand. As Richard reached for Nadine, she took a step back.

"No, tell me this isn't true," she pleaded.

He took a step closer, holding both his hands out to her. "I'm sorry, Nadine. I wanted to tell you myself."

"When?" she asked, her voice shrill. She looked at Sam. "You've wanted to tell me this for what—four or five years? But couldn't bring yourself to do it?"

"I didn't want to hurt you," he said.

Looking at Julie and Sam, she whispered, "It's too late for that, isn't it?"

Herman, sensing her distress, trotted around the coffee table toward her and leaned against her leg, looking up at her.

"How . . ." Her voice cracked, and she cleared her throat, standing up straighter. Herman looked up at her and gave a little whine. She gave him a reassuring stroke on the top of his head. "How old is Sam?"

Julie spoke up. "He'll be five in October."

Nadine's mind began to work backwards. Briefly, her eyes met with the other woman's, and she knew Julie had read her mind: how she was counting back the years to figure out where her marriage was and what had been going on in their lives when this child of Richard's was conceived and born.

Five years ago, Emma was having braces put on her teeth. They'd spent two weeks at a house right on the ocean in Rodanthe in the Outer Banks. They'd been happy. Or at least she had.

She swallowed down her emotions, trying not to cry, but her pride went down first in one big gulp.

Richard was about to say something, but Nadine cut him off. "When did you find the time to have an affair, a child, while working and traveling for your job?" He must be some kind of Marvel superhero. There were only so many hours in the day, and it was clear that he was spending time with his son.

He stammered and ran his hand through his short-cropped hair. "I don't travel anymore."

"Since when?"

"Since the promotion to vice president."

Six years ago. It all fell into place. While she'd believed he was in another city working for two or three days a week, he'd been living with Julie and Sam. Her shoulders sagged in defeat. She felt like the stupidest person on the planet. That old axiom that the wife was the last to know was true.

At that moment, Emma appeared in the doorway, tennis racket in hand, sports bag over her shoulder. "Hey, what's going on?"

Nadine squeezed her eyes shut. *Emma.*

"Emma!" Richard said, surprised.

As Nadine brushed past Richard, he reached out for her, his expression pained. "You don't have to go." His voice was pleading.

She looked at him, no longer recognizing the man she'd lived with for more than twenty years. Pulling her arm out of his reach, she said to their daughter, "Your father will explain everything." And she left the room, not missing the bewildered look on her daughter's face.

In that moment, her devastation turned to outrage at the thought of her daughter being hurt. But there was nothing she could do about it. She wanted to clobber her husband for being selfish enough to put them through this.

She took the stairs two at a time with Herman following her, seeking the refuge of her bedroom. As she ascended the staircase, she could hear Richard's whispered words to Emma, followed by their daughter's wail. "What?"

Inside her bedroom, she slammed the door shut and leaned against it, sliding down to the floor until she sat on the plush carpet, burying her head in her hands and allowing the tears to fall.

Her life as she knew it was over.

# Chapter Three

Richard found her upstairs in the bedroom. He tried to open the door, but she was leaning against it.

"Come on, Nadine, let me in," he said softly.

"Go away."

"I won't go away until we talk."

Sighing, she stood up, swiping at her eyes with a soggy tissue. Herman, who'd been keeping her company, stood but didn't take his eyes off of her. Richard stepped into the room and closed the door behind him. Nadine hopped up on the king-sized four-poster bed. Herman looked at her, and she patted the empty space beside her. The dog looked over his shoulder at Richard, but Nadine said, "Come on, Hermie, it's all right." She knew Richard hated the dog on the furniture, especially their bed, but as he wouldn't be sleeping in it anymore, it no longer mattered. Without ceremony, Herman jumped up and settled beside her, laying his head in her lap. Absentmindedly, she stroked his head, brushing the hair away from his eyes.

Richard stood there with his hands in his pockets. Beneath his tan, he was pale. He looked washed out. Nadine could only imagine how she looked.

Trying not to disturb the dog, she leaned over to grab the box of tissues from her nightstand.

"How did Emma take the news that she has a little brother?" she asked. She needed to pull herself together to be able to comfort their daughter.

He shrugged. "Not well."

"Of course not!" Nadine said. "How did you think she'd react?"

He had the grace to remain silent, but Nadine felt herself just starting to get on a roll.

"I mean, I thought the kid looked familiar when I opened the door but, dummy me, I couldn't place him!" she said. How could she have been so stupid? Herman lifted his head and whined. She buried her hand in his fur, stroking him. "All I had to do was look at the photo on the bookshelf."

"I'm sorry this has caused you pain," Richard said quietly.

He was so damned calm about the whole thing. This was a quality of his that stood on her last nerve from time to time. His feathers never got ruffled. Nothing ever seemed to upset him.

She stared at the crumpled tissue in her hand, trying to find a dry spot but failing. "Is there any chance the child is not yours?"

Deep down, she already knew the answer to that. One didn't have to be a rocket scientist to see the strong resemblance he bore to Richard. When Richard's answer wasn't forthcoming, she looked at him. He stood with his hands on his hips, his confidence pose. She wondered how confident he felt now.

"You love her," she said.

"Not like I love you."

Nadine snorted. "Poor Julie!"

When he didn't say anything, she shook her head, and her laugh was brittle. "I must be a special kind of fool."

"Nadine—"

"You promised me you would never cheat on me again," she said through gritted teeth. "But this is something else altogether."

"Nadine, I—"

"And don't tell me she means nothing to you! You have a son with her!" she said, her voice rising.

"I was going to apologize," he said quietly.

"That's rich of you," she said. "Do you remember the first time you cheated?"

The muscle along his jaw clenched and he lowered his head, looking at the carpet. "Yes."

They had only been married a few years. Emma was two. Nadine found out that Richard had been sleeping with one of the neighbors for a couple of weeks. She'd been devastated. It had precipitated intensive marriage counseling and a move to a different neighborhood.

"Do you remember what I said to you after that first affair?" she asked.

"Yes, but—"

"No buts," Nadine said sharply. "I told you if you ever cheated on me again that there'd be no reconciliation. That it would mean divorce."

Richard reached out, but she shrank back against the headboard. "Nadine," he said, "let's not do anything rash."

She blinked several times. "Rash? You've got a child with another woman!"

"We've got twenty years invested here," he said. "There's no need to throw it all away."

"You should have thought about that when you were sleeping with another woman, fathering a child. How would that work? Would your son be spending the weekends with us?" As much as that child was an innocent, she didn't want a constant, physical reminder of her husband's infidelity.

"I'm sure we could work something out."

She blinked rapidly in disbelief. "You're serious. And what about Julie? I'm sure she didn't come here to discuss a custody arrangement, that we'd have Sam for holidays and weekends." This conversation was so surreal it beggared belief.

"I'll talk to her."

"The same way you were going to talk to me about Sam and Julie? That only took six years."

Finally, her stomach, which had been threatening to rebel, did just that. She managed to scramble off the bed, dislodging Herman's head from her lap, and dashed to the ensuite bathroom. Lifting the lid and seat from the toilet, she promptly vomited into it, feeling the pressure behind her eyes. The vomit spewed forth until there was only bile left.

Richard was beside her, reaching to pull her hair back as he'd done for her during her pregnancy or any time she'd gotten sick with a stomach bug. Lashing out, she pushed him away with her arm. "Don't touch me," she bellowed.

He retrieved a clean hand towel from the cabinet and handed it to her. Without a thanks, she took it from him. Quietly, he left the room.

Finally, when she thought she had no more to expel, she straightened up and washed her face and brushed her teeth over the marble sink with the gold taps.

*All this luxury, what did it mean? Absolutely nothing.*

Feeling somewhat fresher despite the pain in her stomach, she grabbed the roll of paper towels and disinfectant from the bottom shelf of the cabinet and cleaned up after herself. Once finished, she put everything away and washed her hands.

Herman waited in the bedroom, standing and wagging his tail, worried about her. She smiled at him. She could always count on him. She was his person, and had been ever since she'd found him going through their garbage bin four years ago.

Richard stood there as if waiting for her to pronounce some sort of sentence. As far as Nadine was concerned, there was only one way forward, and that was separation.

"Look, we can get through this," he said.

She looked at him sharply and spoke, not caring that her voice had an edge to it. "I don't think so."

"Come on, Nadine."

Nadine's anger blazed. "Wake up, Richard. I could never trust you again." Was he delusional, thinking their marriage could be saved?

"We can go to counseling." His tone suggested that he'd made the decision and that's what they would do.

She looked at him like he'd grown a second head. "What's a counselor going to do? Wave a magic wand?

Have us talk about our feelings? I'm pretty sure you know how I feel."

"We can't throw away over twenty years of marriage." His voice was calm and reasonable. She wanted to punch him.

"*We* didn't throw it away. *You* did it all by yourself."

A thought occurred to her. "What does she want? Why did she show up here?"

Richard blew a short, sharp breath between his teeth. "She wants us to be together as a family, full time."

Nadine snorted. "I bet she does."

"She wants me to divorce you."

"Obviously. Tell her she's succeeded." Nadine was going to make all of Julie's dreams come true.

"She can be persistent," he said with a sigh. Was that regret for the entanglement? Had the bloom worn off of *that* rose? Served him right.

"All this time, you've been raising this boy, and I didn't know a thing," she said. Again, disbelief overwhelmed her. She considered herself to be reasonably intelligent, but now she felt ashamed that she hadn't picked up on what was going on. She leaned against the bed, parking her butt against the mattress. Sadness rolled over her. She thought back to the start of her day, just that morning, when she'd sat at her kitchen table watching the breakfast morning show, eating some fruit, yoghurt, and toast and not having one clue that her life as she knew it was ending that day.

"You're responsible for the boy," Nadine said.

"I know *that*," Richard snapped. "I've never shirked any of my responsibilities." With emphasis, he added, "Ever."

*Well, good for you*, she thought. *You're one upstanding guy.* She rubbed her forehead with her fingers and sighed. "Look, I need some time and space to process all of this. You need to move your things into the spare room tonight."

"You're not going to let me sleep in my own bed?" His voice was tinged with disbelief.

"No." He couldn't be that stupid that he'd think things could go on as usual. Or was it arrogance, pure and simple? She was betting on the latter.

"This is kind of rash, but okay. I'll go to the spare room. Take all the time you need and then we'll regroup."

She clenched handfuls of the bedcovers on either side of her. She almost clenched her teeth. "You're not listening to me, Richard. We will not regroup from this."

"How many times can I say I'm sorry?"

"I don't have the answer for that either."

"What about Emma?" he said.

"What about her?" Nadine asked sharply.

"She's really upset."

Nadine's laugh was brittle. "What did you expect? A handshake? A hearty pat on the back? Of course she's upset, you've not only betrayed me but her as well."

Richard squeezed his eyes shut and patted the air down with both his hands, as if trying to keep a lid on something. "Don't use that word. Betrayal."

"Actually, it's the perfect word," Nadine said evenly. An image of her daughter in her room on the other side of the hall filled her mind. *I need to see her and make sure she's okay.*

"We can work this out . . ." he said, his voice trailing off as if he no longer believed it either.

"I don't think so," she said coldly, brushing past him with Herman following her. She needed to put her own hurt aside and go see her daughter.

She thought about the pot waiting for her in the kitchen that would need a good scrubbing, and the laundry waiting to be folded and ironed. It was going to be an early night: pajamas, a box of tissues, and binge-watching something on Netflix. She was grateful they'd installed a television in their bedroom. She could close the door, climb into her bed, and not have to deal with her husband or the mess he'd made.

She stood outside her daughter's door and knocked softly.

"Go away!"

"It's Mom."

The door opened and Emma's tearstained face came into view. Her eyes and nose were red. Immediately, Nadine pulled her into her embrace and held her tight as her daughter sobbed.

She whispered in her daughter's ear, "We're going to be all right, I promise."

# Chapter Four

B ut everything wasn't all right. At least not right away. She felt upside down. Although her initial impulse the morning after learning about her husband's other family was to remain in bed, she forced herself to get up if only to see Emma off to school. Her teenaged daughter balked, but Nadine remained firm and insisted she go. What would she do at home? Probably the same thing Nadine was tempted to do: wallow and cry, then wallow some more. No, her daughter was going off to college pretty soon. Nadine simply had to get her over this hump. As for herself, she decided a dose of the same medicine applied. She made her bed quickly so she wouldn't be tempted to climb back into it and fritter the day away.

Nadine Cook Eberhardt was a creature of habit and as her husband—soon to be ex—used to tease her, she was a slave to her routine. But now she depended on that routine to keep her distracted enough to function.

Despite all that was going on, they still needed to eat, the bills needed to be paid, and the laundry needed to be done. She threw herself into cleaning out the junk drawer in the kitchen and taking everything out of the cabinets and wiping down the shelves. Then she re-arranged the pantry.

At home, she walked around in a pseudo-fugue state, not quite sure of who she was and how she fit into everything. It was as if she were a puzzle piece trying to fit into the wrong jigsaw. Her own home seemed unfamiliar to her as if she were visiting for the first time. Framed photographs depicting memorable or happy events seemed strange. She felt like a voyeur, staring at someone else's life the way one trawled through online celebrity photos.

What she felt like was an imposter.

From afar, she watched as her husband began to open-ly get involved in his son's life. Richard encouraged her to join them, to "get to know Sam." Nadine was horrified. She had nothing against the boy, but she didn't want to get to know him. Could Richard really be that clueless? The distance between her and her husband grew larger. It seemed inevitable, as if Richard had stepped onto a different path that didn't include her.

But what was worse was that Richard refused to leave the family home. Refused to separate, which made no sense to Nadine as he'd spent years dividing his time between two families.

What worried her most was Emma. Her normally outgoing teenager was now sullen, prone to holing up in her room and slamming doors.

On Nadine's weekly phone call to her mother, the older woman picked up almost right away, with some kind of maternal sixth sense that something was amiss.

"You sound different," Louise Cook said.

"Do I?" Nadine asked.

"What's wrong?" her mother asked, determined, like a hound with its nose to the scent, to get to the bottom of it.

How Nadine wanted to unburden herself to her mother, tell her everything that had happened, how her marriage was in pieces on the floor, like the fragments of an eggshell. More than anything, she wanted her mother to comfort her.

"Nothing," she lied. If she were to reveal her current situation, she might not be able to stop. She felt like a weak dam trying to hold back too much water.

"Hmm," her mother said, unconvinced. "How's Emma?"

Nadine was relieved for the pivot to a neutral subject. She could go on about Emma forever. When Emma was younger, the two of them had spent every summer in Nadine's hometown of Lavender Bay, New York, on the shores of Lake Erie. It had been important to Nadine that Emma have summers at the beach, like she had, and more importantly that she got to know her grandmother and her aunts and cousins well while she was growing up. Back then, Richard traveled constantly for work, dropping into Lavender Bay whenever he could. Nadine had loved those early years, when Emma was gap-toothed and brown as a berry from time spent outdoors, her hair perpetually damp from swimming.

She pushed those memories aside and launched into an account of Emma's end-of-summer activities and her preparations for college in the fall.

"I don't suppose you want to come home for a quick visit," Louise said.

Nadine's first instinct was to say no, thinking about all her obligations, but she found herself saying, "You know what, I'll think about it. I'll ask Emma if she'd like to come, too. It might be nice for you to see her before she heads off to college."

"Really? That would be wonderful! And yes, I'd love to see Emma before school starts," her mother said with such surprise that she must have been expecting a negative reply.

"Good, I'll talk to her tonight."

"What about Richard?" her mother asked, hopeful.

"We just came back from Hawaii. I don't think he can take time off work again so soon."

"All right. Call me and let me know what you decide."

"Will do, Mom."

"I'd love to see you."

Her mother had never gotten used to the fact that two of her four daughters lived away from Lavender Bay. They spoke for twenty more minutes, getting all caught up on news about Nadine's sisters, cousins, and everyone back home. And when she hung up, she realized how much she missed everyone back in Lavender Bay. The thought of going home cheered her up to no end.

*ele*

"Honey, you can't ignore me forever," Richard said to Emma.

Emma narrowed her eyes at him. "I can, and I will."

"I think maybe you should stay in tonight," he said sternly, looking at his plate of dinner. The sigh that escaped him was heavy and put-upon. Nadine almost snorted.

She hadn't put in much effort for dinner. She wasn't interested. There was plain baked chicken, baked potato, and frozen peas. She could throw it together with her eyes closed.

"Richard," Nadine warned. Now was not the time to be punishing their daughter simply because she wasn't speaking to him.

"Nadine, stay out of it," he said firmly.

Nadine squared her shoulders. "She's entitled to feel the way she does."

"I don't care, I won't have any disrespect."

"If you want respect, you have to earn it," Emma snapped.

She stood, leaving her plate on the table, and stormed off with her father calling after her, "Your plate. Pick up after yourself. You're grounded for a week, young lady."

The sound of a door slamming shook the house.

Richard looked at Nadine as if it were her fault.

"Don't look at me," she said.

"Does she have to slam the door?" he asked. "This isn't how adults handle bad news."

*If only it were that simple.* Emma was still a girl-woman and she'd grown up thinking her father was perfect. Now she was dealing with a major imperfection of his: cheating, and the news that after being an only child her whole life, she now had a brother.

"It doesn't help when you go along with her," he huffed, pushing bits of baked potato around on his plate.

"I'm not going along with her. I happen to know how she feels, it's only that I have a lot of life experience behind me to deal with it better." There was a sharpness to her voice, but she didn't care.

Without waiting for any further discussion, she stood and carried her plate of untouched food over to the dog's bowl and scraped the potato and peas into it. Herman, sprawled beneath the table, stood, bumping his back on the underside of the table, and pushed through two chairs to get out.

"Don't get excited," Nadine said. "It's only potato and peas."

Her plan was to go upstairs and pack for Lavender Bay. She'd spoken to Emma earlier about a road trip and her daughter jumped on it, no hesitation. They'd be leaving first thing in the morning.

She wanted to be alone and indulge in thinking of her hometown. There were so many things she wanted to do when she got there. There would be long walks on the beach with Herman. The dog was no fan of the water, but he liked walks. There was her sister's coffee shop, Coffee Girl, where the most decadent desserts she'd ever indulged in were available. And she could hang out with her Aunt Gail, who owned Prime Vintage, the town's antique shop.

"A penny for your thoughts," Richard said, joining her and scraping his dinner, minus the chicken, into the dog's bowl.

She almost snorted. Almost. Her thoughts were worth a lot more than a penny.

"Before I forget, Emma and I are going to Lavender Bay in the morning."

Richard rounded on her. "What? When did you make this decision? When were you going to tell me?"

"I made this decision today, and I'm telling you now."

"For how long?" he demanded.

Nadine shrugged. "I don't know. My plans are up in the air."

"Emma is getting ready to go off to college. I want to spend time with her before she goes. She can't go with you. I forbid it."

Had he always been this controlling? Her laugh was brittle. "She's eighteen, she can do whatever she wants. Personally, I think the change of scenery will do her a world of good."

"I'm still her father."

She remained silent. There was nothing more to say. He was tiring.

"So you're just leaving me high and dry?"

Now she rounded on him. "I want you to leave the house. I've told you that. We need to separate but you refuse. So I'll leave."

"We can work this out."

"No, we can't. And what about Julie and Sam? You've been living over there part time and now what? Just going to chuck them to the curb?"

He ground his teeth.

"You spent years living with two families, unable to make a decision and commit fully to one. I'm making the decision for you. It's over. Go live with Julie and Sam." She stormed out of the kitchen and said over her shoulder, "Come on, Herman, we have to pack."

# Chapter Five

By the time Nadine had crossed the New York State border and headed up the thruway, she'd pushed Richard to the outer recesses of her mind, and even that was too good for him.

She'd decided to do the cross-country drive because she didn't know how long she'd stay in Lavender Bay, leaving her return date open-ended. Besides, she'd need a car to get around. She couldn't—no, wouldn't—depend on her mother or her sisters for transportation.

Next to her, Emma had fallen asleep with her head against the window. And occupying the back seat was Herman, who loved riding in cars. Currently, he sat in the middle, and every time Nadine looked in her rearview mirror, she made eye contact with him, which brought a smile to her face. *If only humans could be more like dogs*, she thought with a sigh.

Nadine was delighted that Emma had chosen to accompany her back to Western New York. It was going to be a great way to spend the remainder of the summer before she headed off to college.

Emma opened her eyes, blinked several times, and sat up and stretched.

"What time is it?" she asked. "And where are we?"

"It's four. And we're in New York, about an hour away from Lavender Bay."

Nadine looked over at her daughter. She'd been experimenting with her hair color since sophomore year. Currently it was an impossible shade of bright red. When Richard complained, especially during the blue and purple phases, Nadine pointed out that it could be worse; she could be experimenting with drugs instead. That had shut him up. Emma was trying to find her way. Those teenaged years were awkward and thorny. Memories of her own life as a teenager made her shudder.

Emma favored heavy, dark eyeliner on the upper lids, and bright red lipstick. Nadine suspected it was an effort to downplay her intelligence. In the eighth grade, Emma had been labeled a "brainiac" and she'd worked hard to present herself against type while, thankfully, maintaining her grades.

Nadine knew she was hurting. Emma had always enjoyed a close relationship with her father. And although anger and hurt had fueled her decision to leave home and travel across the country with her mother, Nadine hoped someday there would be a reconciliation between father and daughter. She couldn't shut him out of her life forever. But she needed some time. Nadine hoped the sun and sand and her extended family would be a good diversion and help them both heal.

"How are you doing with everything?" she ventured.

Emma rolled her eyes. She pulled her feet up onto the seat and wrapped her arms around her shins. "You're not going to ask me that every five minutes, are you? Because I could ask you constantly how you're doing, too."

"Noted."

Emma looked at her mother and widened her eyes for emphasis. "Well, how are you doing?"

Nadine sighed. "I'm coping." It wouldn't be fair to lay her burden on her daughter's young shoulders. She wanted her to be thinking about college and the fantastic future that lay ahead of her. It wasn't Emma's role to be her sounding board.

"Mom, you know you can talk to me. I'm not naïve. I'm pretty sure it was a terrible blow to find out Dad has a son." She turned her head to stare out the window and whispered, "And another woman."

Nadine flinched. It had been a terrible blow, one she wasn't sure she could recover from. What scared her was the uncertainty of her future. Emma's future appeared more stable and certain than her own. She had no idea what would happen next in her life. Everything was up in the air. When she wasn't angry with Richard, she sometimes found herself wondering what was wrong with her that her husband had strayed. But on some nights, when she thought about what she might tell Emma if something like this ever happened to her, she'd remember that he, and he alone, was accountable for his actions.

Surrounding them on both sides of the highway were acres and acres of vineyards as this area was one of the largest grape-producing regions in the United States. She'd practically lived on grape jelly as a child, and she had wonderful memories of Lavender Bay's annual grape festival, held every September.

They traveled in silence for the rest of the ride, which wasn't long. Soon, the sign for Lavender Bay appeared, touting *The quaintest town in America, next left 2 miles.* The large billboard showed the logo for Nadine's hometown: a lake, a lighthouse, and grapes in various shades of lavender and purple. A pulse of excitement coursed through her the closer they got.

"It's good to be home," she said with a smile on her face.

"Can we stop at Aunt Angie's and get coffee and some baked goods?" Emma asked, referring to Nadine's sister's café, Coffee Girl.

"Oh, I don't know. Maybe later."

She hadn't told her sisters she was coming home. Angie was busy running her coffee shop; their mother had reported that she hardly ever saw her or spoke to her as she was working over eighty hours a week. And forget about even talking to her older sister, Maureen. Maureen was fully ensconced in wedded bliss with her picture-perfect marriage to Allan. Their mother had pronounced him a "gem." And he truly was. Nadine didn't need such a stark reminder of how her marriage was crumbling around her. And flaky Deedee was down in Florida, rarely visiting home. It made Nadine sad that they weren't close, but that's how things had ended up. Through the years, the slights, real or imagined, had piled up. She often wondered if it would have been the same if she'd had brothers.

The only one who knew of her impending arrival was her mother, whose house they'd be staying at.

She hoped Lavender Bay would give her some space to think about her life and her future. Because right now, she had no idea what she wanted to do with the rest of her life.

From the highway, she turned onto Main Street which, further on, would run straight through the small business district of Lavender Bay, with side streets branching off on either side. Wanting to avoid the busier section of Main for now, however, she cut over Primrose and then made a left on Vine, then another left on Heather Lane, where her mother lived and where she and her sisters had grown up.

A smile spread across her face at the sight of her childhood home, a small Victorian with gingerbread trim. The cladding was painted in olive green, and the accent colors were maroon and cream. There was a tiny porch to the left of the large picture window, too small to accommodate a chair, but with room enough for her mother's ever-present seasonal decorations. Today, propped up in the corner next to the front door, there was a tall, rectangular black slate bearing the word "Home." In the fall, there'd be a decorative cornstalk, to be replaced in mid-October by a trio of carved pumpkins placed on the side of each porch step. At Christmas there would be tons of festive holiday lights, and the front door would be wrapped in shiny red wrapping paper with white ribbon in the shape of a cross and a big white bow. Her mother had been doing that at the holidays for as long as Nadine could remember.

She pulled into the driveway behind her mother's SUV. The sound of their car doors slamming brought Louise Cook out onto the small front porch. Her smile was broad, and she waved at them, dish towel still in hand as she came down the porch steps. Nadine noticed her mother held on to the handrail as she descended. She also noticed her mother had cut her hair. It was close-cropped and ethereal white. Her mother seemed to get prettier as she aged.

Emma was closest, and she and her grandmother approached each other with arms wide until Emma was engulfed in her grandmother's embrace.

"How's my girl?" Louise asked. When they separated, Louise held on to Emma's hands and took her in. "Look at you! All grown up. A beautiful young woman. You know, it wasn't too long ago that you were asking me for some cookie dough ice cream."

Emma laughed. Nadine and Herman reached Louise, and she immediately threw her arms around her daughter.

Nadine let herself be folded into the warm embrace and breathed in her mother's signature scent: Philosophy's Amazing Grace.

"And you, Nadine? How are you?" Louise whispered in her ear.

Nadine squeezed her eyes shut. "Happy to be here, that's for sure," she said truthfully. At some point, she would have to tell her mother what was going on. Something like a love child was hard to keep secret these days.

She took in her mother's new haircut. "Wow, Mom, you've gone short."

Her mother gave an easy shrug and grinned. "It's wash and wear. I'm tired of doing my hair. This is more convenient."

Herman stood next to her, waiting patiently for his turn. And Louise did not disappoint him. She lavished plenty of attention on him, telling him what a good boy he was. She beckoned him to follow her in with the promise of some treats. At the top of the steps, he stopped and looked toward Nadine, waiting.

Nadine and Emma were removing their suitcases from the back of the car.

Nadine smiled at him. "Go on, Herman, we'll be in in a minute." She shook her head, laughing. Herman disappeared into the house with Louise with a light-footed trot and his tail wagging happily.

As she slammed the trunk closed, Emma asked, "When are you going to tell Grandma?"

Nadine shrugged. "Soon. I don't know."

"I can disappear. I'd like to check out the beach as soon as possible."

"I appreciate that. Maybe tomorrow morning?"

"Sure."

She couldn't help herself that she wrapped her arm around her daughter's shoulders and pulled her close, laying a kiss on her forehead.

"Mom!" Emma said.

Nadine laughed. "Come on, let's go inside and see what they're getting up to."

# CHAPTER SIX

After an easy lunch of hot dogs on the grill and homemade macaroni and cheese, Nadine decided a walk was called for. Even though she was tired and achy from the long drive, she felt it would be a good opportunity to stretch her legs, wander through her hometown, and counteract all the calories from the comfort food her mother was famous for. It was a marvel to Nadine that her mother maintained a trim, slim figure.

"Mom, are you sure you don't want to go with us?" Nadine asked.

Louise scowled. Her attitude had always been, *Why walk when you could drive?* She was not a natural exerciser. "No, thanks. You go ahead. I'm perfectly content to stay here. Leave Herman with me if you want."

"You don't mind?" she asked with a glance at the dog, who was sound asleep against the paving bricks of the back patio. She'd read somewhere that animals didn't travel well. Maybe this was jet lag for him. Plus, she wanted to stop in and see Angie, if possible.

"Of course not," Louise said with a wave. "Herman and I are old friends. Besides, he looks beat."

"We won't be long. We might stop in and see Angie."

The smile disappeared from her mother's face. "If you do, remind her that I still live in Lavender Bay." Her mouth puckered until her lips disappeared.

*Uh-oh*, Nadine thought. Angie was third in the lineup of Cook sisters and four years younger than Nadine. She'd never married, had no children, and had always been about work. The coffee shop she'd opened three years ago apparently consumed every waking moment.

Emma joined her and they headed away from Heather Lane toward the main area of town.

As they walked, neighbors who were tending their front gardens or sitting on their porches called out to them and waved, welcoming them back to Lavender Bay. The air was filled with the scent of fresh-mowed grass and Mrs. McAllister's roses, which she grew in abundance in her front yard.

"Everyone is so friendly here," Emma said. "And everyone knows you."

"That's what happens when you grow up in a place where most of the residents don't leave."

It was different back home. They were friendly with their immediate neighbors, but if you went for a long walk around the gated community in which they lived, there was no one to wave to. No one was ever out front, preferring the privacy of their fenced-in backyards. If you didn't hear the splashes from the pools in the summer, you'd almost think the homes were abandoned.

"Of course, the flip side of that is that everyone knows your business," Nadine said with a sigh.

"Mom, you're not the first person to have marital trouble," her daughter said sagely. "Look at my friend Jenna. Her mother is on her second marriage. Her father is on his third, and the wives keep getting younger!"

Nadine winced and said nothing, not wanting to veer onto the subject of her imploding marriage with her only child. She wasn't a big believer in oversharing. There was still some disbelief that her marriage was over.

"Come on, let's cut over to Maple," Nadine said with a nod in the direction of the street off of Vine, where they currently walked.

Emma laughed. "Mom, you're so transparent. You just want to see *Monsieur Aubert*!" she said, affecting a French accent.

"I suppose," Nadine admitted.

They didn't have to walk far to meet up with Jacques Aubert, or rather the statue of him that had been there since the turn of the last century. The statue had been erected in an empty lot on Maple Avenue. At the time, there'd been a lot of infighting and politics, and he did not end up in the center of the park as some people had wanted. Instead, an early citizen had donated the land next to his house for the statue. Over the last century, it had turned into a small, impromptu park with a couple of benches that required repainting every few years. Volunteers kept the grass cut and the paved brick walkway weed-free. In the springtime, they planted flowers. It was an odd little spot, off on a side street, something only the locals knew about. It was one of Nadine's favorite spots in Lavender Bay. If she were alone, she'd take a seat on a bench, but she figured Emma wouldn't be interested. She'd want to keep moving.

A bee buzzed along the roses circling the statue, and a monarch butterfly flitted from one stem of goldenrod to another. They stood on the pathway and Nadine stared at the statue, an imagined likeness of the man who'd founded their town in the late 18th century.

As the story went, Jacques Aubert had been traveling by boat across Lake Erie from what was now Canada when he drifted off course and ended up here. He found the sunsets remarkable and, according to his personal diaries, never grew tired of them. The light purple-hued skies at nighttime were purported to remind him of the lavender farms back home in France where he'd grown up and thus, he named the area—inhabited exclusively by Native Americans at the time—Lavender Bay.

Nadine and Emma headed to the end of Maple and rounded the corner onto Main. Nadine immediately picked up on the buzz that Main Street couldn't help but have with its mishmash of shops and eateries.

There were no big chain stores in Lavender Bay. If you wanted that, you had to go out onto the main highway. Here in Lavender Bay, small businesses thrived. The townspeople were keen to support the local businesses because no town needed vacant storefronts and empty buildings. It would herald a downward slide.

She smiled as she spotted the familiar storefronts, including her aunt's antique shop, Prime Vintage. Gail was her mother's older sister. Nadine narrowed her eyes to see if her aunt's dog was there. Brutus was a retired bloodhound who'd worked in the south as a tracker. His only job right now was to find the perfect sunny spot every day. Apparently, he'd found it right in front of the door. Nadine smiled and went to cross the street but saw that her aunt had customers and decided to visit her another day. Brutus was out cold and didn't even lift his head as she passed.

Nadine was making her way around the corner onto Oak when she bumped straight into Edna Knickerbocker.

"You really need to watch where you're going," Edna said, putting her hand to her forehead and palpating the area.

"I'm sorry, Mrs. Knickerbocker," Nadine replied. The older woman had always been called "Mrs.," even though she never married.

Edna narrowed her eyes and asked, "Do I know you?"

Nadine nodded. "Sure. Nadine Eberhardt. Used to be Nadine Cook."

"Yes, of course. I didn't recognize you. I haven't seen you in a long time."

"I've been away from Lavender Bay for a while," Nadine said. "This is my daughter, Emma."

"You look like a Cook," Edna said, still running her fingers along her forehead and gently probing it. "Do I have a goose egg?"

Nadine peered at the older woman's face. "Not that I can see."

"Are you back for good or just a visit?"

"Just visiting," Nadine said, hoping the other woman wouldn't ask too many questions.

But Edna went off on a tangent. "I'm just back from Chicago." She shuddered. "I really don't like the big cities. Too much noise. Too much traffic. Too much wind. Too much of everything."

"Were you there on vacation?"

"Nope. My cousin, Johnny Hadley, passed away."

"I'm sorry to hear that," Nadine said.

Edna waved her comment away. "He was almost nine-ty. He had a good and happy life. He's left me plenty to do, though. He made me executor of his will. I've got to come up with a plan for the house he still owned over on Pearl Street."

A dim memory from her past surfaced. "Oh, the old Hadley place." Nadine said.

"That's the one," Edna confirmed. "'The house that takes in strays,' we used to call it in the family. For years, my aunt ran it as a boarding house."

Nadine remembered hearing that when she was young. She'd been fascinated by the thought of all those strangers living in one house. Many times, she would have preferred living with strangers over living with her sisters, parents, and grandparents in her own busy home.

"I'll have to put the old place on the market," Edna mused. "I don't need a house that big."

Edna's fingers returned to her forehead. "Anyway, I'd better get to the doctor to make sure this isn't a serious head injury." Worry etched her features.

Though Nadine was sure that wasn't the case, it was pointless to argue. Edna liked going to the doctor's office. Despite being over eighty, she'd spent most of her adult life needing to be reassured by a medical professional that her death wasn't imminent.

Nadine and Emma continued on their walkabout, picking out other familiar places: Pen Pals, the stationery shop; Fine Print, the independent bookstore; and Bits and Bobs, the sewing and craft store. Nadine's eyes bounced up and down Main Street, taking in all the familiar sights and noting the new stores as well.

A tattoo parlor called the Ink Stain had opened, as well as BAC Security. There was a new restaurant, the Annacotty Room, which her mother had raved about. And directly across from her sister's coffee shop was another coffee shop, Java Joe's. She didn't remember that being there the last time she was home.

"Come on, let's see Angie," Nadine said. She pushed through the front door of Coffee Girl, thinking as she did every time how much she loved the name of the place. When Angie was fresh out of high school, she'd taken a job driving a coffee truck that sold coffee, tea, sandwiches, and pastries. She drove from worksite to worksite, to places of business like the Gibson's Grape Jelly factory out on the highway. She'd earned the nickname Coffee Girl, and people were always glad to see her coming. When she took a week off to go to Florida with her friends for spring break, there'd almost been a revolt.

Angie's coffee shop was housed in a hundred-year-old red-brick Italianate building. It was a long, narrow space with a copper-tiled ceiling and gleaming hardwood floors. There were high tables with polished black walnut chairs and low tables made of the same walnut. A bar ran along the length of the front window for those who wanted to sip their coffee and people-watch. Currently a couple sat in the front window, a discarded, well-thumbed newspaper beside them. The counter ran half the length of one side wall, and it housed a long pastry case and a grouping of glass-domed cake plates. As it was the end of the day, there wasn't much left.

Nadine couldn't see her sister, but she could hear her, as vocal as ever: "Come on, get the lead out, we're leaving on time tonight."

The stainless-steel butler door separating the front of the café from the kitchen swung open, and Angie pushed through holding a tray of clean coffee mugs emblazoned with the Coffee Girl logo. She set the tray down, oblivious to the presence of her older sister and niece.

Nadine elbowed her daughter and grinned. "Come on, let's make our presence known."

Slowly, they approached the counter. Angie had her back to them, stacking the clean mugs on the counter.

It had always seemed to Nadine that the Cook sisters got prettier the farther they got down the line. It wasn't that she herself was unattractive; she wasn't, but she was no match for Angie, with her curves and her red hair and beautiful face. And as for their youngest sister, Deedee, she had movie star looks that left them all in the dust.

Finished with the mugs, Angie spun around to approach her next task when she spotted Nadine and Emma in front of her. First, she blinked several times as if she were seeing a mirage. Then her eyes widened and her mouth fell open. Finally, she came out from behind the counter, arms out, and embraced the two of them.

"What are you doing here?" she asked. "And how are you?" She pulled back and looked at them, focusing first on Emma. "Look at how much you've grown. We've missed you." And then as if a thought had occurred to her, she asked, "Did you get my graduation card?"

"I did, thank you for your generous gift," Emma said, casting a sheepish look at her mother.

Nadine rolled her eyes, thinking she wasn't going to mention in front of Angie how she'd been reminding Emma how important it was to send thank-you notes. You could only do so much as a mother; at some point, they had to learn for themselves.

"What are you doing here? You didn't say you were coming," Angie said.

Evangeline Cook, of all the sisters, was determined to be taken seriously. Growing up, she'd been known as Nadine and Maureen's younger sister. But she'd been set on making her own mark on the world. On her terms.

"There's a lot going on. I'll fill you in later," Nadine said. The coffee shop wasn't the place to inform her sister about her marital drama.

"Come on, come on, let's sit down," Angie said. She looked quickly around at the other tables.

"We won't stay long," Nadine said, knowing of her sister's inability to relax and take a break.

Angie herded them over to a table close to the front window, where she took the seat that would allow her to keep an eye on the shop.

*She's consumed by her business*, Nadine thought. Her sister had never married and had no children, and she supposed in a sense the café was her baby. But she wondered if Angie was happy. She probably didn't even have time to think about abstract thoughts like these.

"Oh gosh, where are my manners," Angie said. "Would you like coffee?" To Emma she said, "We have iced coffees, too."

Emma shook her head. "No thanks. I'm coffee-ed out. We drank a lot on the drive from home."

"You drove?"

"We had to. We've got Herman with us," Nadine explained.

"You brought Herman?" Angie said. "How long are you staying for?"

"For a while," Nadine said vaguely, squirming in her seat. She wasn't sure herself.

Without taking her eyes off Nadine, Angie turned her head slightly and narrowed her eyes as if drawing her own conclusions. Abruptly, she changed the subject.

"Have you seen Maureen?"

"Not yet, she doesn't know we're here. I'll call her tomorrow."

Angie nodded. "Good."

"How's she doing?"

Angie shrugged. "As far as I know, fine. You know Maureen, she's got the perfect life."

Nadine almost winced but didn't. That's what her friends used to say about her and Richard, that they had the perfect marriage. Even Nadine had gone along with that and had eventually believed it.

"What about Deedee?"

"I get a text from her every so often. She's with some acting troupe down in Florida. She likes it. Seems happy. She was going out with a lawyer, but I don't know if that's still a thing."

Angie knew more than Nadine did. It was sad how the four of them weren't close, not the way their mother was close to her sister. As teenagers and young women, Nadine and her sisters had tended to rub each other the wrong way and would spend days or weeks not speaking to one another, despite their mother's insistence that they "get over themselves." It wasn't that they'd ever had some big falling out, but they were different people with different personalities, and each one of them was guilty of nursing those old slights, real or imagined. Nadine and Deedee moving out of state didn't help matters. Their lives had all gone in different directions.

"Still working eighty hours a week?" Nadine asked. This was a constant complaint from their mother when she spoke to her on the phone. How worried she was that Angie was working herself to death.

Angie grinned. "It's not work if you love doing it."

Nadine was happy that she felt this way about her café, and her sister should be proud as she had built her business from the ground up. She was about to say so when Angie's smile disappeared and she hooked her thumb over her shoulder, indicating the business across the street. "Did you see I have competition?"

"I did. Java Joe's," Nadine said.

"As small a town as Lavender Bay is, that clown had to go and set up shop directly across the street from me," her sister griped. Nadine had forgotten about Angie's tendency to take personal offense.

"I'm sure he didn't open his café with the sole intent of aggravating you, Angie," Nadine said, trying to be the voice of reason.

Angie snorted. "Well, I know that, Nadine. But how much of an idiot is he to try and start a coffee shop right on the same block? Why didn't he go somewhere else in town?"

Nadine didn't know if this was a rhetorical question or if her sister really wanted an answer. She didn't offer an opinion.

There was the sound of dishes crashing to the floor in the kitchen, and Angie jumped up. "I better see what's going on."

"Of course."

"I'll catch up with you later," Angie said and before they could say goodbye, she was pushing through the butler door to the kitchen.

"Come on, Mom, let's go," Emma said, standing up and pushing her chair in.

"Sure. Let's walk over to the beach," Nadine suggested.

The air was heavy with humidity, and Nadine could feel her hair beginning to frizz. Emma pulled a hair tie off her wrist and quickly and expertly whipped her hair off her face and into a chic-looking messy bun. Nadine tried to remember if she was as put together and confident at that age, and somehow didn't think so. She remembered being very shy as a teenager.

"Why, I don't believe it! As I live and breathe! Is that you, Nadine Cook?" called out a voice that had a little bit of a croak to it.

Nadine turned to see Lavender Bay's oldest resident, Grace Gibson. Grace didn't let the fact that she was almost one hundred years old hold her back. She wore white capris with hot pink piping and had a pair of silver sequined sneakers on her feet. Nadine hoped when she was elderly, she had fabulous hair like Grace's: thick, silvery, and with a nice wave. It complemented her bright blue eyes.

Grace was the daughter of the founder of Gibson's Grape Jelly She'd never married, and lived in the oldest and grandest house in Lavender Bay. For as long as Nadine could remember, Grace had almost always had a smile on her face. Maybe the secret to a long and happy life was remaining single. She'd have to think about that later on when she was alone.

Nadine leaned toward the diminutive woman and kissed her lightly on the cheek. She smelled of Chanel No.5, as always. Nadine's mind drifted off, a small smile forming on her lips. When she was fourteen, she used to go up to Grace's home and dust for her. She'd had a treasure trove of knickknacks: lots of Hummel figurines, Precious Moments statues, and Lladro. But the Napcoware head vases had been Nadine's personal favorites. She'd been intrigued with these, with their pearl earrings, their lustrous hair, and that thick line of black eyeliner painted on the eyelids.

"Oh dear, I think we've lost you," Grace said, waving a thin, gnarled hand with a signet ring on one finger in front of Nadine's face.

"Mom!" Emma said sharply to get her attention.

"I'm sorry," Nadine blustered. "I was just thinking about how I used to come and dust for you after school."

"That's right!" Grace said, her eyes sparkling.

"I used to love those lady head vases," Nadine said.

"I didn't know that," Grace said.

"Lady head vases?" Emma said.

"Have your mother bring you up to the house someday and I'll show you my collection. I've been collecting them since the 1950s."

"There were a lot of knickknacks to dust," Nadine said with a laugh.

"And it was worth every penny to have you do it," Grace said.

"You said back then that you didn't know how much time you had left, and you didn't want to spend it dusting," Nadine said.

"It seems to me that the Good Lord has forgotten me," Grace quipped with a glance heavenward. "Not that I'm in any hurry to leave my wonderful life, but I think people are beginning to talk."

Nadine and Emma burst out laughing.

"Anyway, it was wonderful to see you again. Stop by and see me anytime," Grace said. "Ada is still making those wonderful lemon bars."

"Is Ada still with you?" Nadine asked. Ada Katz had been with Grace for a long time, as a cook and companion. She'd been there already when Nadine went up the hill to dust after school thirty years ago.

"Of course. I think the Lord forgot about her, too," Grace said, smiling.

"Say hello to her for me," Nadine said.

"Will do," Grace said. "Now, I must keep moving. If I stand for too long, my joints start to get stiff." She looked at Emma. "Young lady, it's a great life if you don't weaken."

Emma smiled. "I'll tuck that away for future reference."

"Good girl."

They parted ways, with Nadine and Emma heading north along Pearl Street, which ran parallel to the beach, and Grace going south, heading toward her home.

"Can you imagine living in these big houses with the beach in your backyard?" Emma asked, her eyes wide as her gaze swung from one house to the other.

Emma had been enthralled with the beach ever since Nadine and Richard first brought her here as a two-year-old. Every summer when they came home, it would be the first thing Emma would want to do. When they'd visit Maureen's and all the kids would be in the pool, Emma would lean into Nadine, her lips blue, her wet hair slicked back, water dripping off her bathing suit, and whisper, "Can we go to the beach?"

All the homes on the street were older Victorian-style houses replete with gingerbread trim and painted the obligatory three colors. As they walked along, they could hear the surf from behind the houses, which backed onto the shore. As long as Nadine lived, she'd never get tired of that sound. And when she came home, she always realized how much she missed it.

With the sound and the scent of the beach, she realized this would be a place where she could sort out her life. Figure out her problems and decide where she wanted to go from here.

Whether consciously or not, she found herself heading in the direction of the Hadley house Edna Knickerbocker had mentioned, and when she reached it, she paused on the cracked sidewalk. It was such a grand house! It was almost three stories if you included the top-floor attic. It had a deep front porch with wide steps. Above the porch was a balcony off one of the upstairs rooms. The faded paint was the color of cocoa, with cream and green accents. A bay window on one side of the house, toward the rear, must offer a partial view of the beach and the lake beyond.

What was it about a house that you could always tell if it was uninhabited? Had it lost its soul? Its spark for life? Despite the architectural prettiness of the house, it seemed forlorn. It seemed how Nadine felt: alone, lonely. At that point in her life, it was hard to separate the two. Edna Knickerbocker's words rang in her head: *it was a house that took in strays.*

"It's sad that the Hadleys didn't remain in the house," Nadine said, more to herself than anyone.

"Mom, people move. They do it all the time," Emma said, one hand on her hip, her knee bent slightly as she studied the house.

Were they a rare breed, people who remained in the same house for forty, fifty years? Nadine's own mother had lived nowhere else since she'd married but the tidy little Victorian on Heather Lane.

"If I had the money, I'd buy that house," Emma announced.

"You would?"

Emma nodded, her arms folded across her chest, the short sleeves of her T-shirt laid smooth along her slim shoulders, her collarbones neat and symmetrical. Sometimes Nadine could only stare at her daughter, stunned that this other person, in all her perfection, had come forth from her. It was mind-boggling.

"I'd love to live on the beach, or near it. Especially this one," Emma was saying.

"Why's that?"

"I have great memories of our summers here by the lake," Emma said with a laugh. "Why wouldn't I want to live here?" She paused, kicking at some loose sand on the sidewalk. "It's one of my life goals: someday, I'm going to live on a beach."

It bothered Nadine that she didn't know this fact about her only child. How had she not known that? What else didn't she know about her daughter?

Early in their marriage, she'd been hopeful that she and Richard and Emma could move back to Lavender Bay, but Richard had never been keen on the idea of living in Nadine's hometown. *The things we sacrifice,* she thought. All in the name of love.

"Come on, we better head back. Your grandmother will wonder what happened to us," Nadine said, pivoting. As they walked in the general direction of home, she looked over her shoulder at the house, one might almost say longingly.

# CHAPTER SEVEN

That evening, Louise fired up the grill.

"Did you see Angie?" she asked, holding a plate of raw burgers in one hand and a grill spatula in the other. She was decked out in canvas shorts that went to her knees and a sleeveless T-shirt with a scalloped lace trim over the bosom.

"Mom, here, I can man the grill," Nadine said, relieving her mother of the plate and the spatula.

"Thanks, honey. Maybe Emma could help me set the table?"

"Sure, Gram."

"And yes, we saw Angie briefly. She was too busy really to talk. Hopefully, we'll catch up later," Nadine said.

"Did she say anything about Java Joe's across the street?" her mother asked.

"She's not happy about it."

Louise pursed her lips and shook her head. "That's a rant she can't seem to get off of. Honestly, she sounds like a broken record. It's like she's taking it personally," she huffed.

"Let me grill these burgers and we'll talk about it later," Nadine said, anxious to get outside and get started. Her stomach growled.

When she stepped out back, she took in a deep lungful of air. That's what she needed, fresh air and lots of it.

She loved her mother's backyard. Although small, everywhere you looked, there was something to look at. Louise was an avid gardener, and every available space had been utilized. A paved brick walkway looped around the garden. The grill sat on a bed of stones with paving bricks right in front of it, like a mat. Nadine laid the burgers on the grill and sat down in the chair next to it, crossing one leg over the other, content to sit and chill for a minute. She looked around, enjoying the hostas, the astilbe, the lilac bush that had been a gift from her grandmother. There was a small boulder that her father had moved from the beach, surrounded by plantings of black-eyed Susans and daisies. Wind chimes hung from the roofline, but there was no breeze that day and they were still. The sun was getting low in the sky, and the shade just about reached her. The smell of the burgers and the sizzling sound they made on the grill made her stomach growl louder.

A few birdhouses painted in shades of gray, green, and brown lined the back fence. She didn't have to turn her head to know that on the table on the patio were a pair of binoculars and a book about birds.

Shortly, she carried the plate of burgers inside and asked, "Mom, who is going to eat all these?" There'd been five on the plate.

"One for each of us and two for Herman," Louise said.

Herman came running from the other room, came to an abrupt halt in the doorway, and turned around and walked backward into the room.

"Beep, beep!" Emma said with a laugh.

"Why does he do that?" Louise asked.

Nadine shrugged. "I don't know."

"He even looks over his shoulder when he's doing it, like he's backing into a driveway." Louise said. "You like hamburgers, don't you, Herman?"

Herman wasn't fussy when it came to human food. He liked it all. He was an equal-opportunity eater.

The three of them gathered around the table, and Herman settled down with a groan of protest against the wall. Nadine had trained him early on about begging from the table or table surfing. Still, he was vocal about his disagreement over this from time to time. She suspected he was now trying to elicit sympathy from her mother. And by the look on her mother's face, it might be working.

Louise tore off a small bit of hamburger.

"Mom, don't," Nadine warned, her voice low.

Herman seemed to know that the discussion was about him and lifted his head.

"Just this one time, that's all," her mother said with a smile.

"No."

Louise scowled and looked sympathetically at Herman. "I'm sorry. She's a meanie. But after dinner for sure."

With a sigh, the dog laid his head down between his paws.

"Come on, let's eat," Louise said, nodding toward all the food on the table.

There was a bowl of potato salad with sliced hard-boiled egg and a sprinkling of paprika. Next to it sat a bowl of tuna macaroni salad and a tossed salad with chopped tomatoes and cucumbers dressed in a light vinaigrette. All the bowls were vintage pink Pyrex that Nadine remembered from her childhood. She was pretty sure they'd been her grandmother's.

"You don't eat like this every night, do you, Mom?" It seemed like a lot of work. Nadine loved cooking for her family, especially when all the planets aligned and the three of them were home together. But those occasions were rare. And sadly, they would be no more.

"Oh goodness no," Louise replied. "It's just nice to have someone to cook for."

"I ran into Edna Knickerbocker," Nadine said. "She told me that Johnny Hadley died."

Louise scrunched up her nose in sympathy. "I'd heard that."

"Remember the old Hadley place?" Nadine asked, dumping a scoop of potato salad on her plate. She passed the bowl to Emma, who sat next to her. She worried the girl wasn't eating properly. But her daughter ignored it, her plate home to only a burger with cheese, lettuce, and tomato.

"I do. Old Mrs. Hadley used to take in lodgers." Louise chewed thoughtfully before adding. "I suppose Edna will sell that place now."

"I told Mom that if I had the money, I'd buy it," Emma said enthusiastically. Nadine looked at her daughter. The wheels in her brain began to spin, albeit slowly because it felt like all the wheels had come off of her bus recently.

"Wouldn't we all?" Louise said. "But I don't know. That close to the beach? It would be a constant battle with the sand." She surveyed the offerings on the table before deciding on the macaroni salad. As she scooped some out onto her plate, she said of the old house, "Torturous."

That wouldn't bother Nadine one bit. Living in a landlocked state had made her miss the water. The sand. The smell. The cry of circling gulls. Sometimes, she longed for it. The missing it was never so acute as when she returned from a visit to Lavender Bay. But with time and how busy she was with all her activities, that homesickness always faded.

She reached for the ketchup and mustard and put generous amounts on her burger before replacing the top bun. "Not to mention the cost of renovating an old house. It's always more than you think it's going to be." She and Richard had found that out the hard way with their first house, which they'd renovated themselves. It had needed a lot of work when they bought it. Although admittedly, Nadine had loved every minute of it. Every time she looked around at it, she was reminded of all the tender loving care they had put into it. But Richard soon grew bored with it and after several promotions, pushed to move. When they purchased their second house, it had been a new build from the ground up. And although everything was brand, spanking new, it did not possess the character and charm the first house had. She had no sentimental attachment to their current home, not like she had with the first, where Emma had spent the first few years of her life.

"Johnny Hadley never lived in that house as an adult," Louise said, referring to the Hadley place. "After he graduated from college, he left for Chicago. He used to rent it out but as he got older, he couldn't be bothered. At one time, long ago, it used to be a boarding house."

"I know, that must have been interesting," Nadine said. How much fun it would have been to be the landlady of the house, looking after all those people and their problems. The mother in her liked looking after people and animals.

"That wouldn't be for me," her mother said, waving her hand in the air, the one holding her burger. She set her burger down on her plate. "All those strangers in your house? No, thank you. I could barely handle four girls, especially during the teenage years." She looked over at Emma and smiled. "No offense, sweetie."

"None taken, Gram," Emma said with a laugh.

"Dad did better with us girls," Nadine said with a smile at the memory of her father.

"Your father was very laid back," Louise Cook reminisced. "The house could be burning down around him, and he'd ask me what was for dinner."

"How long was the boarding house in operation?" Emma asked.

"Mrs. Hadley operated it from the time of the Depression and was still operating it when I was a young girl."

Nadine couldn't believe that a town the size of Lavender Bay required a boarding house. "What happened?" she asked.

Her mother helped herself to some more salad, put the bowl down, and looked at her. "What do you mean?"

"I wonder why it stopped operating as a boarding house."

Her mother shrugged. "I don't know. Mrs. Hadley became too old. She died. Boarding houses became less popular. I don't even know if they're legal anymore." She laughed. "Why all this curiosity about the Hadley house?"

Now it was Nadine's turn to shrug. "Just interested, that's all." She turned her attention to her dinner. But even as she dug her fork into her potato salad, she was aware of a nagging sensation at the back of her mind.

Emma abruptly stood up from the table, startling Nadine. "Can I go to Aunt Maureen's house?"

"Sure. But if they're busy, come back here."

Nadine's sister Maureen had two sons, and a daughter a year younger than Emma. It amazed Nadine how Emma and Ashley always seemed to pick up right where they left off, no matter how long they'd been apart. They FaceTimed each other and were on social media together. She wished it were that way with her own sisters. It seemed that with every reunion, there was that initial awkward stage where they had to get to know each other all over again.

Emma bolted, but Nadine called out after her.

Emma returned, sulking. "What?"

"Clear your dishes. We're not the hired help."

Blushing, Emma cast a glance at her grandmother and muttered, "Sorry, Gram."

Louise waved her away. "Don't worry about it. Leave your plate on the counter and go off to Maureen's. They'll be happy to see you."

Emma smiled, removed her dishes, and carried them to the counter nearest the dishwasher. She bounded out the door with a quick wave.

"Not too late," Nadine called after her.

Nadine and her mother did a quick cleanup. Once the dishwasher was loaded, Louise announced that there was a strawberry-rhubarb pie for dessert.

"I haven't had that in a long time," Nadine said.

Her mother cut two generous slices, and Nadine took vanilla ice cream from the freezer and laid a scoop on each piece of pie.

They sat down together, and as Nadine took her first mouthful, her mother regarded her own fork, turning it around in her hand and staring at it.

"Why don't you tell me the real reason you've come back to Lavender Bay," she said.

Nadine slumped forward in her chair, elbows on the table. She sighed. "What makes you say that?"

Louise laughed. "I'm your mother, Nadine, I've known you longer than anyone. And one thing I know about you is that you don't do anything spur of the moment. You're a planner. Always have been."

Nadine drew in a deep breath. She hadn't considered that.

Louise continued. "When you called me and told me you were on your way, you can imagine my concern."

"Of course." Was she that predictable, that easy to read? No wonder Richard had looked elsewhere. She wasn't exactly exciting.

"Is it Emma?" Louise asked quietly.

Nadine shook her head. "No, Emma's fine." At that point, Emma was the only bright star on her horizon. "It's Richard."

Louise's brow furrowed. "Richard? What's wrong with him?"

"There's nothing wrong with him. It's what he's done."

Nadine poured forth the whole sordid affair. Her mother sat there, her head tilted slightly and her mouth hanging open as she digested all that Nadine told her.

At first, there was shock, then disbelief and finally, outrage.

"I'm so sorry, Nadine," Louise whispered. She stood and gathered the pie plates, the pie half-finished and sitting in pools of melted ice cream, and announced, "We need something stronger than pie. I'll be right back."

She cleared the plates and returned, a container of ice cream in each hand with two spoons.

"Butter Pecan or Cherry Panda Paws?" she said, holding up the two cartons.

Knowing her mother's favorite was Butter Pecan, Nadine said, "Cherry Panda Paws."

Louise handed her the ice cream and a spoon. Nadine wiped her eyes and her nose and then peeled the lid off the carton, took her spoon, and dug in.

"I don't know if eating ice cream will solve my problems," she said. "But it definitely tastes good."

They sat in silence for a bit and her mother swallowed a spoonful of ice cream and said, "You know, Nadine, you could always move permanently back to Lavender Bay."

# Chapter Eight

Nadine was up with the sun, as her grandmother used to say. The previous night, she'd tossed and turned for a while and when she finally fell asleep, she'd slept like the dead and still woke up exhausted. Now she was anxious to get up and get the day started. Herman stirred where he slept at the foot of the bed, groaning. He wasn't an early riser. But when Nadine stood, he jumped up, alert.

"It's okay, buddy, I'm only going to the bathroom."

He seemed to understand and sat there at the foot of the bed, waiting.

As quietly as she could, she padded to the bathroom, did a quick washup, and brushed her teeth. Back in her room, she dressed quickly, deciding an early morning walk on the beach was called for.

"Come on," she said, holding up the dog's purple lead. "Walk?"

He wagged his tail in response and leaned against her, pushing his head against her hand.

She rubbed the top of his head and leaned down and kissed him. "Did anyone ever tell you what a great comfort you are?"

He wagged his tail some more.

As they walked out of the bedroom, she whispered to him, "I think you know more than you let on."

Before they'd said good night the previous evening, her mother had told her that she was welcome to stay as long as she liked.

They walked down the staircase, and Nadine was thankful that it was carpeted so as not to wake any-one. She bypassed breakfast, her stomach still feeling queasy after all the ice cream she'd eaten the previous night. She clipped the lead to Herman's collar, and together they went out.

The street was quiet. There was only the sound of the birds chirping their morning greeting. The air was pleasantly warm, the promise of a hot day ahead of them.

She'd always loved this time of the day, when everyone else was still asleep and she had the world to herself. All of the houses they passed were darkened, curtains and blinds drawn, not yet open to the world. Herman loped along comfortably at her side as they headed toward the beach.

When they reached the beach they saw only one other person, an elderly woman some distance away picking things out of the sand that she then tossed in a tall paper coffee cup. Beach glass, perhaps? Seashells? Herman tugged on the lead, insisting they walk toward the shoreline. Nadine unclipped the lead from his collar and let him off. He had one destination in mind: the water. Herman loved the water. At home, they had an in-ground pool, and no one got more use out of it than Herman. It was one of the many things she loved about him: his carefree spirit. As he romped in the surf, his face full of joy, Nadine did a three-sixty of her surroundings. Not much had changed since she moved out of the area. The same houses lined the beach, only now some had been spruced up, the paint color changed, and some had fallen into disrepair, which was always sad to see. Her eyes traveled east, facing the rising sun, as the land sloped gently, and the town was laid out for all to see. The familiar landscape gave her a boost, which was desperately needed.

After a while, Herman emerged from the water and returned to her side, shaking off water right next to her, drenching her.

"Thanks," she said wryly. She reattached his lead and they headed off.

As they left the beach, she said, "Come on, let's see if we can find a cup of coffee." She wasn't sure if Angie opened this early, but she didn't mind walking up to the town to find out.

Their walk was meandering. She gave the lead slack when the dog wanted to investigate things, which was often. He must have sniffed at every shrub, flower, and rock on the way into town. She didn't mind; it gave her time to think, something she'd been doing a lot of lately.

What was she going to do with the rest of her life? Returning to her and Richard's house was not an option. It used to be a home, but now it was only a house shared by two people who used to love each other. There really was no reason to return, especially since Emma was going off to college. If Emma was still at home, it would have been a no-brainer; she would have returned and figured something else out. She had been out of the workforce a long time. She'd liked keeping a home and taking care of her family. The idea of looking for a job at the age of forty-four with an empty resumé did not thrill her.

As she waited for Herman—who had his nose stuck in a privet hedge—she realized she had a lot of important decisions to make. As much as this scared her, there was a small part of her that felt that this newfound freedom was absolutely delicious. She could do whatever she wanted, with no one other than Emma to consider. She could live wherever she wanted in the world. That, too, was a no-brainer. She was going to live in Lavender Bay. Her mother's suggestion had kept her up all night, and she knew it was the right choice.

Eventually, she and Herman found themselves back in town, shops still closed as it was only six thirty in the morning. Her first stop was her sister's café, but it was still dark, and the sign said they didn't open until seven. But across the street, Java Joe's front door was wide open, the sandwich board was already perched out on the sidewalk, and the lights were on inside. Along the current of warm air, the smell of fresh-brewed coffee and grilled food traveled to her, her stomach gurgling in response.

"Come on, let's get coffee," she said to Herman. Despite the fact that there was hardly any traffic on the street that early in the morning, she still looked both ways when she crossed, the dog at her side. After she secured Herman's lead around the lamppost outside the café, she stepped inside of Java Joe's.

There were two people in the coffee shop; apparently, she wasn't the only early riser out and about that morning. The inside of Java Joe's definitely had a masculine feel. It was all dark wood and brass and copper fixtures. Chrome tables with Formica tabletops and black vinyl chairs filled the place. The wide plate-glass window in front looked directly across at Coffee Girl.

Momentarily sheepish, Nadine hesitated. But the aroma of coffee was too appealing, and her feet propelled her to the long counter. There were a few pastries and cakes in the display case, but nothing like the assortment her sister offered. Overhead, a menu painted on distressed wood hung suspended from chains. A quick scan showed a variety of breakfast sandwiches. Her mouth watered.

"Can I help you?" a deep voice asked, startling her. The big man who'd emerged from the back room had a neat beard and multiple tattoos. He was intimidating.

"Um, sure," she said, scanning the menu, grateful there was no one behind her in line. "I'll have an Americano and a bacon-and-egg sandwich. On a croissant." There were other, more adventurous choices, but she decided to keep it simple. As she waited, she stared out the window. The traffic was beginning to pick up.

He handed her her order in a brown bag and the coffee in a takeout cup, and she turned and exited, relieved to find Herman waiting patiently for her on the sidewalk.

"Hey, handsome, how about some breakfast?" She opened the bag and pulled out the sandwich, unwrapped it, ripped off a big chunk, and tossed it to the dog, who caught it in his mouth. When she looked up, she spotted her sister Angie standing in front of Coffee Girl, her hands on her hips.

She was not smiling.

*Oh boy.*

Quickly, she shoved the rest of the sandwich back into the bag and untied Herman from the lamppost, the two of them trotting across the street.

A thunderous look covered Angie's face.

"Hey," Nadine said, deciding to downplay things.

"I don't believe you!" Angie started. "You're not back in town for two days and you're giving your business to my competition? *Thanks.*" Angie's temper matched that fiery red hair of hers.

"Now wait a minute," Nadine said. "My intention was to stop here, but you weren't open." It was a bit early to be attacked like this. All over a cup of coffee and an egg sandwich.

"You could have waited. I was running late," Angie said. "My freezer is on the fritz, and I had to empty everything into the sink."

"How was I to know that?" This was how it was with her sisters. Sometimes, it only took a cup of coffee to set things off.

"Even so, why would you drink coffee from the enemy?" Angie asked.

Nadine thought her sister was being dramatic but kept that opinion to herself; she had enough drama in her own life. She glanced over her shoulder at Java Joe's, watching as a couple entered the building.

"Does he know how you feel about him?"

"This isn't some romantic comedy on Netflix, this is about some brute trying to muscle in on my business," Angie said hotly.

Nadine frowned. "Does he feel the same way?"

"I have no idea. Our conversations have never lasted long enough for me to determine how he feels."

"But I bet he knows how you feel," Nadine said, venturing a guess.

"Of course," Angie said with a sniff. She pulled a large set of keys from her pocket. "Look, I've got to open up. I'll talk to you soon."

Nadine said goodbye and wondered if that was true. It seemed Angie was too busy to talk at all.

She stood on the corner of Maple and Main and finished her breakfast sandwich, handing the last chunk to Herman, who gobbled it from her hand, leaving a trail of slobber in his wake. She wiped her hand on the napkin from the bag. She gulped the rest of the coffee, which had now gone cold. She'd never admit to Angie that the sandwich and the coffee were delicious. No sense in stoking *that* fire.

After she threw the cup and bag into a garbage bin, she and Herman started in the direction of her mother's house, but she felt compelled to detour past the Hadley home on Pearl Street. She couldn't account for the pull, but she'd thought about the house during the night as she tossed and turned. It certainly was more pleasant to think about an old boarding house than her own problems. The distraction was good.

It wasn't far from the center of town. She headed down to the end of Main Street and then made a right on Pearl, heading north. Soon she found herself standing on the sidewalk in front of the Hadley house. She could so easily see it being a boarding house all those years ago. It had a sturdiness and familiarity to it. She wondered about the boarding house residents. What had that been like? Why had Mrs. Hadley resorted to running a boarding house? To own a house right on the lake would have indicated some money at some point.

Herman sat patiently next to her, staring at the house. She looked down at him. "What do you think?" In a million years, she would never be able to explain the pull of this house. She tugged her phone from her back pocket and took a quick photo. She bit her lip.

"Come on, Herman, we've got to get back," she said. Hurriedly, she trotted toward home, anxious to call Edna Knickerbocker before she lost her nerve and changed her mind.

No one was up yet at her mother's house, the downstairs quiet and still. There was a small writing desk in the alcove beneath the stairs. Nadine rummaged through the drawer, searching out her mother's address book. She opened it on top of the desk, flipping through the pages and finding the number she sought. She picked up the handset of the desk phone and began to dial.

It was answered on the third ring.

"Hello?" said a groggy voice.

"Mrs. Knickerbocker?" Nadine said.

"Who's calling this early in the morning?"

"It's me, Nadine Eberhardt." Excitement gripped her. "I'd like to talk to you about buying the house on Pearl Street."

# CHAPTER NINE

Nadine was alone in her mother's house. Emma had gone off with her cousin Ashley to the beach, and Louise had gone grocery shopping. Nadine had been busy in the kitchen, and the house smelled of freshly baked Watergate cake. Currently, Herman stood in the front window, barking at something outside.

She sat in the living room, talking on the phone to Richard.

"Hello? Richard? Are you still there?" Had he hung up on her?

"Yes."

"Did you hear what I said?" she asked. She'd signed an agreement to purchase the old Hadley place from Edna Knickerbocker a few days ago. The house was being evaluated by a realtor, and she'd already consulted her mother's attorney.

"I heard every word." His voice was low and quiet.

"And?" she pushed. This conversation needed to be had. Over the phone wasn't ideal, but there was nothing she could do about that. She'd be returning soon enough to pack up her things and move permanently to Lavender Bay.

Herman moved from the front window to a side window and barked again.

"How could you make such a purchase without consulting me first?" he asked.

She almost shot back, *How could you have a child with another woman?* but she refrained, thinking at some point, she was going to have to move on from his transgression. She didn't want that negative energy leaking into her new life. She wanted a clean slate.

Purchasing the house on Pearl Street had been an impulsive move. She'd paid a cash deposit for it, moving some funds from their joint accounts to a brand-new bank account in Lavender Bay without giving it a second thought. The remainder of the funds needed for the purchase remained in her new bank account. In the past, she would never have done anything like that or made a big purchase without consulting her husband. But not this time. Besides, Richard had their marital home, which at over five thousand square feet was worth almost three times the cost of the old boarding house. He could keep the house; she had no intention of returning to it except to gather her belongings.

"Nadine?"

"I'm going to need somewhere to live," she pointed out.

"You have a home! Right here, with me," he said, exasperated.

"But you live there."

"That's the idea. Two people who are married usually live together."

Nadine sighed. She hadn't thought he'd cling. He'd never been the clingy type. She'd been convinced he'd take off to live with that other woman and their son.

When she didn't say anything, he spoke again. "Come home, we'll go through intensive marriage counseling and get our marriage back on track."

"Like we did before? Before you cheated again?" she asked. To say those words out loud, that plain truth, seared through her.

His exasperated sigh traveled down the phone line.

Nadine laughed although there was nothing funny about their situation. "Come on, Richard, what did you expect? Did you think I'd be good old Nadine? Always ready to take the high road and forgive?"

"Yes."

There it was, simple. She wasn't going to be anyone's doormat. Not anymore.

"I forgave you once, but you've made a fool of me."

"No one has to know," he pleaded.

She snorted. "It's going to be a little hard to hide Sam. Where would you keep him? How would you explain that?"

"Don't be like that."

"Tell me, how should I be?"

"Come home, give me another chance," he said.

"No."

"What about Emma? Don't you care how this will affect her?"

Anger coursed through Nadine. "How dare you bring Emma into it? How did you think having an affair and a child with another woman would affect her? Let's be honest, when you were playing around, you never gave Emma or me a single thought. So cut it out."

"Nadine—"

"There's nothing more to say. I bought this house because I need a place to live. Get over it." She paused and added, "And please don't contact me anymore unless it has something to do with Emma or the divorce."

Nadine was still fuming ten minutes later when her mother walked in the door with Maureen. She was sitting on the edge of the sofa, taking some deep breaths and trying to calm down. It had worked until she saw her sister. She'd been home almost a week, and this was the first time she'd seen Maureen.

"Nadine!" Maureen said, coming toward her with her arms outstretched.

Not a strand of Maureen's glossy chestnut hair was out of place, and her makeup was flawless. Not a blemish to be found, and hardly a line anywhere. Her put-together look appeared effortless, and her subtle perfume smelled expensive. Nadine was envious. She knew she had purple circles beneath her own eyes and although she'd washed her hair the previous day, she'd done nothing with it and now it hung flat and limp around her face.

She stepped into her sister's embrace. She'd been back in Lavender Bay for a week, and her sister hadn't even stopped by to say hello. *Too busy with her perfect life.* But she was ashamed to admit that she hadn't called her sister either.

When they pulled apart, Maureen studied her, a frown forming on her perfect complexion.

"Mom told me about Richard. I'm sorry to hear this," Maureen said.

Nadine pulled away, muttering, "That's life." It wasn't fair to take out her frustration with Richard on her sister, especially since Maureen had nothing to do with it.

The three of them headed to the kitchen and pulled out chairs from the farmhouse table that took up a big portion of the room.

"Mom said you bought the old Hadley place," Maureen said, taking the chair across from Nadine.

"I did," Nadine said.

"It'll be great to have you back in Lavender Bay."

Nadine hoped so, too. Maybe she could get back on track with her sisters.

She rolled her shoulders and twisted her neck, trying to relax.

"I still can't believe you bought the house!" Louise said. "You're not my impulsive child."

"No, Deedee is," Maureen said with a laugh.

"I'm thinking of turning it into a bed-and-breakfast," Nadine said.

Louise and Maureen stared at her. "Are you serious?" Louise asked.

"I am. How hard could it be? You serve breakfast and make sure the rooms are clean." Even as Nadine said these things, she realized how lame they sounded and that it probably involved a lot more than that. Nothing in life was easy.

Louise's expression was one of concern as she frowned. "Oh, I don't know about that. I don't think you can simply hang out a shingle and call it a B & B. I'm sure the state has all sorts of rules and regulations."

Nadine hadn't thought about that, but she covered up and said, "I know. I'm already looking into that." Switching subjects, she asked Maureen, "How are Allan and the kids?"

Maureen waved a hand breezily. "Great. Busy with work and school. You know how it is."

"I do," Nadine said. Although she'd only had Emma, she'd longed for more children. But many failed attempts at IVF had left her raw, and she'd decided to focus her attention on the child she did have. Richard had been disappointed as he'd wanted another child as well.

Maureen left with a promise to get together soon.

Nadine watched her sister leave, wistful, and mumbled, "Maureen's so lucky."

Her mother had her back to her, but she said over her shoulder, "Don't be so sure your sister's life is so perfect."

# Chapter Ten

They'd unpacked everything. Nadine looked around Emma's dorm room and sighed. It was hard to believe the little girl who loved swimming and the beach was now heading off to her own life. They'd left the night before from Lavender Bay, stayed at a motel not far from the college, and the two of them were up early to move Emma into her dorm.

There was nothing more to do. The bed was made, posters were put up on the wall, and all of Emma's clothes had been put away. The dorm-sized fridge was stocked, and they'd set up the small microwave on the corner of the desk. Looking at the space, Nadine realized that this was the first time in her daughter's life where she would be living somewhere other than with her parents. It made her stomach churn and roil. She could feel the bile at the back of her throat as the worries plowed through her mind: Would she be safe? Would she eat properly? Would she get involved with the wrong crowd?

It was time to go, but she was having a hard time leaving. Emma stood on the other side of the room talking to her new roommate, a lovely Indian girl named Suni, whose mother Nadine had met and instantly liked. That was a relief. She'd heard horror stories from her friends about roommates from hell.

Emma bounced over to her. "Mom, Suni and I are going to go and check out the campus."

That was Nadine's cue to exit. She nodded quickly as her chin quivered.

"Of course." She gazed around the room, unable to look at her daughter, and said, "I think that's everything. Of course, if you need anything, call me. Or Dad. He'll be here next weekend."

Emma put her arm around her mother. "Come on, Mom, I'll walk you to your car." As they headed out of the room, Emma looked over her shoulder at her new roommate and said, "I'll be back in a few."

"No worries," replied Suni. "It was nice meeting you, Mrs. Eberhardt."

"Good luck to you, Suni," Nadine said as she left.

She and Emma walked side by side out to the parking lot. Nadine bit her lip to stem the flow of tears that threatened to let loose. They paused beside the car.

"Well, I guess this is it," Emma said. She looked around the parking lot, avoiding making eye contact with Nadine. She lowered her head.

Nadine realized it was just as hard for Emma as it was for her. That thought made her firm up her resolve not to turn into a blubbering mess in the parking lot and make it more difficult for her daughter.

"Okay, honey, I'd better go. Don't keep Suni waiting." Nadine pulled her daughter into her arms, hugging her tight. She closed her eyes and breathed in the scent of her only child. It felt good to hug and to be hugged.

When they pulled apart, Emma said with a wobble, "I'm going to miss you."

Nadine forced a bright smile even though she felt like crying on the inside. "As luck would have it, I'm closer now that I'll be living in Lavender Bay." It was still a bit of a drive, but it was doable in one day. She reached over and tucked a strand of Emma's hair behind her ear, something she'd always done when she was little. "I am so proud of you and the person you're turning into." There was a little quiver in her voice as she said, "I couldn't be prouder of you if I tried."

"Do I have to see Dad next weekend?" Emma asked, crossing her arms over her chest.

Nadine sighed. Emma had not been in touch with her father until recently. At one point, Richard accused Nadine of poisoning their daughter against him. She didn't waste her breath explaining that he'd managed to do that all by himself. But Emma had spoken to him twice on the phone and had agreed to have him come for a visit.

"Emma, you don't have to do anything you don't want to do," Nadine said. "But he is your father. You have to decide if you want to be a person who forgives or the kind who holds a grudge. Because I can assure you that the latter requires a lot of anger, and that is no good."

"But Mom—"

Nadine held her hand up. "I know. What he did hurt us all. But there's no doubt in my mind that he loves you very much. That never changed. And it never will. And even though it ended our marriage, it is between your dad and me."

"I know, but I can't stand the fact that he hurt you."

Spontaneously and full of gratitude, Nadine threw her arms around her daughter. "Have I ever told you how much I love you?"

Emma laughed. "All the time."

"I'm telling you again." Nadine looked toward the dormitory building, thinking Suni was probably wondering what was taking so long. "Give him a second chance, because we all make mistakes. Big ones. Little ones. And ones in between."

Emma nodded. "Are you going to be okay?"

"Me?" Nadine asked with more cheeriness than she felt. "Of course. In a few weeks, I'll have a house on the beach. And I'm back home with my mother and sisters in Lavender Bay."

"All right, Mom."

"Come on now, hug me one last time and go find Suni."

They had one last hug and Nadine planted a kiss on her cheek. "Goodbye, honey, take care of yourself."

"I will."

Nadine got in her car, and smiled and waved as she pulled away. In her rearview mirror, she could see Emma standing there on the sidewalk, waving goodbye.

She tooted the horn one last time, and soon Emma was out of view. The GPS directed her to the thruway entrance, and Nadine was proud that she'd managed to hold it all together that morning and not alarm her daughter with hysterics and drama. But as she pulled onto the thruway, she burst into tears.

# CHAPTER ELEVEN

Three weeks after she dropped Emma off at college, Nadine closed on the house on Pearl Street. Once the keys were handed over, she had to admit to a bit of excitement and enthusiasm. This was the first piece of property she'd owned in her own name. If she never felt like a grown-up before, she certainly did now. She was more than ready to roll up her sleeves and get to work.

Her mother had wanted to take her to lunch to celebrate but Nadine begged off, saying that she wanted to go over to the house immediately. But she promised she would join her for dinner.

It was a beautiful September day. Everything had a golden-hued cast over it. The trees were still lush and vibrant green. The lake's temperature was still warm as August had been unusually hot. All the children in Lavender Bay had gone back to school, leaving the streets and beach quiet. It was a pleasant time of year.

With the keys in hand, she stepped up onto the front porch, noting the gunmetal gray paint on the wooden floorboards. She would leave them as such. For now. The house had been vacant for years although Edna assured her that every few months, she'd done a walk-through to check on things for her cousin. Now, Nadine was anxious to do her own walk-through and open the windows and let the fresh air in. She was anxious to get her project off the ground.

She'd spent the previous three weeks throwing herself into research about opening a B & B, talking to all kinds of officials, from the zoning board to the County Department of Health. She couldn't do anything until she owned the house outright, for obvious reasons. New York State did not allow the use of more than five bedrooms for an operational B & B, which was fine as the house only had that many, and she'd be using one for herself. Finally, she'd consulted an attorney who specialized in start-up businesses. Right off the bat, she'd need a business license, a health department permit, fire safety inspection, and a food service permit. The paperwork she'd gathered up to that point was not for the faint of heart. But she'd put her head down and soldiered through. Besides, all of it had taken her mind off her ending marriage and the fact that she was an empty nester.

There were still a lot of things to do: get certified in CPR, get insurance, set up a Tripadvisor account, organize ways to accept credit card payments. Every day, she thought of another thing that had to be done, and her to-do list grew longer and longer. Her plan was to open by Christmas but every time she looked at her list, it seemed impossible. She was dropping a substantial amount of money into the place already and she hadn't even had her first guest. The following day, she had meetings set up with a home renovator and the town's fire safety inspector.

Holding her breath, she unlocked the front door.

For a moment, she stood in the wide front hall with its ornate staircase and looked around, hardly believing that it was hers. She knew the layout of the house by heart. At the back of the first floor was a servants' staircase leading to the upstairs and the attic. To her right was the dining room with built-in china cabinets and the original hardwood floor. Behind the dining room was a large kitchen. To her left was the parlor with a fireplace and mantel, and a large front window that looked out onto the porch. Past the parlor was a library with floor-to-ceiling shelves and a pair of French doors overlooking the back porch and beyond that, Lake Erie.

She was immediately greeted by a sour smell, probably from the windows being closed all summer. Before she looked at another thing, she went to the parlor and threw open the two windows. They were the old-fashioned kind, with a rope and pulley. In one spot, the rope appeared to be rotting. Pausing, she pulled a notebook out of her purse and added *fix ropes and pulleys on windows* under the heading "Jobs to be done." She heaved a big sigh. But her momentary disenchantment and the continual worry that she might be in over her head was soon forgotten as she spotted the lake out the back window.

From where she stood in the parlor, she looked straight through to the empty library and out the back porch to Lake Erie. Across the lake, Canada was visible, hazy and distant. Forgetting about her tasks at hand, she stepped out onto the back porch and breathed in the smell of the beach, her eyes closing. A smile spread across her face.

*Home.*

An old swing hung on the southern end of the porch; the lake lay to the west. Cautiously, she tested out the swing and once she was certain it was safe, she leaned back and enjoyed the view of her new backyard. How lucky was she?

Hydrangeas grew in abundance on the other side of the porch rail, the soil being sandy and perfect for those flowers. There was a small backyard that led directly to the beach. She could see many morning walks for her and Herman.

Although she would need to furnish the empty house, that would have to wait until the renovations were done. She had all the time in the world.

She spent the afternoon going over every nook and cranny of the house, memorizing the rich details of the structure that had stood there for more than a hundred years. From the ornate wooden staircase with its scrolls and newel post to the large stained-glass window on the staircase landing depicting a pineapple, to the upstairs bedroom at the back of the house with its two windows, one facing west and the other, a bay window, facing south, giving the room an expansive view of the lake and the beach. She lingered there for a few moments, taking in the incredible view.

Finally, as the sun began to sink into the horizon on the lake, she made her way downstairs, remembering that she was to join her mother for dinner to celebrate. At the front door, she paused.

Looking around at her new home, she didn't see all the work that needed to be done. She didn't see the floors that needed to be refinished, the windows that needed to be fixed and washed, the kitchen floor that needed to be replaced, or that tea-colored stain on the outside parlor wall. What she saw was her new home.

It was the first day of her brand-new life.

# PART TWO

## LENORE

# Chapter Twelve

## September 1931

Lenore Wainwright had just stepped into the kitchen when she spotted that rascal, Billy Stodge, approaching the windowsill or, more specifically, the chocolate cake that had been set on the drainboard in front of the open window to cool. The room smelled of chocolate and baked sugar. It was heady. Mother and Dad would want a slice for lunch but if Billy had his way, there'd be no cake for anyone except Billy. It was a new recipe that didn't require eggs, milk, or butter. Eggs and butter were rationed, along with other food items, which was a challenge when trying to feed people.

Billy Stodge was the bane of her existence. He took anything that wasn't nailed down. Despite this, Lenore cut him a lot of slack. His father was a drinker and his mother was, well, overwhelmed. That was the only way Lenore could describe it.

The boy hadn't observed her yet. Staying out of view, she took the morning newspaper that had been left on the chair by the stove, indicating it had been read by all parties and could be used for the fire, and folded it in half. With the newspaper in hand, she put her back up against the wall next to the window. As soon as Billy's hands slid through the open window, she leaned over and gave them a swat with the newspaper.

"Ow!" came from outside.

Lenore lifted up the sash and leaned out the window. "That didn't hurt, Billy. But if I catch you near my cakes again, I'll take a switch off the birch tree and use it on you!"

Billy was backing up, rubbing the top of his hand. A scowl formed on his face.

She sighed, looking at him. He was only a child. It wasn't his fault that things weren't ideal at home.

He took off like a shot, heading toward whatever else was next on his list of mischief and general getting up to no good.

Smiling, she wiped her hands on her apron. She might as well give Hilda a hand and start putting the lunch together. She'd made Hoover stew after seeing a recipe for it in a magazine at the library. It consisted of macaroni, sliced hot dogs, tomatoes, and canned corn. There were two slices of bread, which would be reserved for her mother and father.

Hilda entered the kitchen as Lenore pulled out the china plates from the cabinet. Just because they had to skimp and save on meat and other things, that didn't mean they couldn't eat off the fine china, if only to cheer them up.

"Did I just see that Billy Stodge running through the yard?" Hilda pulled her apron off the hook and donned it, tying it.

Lenore rolled her eyes.

With a glance toward the window, Hilda nodded and said, "Let me guess. He was eyeing up the cake."

Lenore laughed. "Yes. But I caught him in the nick of time." She paused, rubbing her chin, thinking. "Maybe I should have given him a slice to take home." Now she regretted that she hadn't.

Hilda shook her head with a laugh. "You're too good, Miss Lenore. What that child needs is a good spanking."

"We must remember that he is still a child," Lenore pointed out.

Hilda took down a jar of preserves and went to open it, but Lenore interceded. "Let me do that."

"All right then," Hilda said easily, handing her the jar.

The previous summer, Hilda had taught Lenore how to can fruit. Right behind the white picket fence out back was a small orchard of fruit trees: apples, cherries, and peaches. At harvest time, any fruit they didn't use or preserve would be gathered up in bushel baskets and set on the front porch for people to help themselves.

Before the Depression, Lenore remembered when two to three cuts of meat were served every day with plenty of potatoes and vegetables. Her father was the mayor of Lavender Bay, and these days, he wanted to set an example by skimping and saving and eating less meat, like everyone else.

He had frozen his own annual salary when he learned that two men of the town hall were to be let go. These men had eight children between them. When people got wind of the fact that he resoled his shoe with a piece of cardboard, it had further endeared him to the electorate.

And like everyone else struggling during these unprecedented economic times, they made do. They ate watered-down soup. They cut back on sugar. They wore the same clothes over and over, repairing holes and tears to get further wear out of it.

Although Lavender Bay wasn't hit as hard as the larger American cities, there were subtle signs that it, too, was suffering. The Gibson's Grape Jelly factory had asked the workers to take a pay cut to save their jobs. There weren't the long lines of people snaking around city blocks, waiting for the soup kitchens, but the church in town provided a hot meal every day at one in the afternoon for those that had lost their jobs. Those men too embarrassed to take part went around privately to houses, never to the front door, always to the back, in search of a little bit of food or some work to be done around the house. Most people, including the Wainwrights, couldn't afford to hire someone to clean out the gutters or paint the picket fence out front. But they did give whatever they could in the way of food.

This past summer, with Hilda's guidance, Lenore turned over a small portion of the backyard for a vegetable garden. They ended up with carrots, radishes, and tomatoes. The corn had failed.

Hilda Wolf had been with the Wainwrights for as long as Lenore could remember. She was a tall, solid woman with a long, narrow face. But she was getting on in years and had terrible arthritis in her hands and wrists. Lenore loved working in the kitchen, much to her mother's dismay and her younger sister's ridicule, but she was happiest when she was cooking and baking. And even though her mother reminded her regularly that there was "help" to do that sort of work, Lenore carried on. She let Hilda do the easier tasks, like walking to the shops, as Hilda was social and loved to meet people, while Lenore stayed behind, figuring out what to do with leftovers or the ingredients they had on hand.

Lenore helped Hilda carry the platters into the dining room, where the family took all their meals. Her father and mother were already seated at the table.

"Lenore, is it true that there's a chocolate cake for dessert?" her father asked, his expression hopeful.

Lenore laughed. "There is, Dad. I found a new recipe and it has no eggs, butter, or milk."

"It sounds ghastly," her mother said with a horrified expression.

"It's a wonderful thing to be your father, Lenore," Mr. Wainwright said, beaming.

At the opposite end of the table, Lenore's mother scowled. "Leo, for a man of your standing, you talk pure foolishness sometimes."

His response was to laugh as Lenore circled behind him. She couldn't help it that she leaned over him and kissed the top of his head. This elicited more laughter.

"What on earth?" Lenore's mother shook her head.

"It's all right, Mother, Dad doesn't mind," Lenore said, breezing out of the dining room.

"But I do!" Eleanor Wainwright called out after her.

Lenore passed her younger sister, Laura, in the hallway. Laura Wainwright was a great beauty, golden-haired and with eyes the color of the palest cornflowers and a pair of dimples bracketing her smile, while Lenore had hair that was dull brown in color and eyes that were more gray than blue.

"Good morning, Lenore," Laura said in passing.

"Morning? Wake up, Laura, its lunchtime," Lenore teased. She did not stop on her way to the kitchen to hear her sister's response, if she'd had one.

Lenore returned to the dining room with the two slices of bread she'd saved for her mother and father. She set a bread plate next to each of them.

Before she'd left the kitchen, she'd made sure Hilda was sitting down with her own plate of lunch. She couldn't see why Hilda couldn't join them in the dining room, but both Hilda and Mrs. Wainwright would have been aghast at such a suggestion.

She no sooner sat down than the doorbell rang.

"I'll get it," she said, pushing her chair back and laying her napkin on the table next to her plate.

Her mother pursed her lips. "Who calls during luncheon?"

"Maybe they don't eat luncheon at this time," Lenore said. As she walked out of the dining room, she called back to the kitchen, "I'll get it, Hilda."

"Sometimes I wonder who the help is around here," her mother muttered.

Lenore opened the front door wide.

On the front step stood a clean-shaven man, thirtyish, with sandy brown hair and dark eyes. The bright afternoon sunlight picked up the gold strands in his short hair. An old scar sliced through his eyebrow and ran down the side of his face, but it did not detract from his handsomeness. In fact, Lenore thought it added to it. He removed his fedora as soon as Lenore appeared. His overall look was rugged, though his clothes were pressed and clean.

"Good day," he said. "I'm here to see Mayor Wainwright."

He was attractive, that was for certain, and Lenore couldn't help but wonder what kind of business he had with her father. People called at the house all the time, mostly politicians or people seeking help: widows needing food for their children, men looking for jobs, anything. Her father did his best to accommodate them all. But this man looked neither like a politician nor someone who was even hungry.

"May I ask who's calling?"

"John Hadley."

"One moment, please." She left the door half open, feeling it would be rude to close it on him.

Back in the dining room, she told her father, "Dad, a John Hadley is here to see you."

"Tell him to come back—" her mother started.

"No, no, Lenore, bring him in. I've been waiting for him," Leo Wainwright said, standing up. To his wife, he said, "Set another place at the table for him."

Mrs. Wainwright stood and headed off to the kitchen to tell Hilda.

Lenore returned to their visitor, doing as her father had asked. "Please do come in, Mr. Hadley, and join us for lunch."

Following her in, hat in hand, he said, "I couldn't impose, Mrs. . . ."

Lenore reddened, stopped, turned, and said, "It's Miss. Lenore Wainwright." It was an honest mistake. At twenty-five, she supposed she should be married by now. Much to her mother's dismay, she wasn't. But she wasn't going to marry just anyone for the sake of getting married, also to her mother's dismay.

He nodded. "Miss Wainwright."

"And you're not imposing. I'm afraid Dad will insist, and he's used to getting his way."

"All right then," John Hadley said with a laugh.

Lenore decided she liked this man. There was something solid about him. Like you could rely on him every which way and on Sundays, too. Lenore figured he was about ten years older than she, although there was an air of gravity about him that made him seem older, as if he had a lot of life experience behind him.

As soon as they entered the dining room, the mood improved. Laura sat up straighter and smiled, and even Mrs. Wainwright stood and extended her hand, then offered him the seat next to her, between her and Laura.

"John Hadley, it's good of you to come all this way," Mayor Wainwright said, shaking his hand.

"I'm sorry to bother you at home, sir, on a Sunday of all things."

"Nonsense. I'm relieved to see you. With our former chief of police dying so suddenly, our officers were left without leadership."

"My condolences," Mr. Hadley said quietly.

So this was the new chief of police, Lenore thought. He almost seemed too young. But again, there was an air of sober maturity about him. Their previous chief of police had fallen ill with something rare; Lenore couldn't remember the name of it. But he'd been dead within three weeks, and the town's police force was made up of only a few men, all too young to assume the position of authority. Unfortunately, those few in Lavender Bay who were up to no good knew of it and took advantage of it.

"You can start right away?" Mr. Wainwright asked.

"Of course."

With a nod toward the scar on the man's face, Mr. Wainwright said, "The Great War?"

"The Meuse-Argonne Offensive."

Leo Wainwright cleared his throat. "My younger brother was killed at the Somme."

"Again, condolences," John Hadley said quietly.

"Hopefully, we'll never go through anything like that again," Leo said.

"Agreed."

Sensing the gloom and despair that threatened to follow, Mrs. Wainwright said, "Come on and sit down. Eat something. Tell us a bit about yourself, Mr. Hadley."

Lenore's mother didn't like unpleasantness of any kind. She was all about putting on a brave face and being bright and cheery. Lenore had only been eight or nine when Uncle Tommy had been killed, and her father had retreated to his study for months. It had taken a long time for the gloom to lift. At the time, her mother had countered her husband's sadness with a forced cheeriness.

Hilda had set another place setting, and John Hadley took the chair between Laura and Mrs. Wainwright, directly across from Lenore.

As soon as everyone was situated, Mrs. Wainwright stood and filled his plate with Hoover stew, apologizing that like everyone else, they were tightening their belts because of the economic crisis the country currently faced. Lenore passed him the small plate of bread-and-butter pickles.

He looked across the table, made eye contact with Lenore, and smiled.

Her heart rate picked up a bit. *Don't, Lenore,* warned a voice inside her head. *Don't go getting notions. It never ends well for you.*

Despite the initial talk of the war, lunch turned into a pleasant affair. Mr. Hadley was both well-educated and well-traveled. And to Mrs. Wainwright, this made him in desperate need of a wife. He hailed from Illinois, and currently worked for the Chicago police department.

He'd never spent time on the east side of the country, except when he'd taken a troop train to the East Coast for transport to Europe during the war.

"Mr. Hadley, what made you decide to come here, to Lavender Bay?" Mrs. Wainwright asked, refilling his water glass from the crystal pitcher.

"I grew up in Chicago, near Lake Michigan, and I thought Lavender Bay sounded like a nice place to live and work."

"Truer words were never spoken," Mr. Wainwright said wholeheartedly.

Mrs. Wainwright turned to her eldest daughter. "Lenore, will you ask Hilda to bring in the chocolate cake and the coffee?"

Lenore pushed back her chair and stood. As she did, John Hadley pushed back his chair and stood as well.

Lenore smiled, appreciative of the gesture. "Don't get up, Mr. Hadley. Or you'll be up and down like a jack-in-the-box all during lunch."

He let out a short bark of laughter in response.

Warmed by his reaction, Lenore went off to the kitchen for the coffee and dessert. Hilda stood at the sink, washing her own lunch dishes and setting them on the drainboard to dry. On the stove, the blue enamel coffeepot began to bubble and hiss, filling the air with the aroma of freshly brewed coffee.

"Oh good, you've put the coffee on," Lenore said. She pulled down china teacups, saucers, and matching dessert plates from one of the cabinets.

"Who's the company?" Hilda asked.

"A Mr. John Hadley. The new chief of police," Lenore answered.

"It's about time, too. Some miscreant broke the window of the hardware store last night."

"Oh no, they didn't," Lenore said.

"They did. Broken glass all over the place," Hilda said.

Lenore cut six slices of cake, laying them out on plates and setting them on a tray, leaving one plate at the table for Hilda.

"Is that coffee ready?" Lenore asked.

"Almost."

"I'll carry the tray in, if you bring in the coffee." Hilda nodded.

As Lenore carried in the tray with the sliced cake, she noticed John Hadley saying something to Laura, sitting next to him. In response, her sister giggled and looked up at him from beneath her dark velvet lashes.

*You little minx*, Lenore thought. Didn't she have enough suitors? They practically lined up around the block every night to call on her. It was a bonus that she was the mayor's daughter.

"Couldn't Hilda bring the tray in, Lenore? You're not a kitchen maid," her mother grumbled.

"It's no bother, really, I was there. Hilda will bring in the coffee," she said.

Lenore set down the tray and her mother handed out the plates of cake, passing them left or right, apologizing to Mr. Hadley that they had no fresh cream. As Hilda entered with the coffee, now in the matching china coffeepot, Lenore eyed the table to make sure there was milk and sugar. The coffeepot was pretty to look at, but did not keep the coffee as hot as the enamel one on the stove. But her mother wouldn't hear of the old blue enamel pot sitting on her dining room table. The only solution was to pour the coffee fast and drink it quickly.

Lenore fixed her coffee, passing on the sugar. She and her mother had given it up in an effort to conserve it.

Laura put two teaspoonfuls into her cup, and Lenore gave her a sour look.

Once everyone had a slice of cake, they went quiet as they dug in.

Despite the lack of butter, milk, and eggs, the cake was delicious, and that pleased Lenore.

"My compliments to the baker," Mr. Hadley said, pushing his plate away. He hadn't left so much as a crumb behind.

Lenore felt the heat creep up to her cheeks. She knew without looking in the mirror they would be stained scarlet.

"That's Lenore," Mr. Wainwright said. "She's the resident baker."

Mr. Hadley bowed his head toward her. "Again, my compliments."

"Thank you, Mr. Hadley," Lenore managed to croak out. Smiling, she finished her own piece of cake. There was satisfaction in cooking and baking for people who appreciated it.

As the dinner wound down, Laura, still smiling at Mr. Hadley, disappeared from the room with Mrs. Wainwright as the mayor and Mr. Hadley settled down for another cup of coffee and a cigar. Anticipating this, Lenore removed the cigar box from the fireplace mantel behind her father, opened it, and offered one to Mr. Hadley. He took one and looked up at Lenore and smiled.

"Thank you."

She handed one to her father and set the box down next to him. She began to quickly clear the dishes from the table as it was Sunday and they usually spent the afternoon playing cards. In the past, local politicians would gather in their parlor every Sunday from late afternoon to late evening, trying to solve the problems of Lavender Bay. But the dual effects of Prohibition and the Depression had ended that. And as one business closed after another in Lavender Bay, the meetings soon turned grim.

As she and Hilda cleared the last of the dishes, her father and Mr. Hadley finished their cigars. She helped Hilda with the washup and they left the dishes to dry. She returned to the front parlor and pulled the card table with its green felt top out from behind the sofa, setting it up in the center of the room. The window faced west, and it was nice to see the colors of the sky when the sun set. She retrieved a deck of cards and laid them on the table. From the closet beneath the stairs, she pulled out the matching wooden chairs that went with the table.

John stood in the hallway. "I best be going."

His gaze lingered a moment on Lenore, and she said hurriedly, "Why don't you join us for cards?"

He hesitated and she added, "I'm sorry, maybe you have other plans."

"No, I didn't want to impose on your hospitality any more than I already have."

"Not at all." She nodded toward the parlor. "Go on in and take a seat."

Lenore joined Hilda in the kitchen, where another pot of coffee was being brewed. Her thoughts were focused on John Hadley.

As if reading her mind, Hilda said, "He's kind of young to be the chief of police. He still looks wet behind the ears."

"He served in the war," Lenore informed her.

"Ah well, that would make anyone old before their time," Hilda said, and no more was said about John

Hadley's suitability for the job he was about to undertake.

# Chapter Thirteen

As Lenore carried the coffeepot into the parlor, she was disappointed to see that Laura had secured a seat right next to John. The doorbell rang, and she set the pot down on the sideboard when it became apparent that her sister had no intention of answering it.

Alistair Young stood on their porch. Although a year older than Lenore, he'd been a childhood friend. If she was honest with herself, she'd say she was disappointed in his arrival, as it would distract her from John.

There was nothing to be said against Alistair. He was a clever, articulate man, if a little soft-spoken. But Lenore felt nothing more than friendship toward him. When she looked at him, the passion meter didn't budge at all.

It was proving to be a different story with John Hadley. She'd only just met him, and he made her feel jittery, like a stammering schoolgirl, but he also made her feel quite feminine. And that was a pleasant sensation.

"Hello, Lenore," Alistair said quietly.

"Hello, Alistair, are you well?" Lenore asked politely.

"I am, thank you," he said. Although Alistair looked meek, he was anything but. His nature was very principled.

"Won't you come in? We're about to sit down to a game of cards."

Alistair was tall, lean, and angular, with a prominent Adam's apple. Even his elbows looked sharp and pointy. There was something about his appearance that suggested he should be wearing glasses, as he always looked as if he'd left them somewhere. But it was well known that he had vision like a hawk. He was a teacher of English over at McKinley High School, formerly John Adams High School, but the name had been changed to honor the assassinated president.

He stepped into the parlor but hesitated when he spotted John Hadley seated at the card table with Laura.

"Come in, Alistair, don't be shy," Lenore's mother cooed from her place on the sofa. Mr. Wainwright sat next to her, leafing through the newspaper. In the corner behind them, the radio was on low volume.

On several occasions, Mrs. Wainwright had suggested that the schoolteacher would make a fine husband for Lenore. To which Mr. Wainwright would always scowl and say, "No, he's not the right man for our Lenore."

The four of them sat at the card table, and Lenore introduced Alistair to John. She picked up the deck of cards. "We have a foursome if we want to play pinochle."

Laura scrunched up her nose in disgust. "Not pinochle. I hate trying to remember which card has been played. How about hearts?"

"That's fine," Lenore said evenly. It made no matter to her, and it saved her from having to get up and get the pinochle deck out of the sideboard.

Although Laura had secured the seat next to John, Lenore had taken the seat directly across from him, which allowed her to study his features. And what fine features they were! The tanned, broad forehead. Those eyes! They were eagle sharp and looked as if they didn't miss anything. The aquiline nose, which gave him an almost aristocratic look. She wondered if she was being foolish with thoughts like these.

"What are your thoughts on Prohibition, John?" Alistair asked as Lenore shuffled the cards.

John appeared thoughtful before saying, "I'm sworn to uphold the law no matter my opinion."

"Hear, hear," Leo Wainwright said behind them, lowering the newspaper.

Mrs. Wainwright added, "Spoken like a true diplomat!"

John laughed, and as Lenore passed cards around the table, she looked up and caught him staring at her. His eyes searched her face and, blushing, she looked away.

"I have a feeling that you might win this game, John," Laura said, leaning toward him and rewarding him with a dimpled smile. He gave her a small smile and returned his attention to the cards in his hand.

Lenore tried not to roll her eyes. "Laura, you're first."

Laura took her turn, then devoted her attention to John.

They played several rounds, and Lenore was tied with John for the lowest score. Alistair was hot on their heels, and Laura was a distant fourth.

"What do we think of the presidential election next year? Do we think Hoover has a chance of getting re-elected?" Alistair asked as John dealt another hand. That was one thing Lenore did like about her friend: he was intelligent and interested in talking about current affairs.

Laura pouted. "We're not going to talk about politics, are we? Gosh, that's no fun."

Behind them, her father piped in. "Pay attention, Laura, you might learn something."

With a bored voice, she said, "Oh, Daddy."

John readjusted the cards in his hand. "It remains to be seen. If things don't improve economically, I'd say he'd have a tough time."

"Who would challenge him? Al Smith?" Lenore asked. The former governor of New York had run unsuccessfully against Hoover back in '28.

John shrugged as Alistair took his turn. "There's rumors going around that Roosevelt might seek the nomination," he said, referring to the current governor.

"Would the country elect a man in a wheelchair?" Mrs. Wainwright asked.

"He's still able to think," Lenore said. "And as long as he's intelligent enough, why shouldn't he run?"

"Whoever challenges Hoover will have to come up with some kind of economic plan to pull the country out of the Depression," said Alistair.

"Correct," John said.

"If that includes programs for helping the unemployed, what of that?" Alistair asked. Lenore knew better than anyone that her friend was all about helping people out, but he also loved playing devil's advocate.

"Just because the administration helps people out doesn't mean we're turning into a socialist state," John said. "This is the worst economic crisis our country has ever had, and people might need a hand up to get back on their feet. There's been a lot of suffering." He went quiet as he studied his cards.

Alistair nodded and Lenore looked at John, feeling a sudden upswell of affection for him. In addition to being good looking, he was kind, too. It was a heady combination.

"Do let's change the subject," Laura whined. "Did anyone see Chester Gavin's new automobile? It's navy blue!"

"It must be nice to be able to afford a brand-new automobile when there are so many people going hungry," Alistair said.

"It's not Chester's fault," Laura said. "It's not his responsibility to feed everyone."

"Of course not," Lenore said to placate her. Laura would begin to pout if she thought she was being challenged, and then the game would be ruined.

Laura laid down her cards on the table. "I don't feel like playing after all. John, would you care to go for a walk with me?"

"Actually, I should get going myself. I've got some things to do," he said.

"On a Sunday?" Laura asked in disbelief.

"Laura," her mother scolded. "It's none of your business what matters Mr. Hadley needs to attend to."

Losing two of the players brought a premature end to the card game, and everyone stood up at once. As Lenore watched John prepare to take his leave, her mother said, "Alistair, would you care for tea or coffee?"

"No thank you, Mrs. Wainwright. I must get going myself. Papers to correct and all that."

From the front porch, Lenore and Laura bid the two men goodbye and watched as they walked off together in earnest conversation. Lenore had been satisfied that although John had been polite to Laura, he didn't seem enamored of her like other men.

Lenore left Laura standing on the porch and went inside to remove the coffee cups from the parlor. As she entered the kitchen, she found Hilda in her chair by the stove, darning a pair of socks.

"That Mr. John Hadley appears to be a fine specimen," Hilda said.

"I suppose if one were looking at him under the microscope," Lenore teased. No matter what, she would not be baited into giving her opinion on the new law enforcement official. Those thoughts she wanted to keep to herself. They were too delicious to share.

Hilda rolled her eyes. "Can you be serious? You need to be marriage minded. It's time you started looking for a husband."

Why did marriage have to be the end goal in a woman's life? If it happened, it happened, and if it didn't, that was fine, too. Because Lenore Wainwright was content with her lot in life. She was never going to set the world on fire, she'd just like to make a bit of difference in her own corner of it.

# Chapter Fourteen

## October 1931

There had been frost the second week in October followed by unusually warm weather. Currently, the windows in the house were thrown open to let in some fresh air. It wouldn't be long before storm windows would be put on until the spring. Lenore hated unopened windows. She'd been busy washing down woodwork in the front of the house, crawling along the baseboards on her hands and knees with a kerchief tied around her head to keep her hair clean.

Just outside the back door, two men who were down on their luck ate sandwiches of bread and butter and a little leftover Hoover stew. They sat on the top step, shoveling food into their mouths, silent, no conversation.

Not only did residents from town show up at the back door from time to time, but men riding the rails turned up with increasing regularity. The trains ran along the Great Lakes, carrying hobos in search of work and a meal wherever they could find it. Gibson's Grape Jelly factory was known to offer these men occasional day work doing odd jobs around the factory, providing them with some necessary dollars and a meal at the company's canteen. The ones that showed up at the Wainwrights' back door pocketed what little fruit was left from the orchard, grabbing an apple or a peach, if it wasn't too rotten, and taking it with them. Lenore couldn't blame them.

She stepped between them, holding the coffeepot.

"Would you like more coffee?" The scent of unwashed human lingered around them. They were both in need of a bath and a shave.

One of the men held up his tin mug, which was his own. "If you don't mind."

She recognized him. He was a resident of Lavender Bay. A single man, he'd been hired by the grape jelly factory in the summer of 1929, before the economic collapse. It was pitiful to see a young man reduced to such a sad state of affairs.

She topped off their mugs.

The other man looked at her and announced, "Lady, you've earned your bed in heaven."

She smiled. "I don't know about that. But eat your fill. I have a little bit of cake you can take with you."

They smiled and went back to finishing what was on their plates. She pulled the cake out of the larder and cut two thick slices, wrapping each in wax paper. The doorbell ringing interrupted her, and she set the two slices of cake aside.

She wiped her hands on her apron and headed to the front door. The doorbell rang a second time before she reached it.

No one was home but her. Hilda had walked up to town. Her father was at his office and wouldn't be home until midday, and her mother had taken Laura out dress shopping. Her younger sister had whined and moaned about how she hadn't had a new dress in more than a year, and her mother caved and said they'd see if they could get something marked down.

When she opened the door, she was surprised to see John Hadley standing there. Of all people, she least expected him, especially late in the morning on a weekday. Since he'd arrived in Lavender Bay, he joined them for Sunday dinner on a regular basis. The previous weekend, he'd had two servings of her tomato soup cake.

He must have come to his senses and realized, like so many other men, that Laura was the one for him. The previous evening, Lenore couldn't help but overhear Laura on the front porch with her newest suitor, the fella already declaring his undying love and proclaiming that he couldn't live without her. At the time, Lenore had rolled her eyes, wondering if this was the sort of palaver couples talked about. Maybe she wasn't missing out on anything at all. Maybe she was better off alone.

"Mr. Hadley, this is a pleasant surprise," she said. Though she wished she'd had a chance to remove her apron and headscarf, and brush her hair and splash cool water on her face. She must look a wreck.

"Unexpected, I expect," he said.

"Do come in," she said, opening the door wide.

He followed her in.

"I'm sorry, I was in the middle of something," she said over her shoulder as she led him back to the kitchen.

"I'm sorry if this is a bad time," he said.

"Not at all, come on back. I'm the only one home right now," she said. In the kitchen, she pulled out a chair for him and he sat in it, not stating his business.

"Would you care for some coffee?" she asked. Sensing his hesitation, she added, "It's a fresh pot."

"I'd love some."

She took down two cups, poured the coffee, and put the mugs on the table. She put the creamer and sugar within his reach. Once she'd laid spoons on the table, she said, "Excuse me for one moment." She picked up the slices of wrapped cake and headed out the back door, handing them to the two men, who stood waiting at the bottom of the steps.

They waved goodbye, said their thanks, and she wished them well.

When she returned, the wooden screen door slamming behind her, John said, "Who do you have out back? Is that where you keep your suitors?"

*As if.* "No, there were two men who were looking for a meal." This was a regular occurrence. People were hungry. It was the times.

His expression darkened. "Lenore, please be careful."

These men that traveled along the railroads were drifters and for the most part, Lenore was always careful. There were usually other people around. Most of the men were only looking for a meal. There had been one incident, last fall, when a man had entered the kitchen and she'd caught him going through Hilda's purse. She'd chased him out, brandishing a rolling pin.

But who did John Hadley think he was, coming into her kitchen and telling her to be careful? She bristled a bit, lifting her chin and her shoulders, and he chuckled.

"I take it you're not used to someone telling you what to do, Lenore," he said, taking a sip of coffee.

There it was again. Her name rolling off his tongue like he'd been saying it all his life. She tried to ignore the pleasant prickly sensation that rolled down her back, but it was practically impossible.

Unsure of quite what to do or say, she joined him at the table with her coffee the way she liked it: black. She liked to save the sugar and milk for baking, that way there was more to go around.

The silence stretched out between them. Why was he here? He knew her father would be at his office during the weekday. Had she missed something? She jumped up and said, "Would you like some cake? I've got a little bit left."

He stood as well. "No, thank you."

Why did she feel this was a surprise test she had not prepared for? He looked ever so handsome, and relaxed in a maddening way as if drinking coffee in the kitchen with her was the most natural thing in the world.

Confused and exasperated, she tucked a stray strand of hair out of sight beneath her scarf, wishing he hadn't stopped by on heavy-cleaning day. And wishing she hadn't decided upon rising that the woodwork in the house needed a good scrub.

Taking a step back, she said, "I'm sorry, Mr. Hadley—" She was pretty sure she was imagining the pulsating heat she felt passing between them.

"Please, call me John." His gaze was unnerving.

"Look, John," she started, closing her eyes and scratching her forehead with her forefinger and middle finger. "Laura isn't here, and I don't know what time she will be home."

He took a step toward her. "I didn't come to see Laura."

"Dad won't be home until midday for his lunch. Did you want to wait, or . . . ?" Her voice trailed off. That was a ridiculous suggestion as her father wouldn't be home for another two hours. Surely, John Hadley had better things to do than sit with her in the kitchen all day. Wasn't he supposed to be keeping Lavender Bay safe?

She backed up until she hit the edge of the counter.

John's eyes were alight with mischief and merriment, and she didn't move from her position. She couldn't. Something was happening here, but she was afraid to name it. She hoped she wasn't the butt of some joke.

"I need to ask you a question," he said, coming close enough that she could have reached out and touched him, close enough for her to see the lines beginning to form at the corners of his eyes and the fine details of the scar that marked him as having fought in the Great War.

She laughed nervously. "It sounds serious."

"Nothing to worry about, I assure you."

She bit her bottom lip. John's gaze traveled to her lips, lost focus for a moment, and then he lifted his gaze until their eyes met.

"Lenore," he started again. "Are you seeing Alistair Young?"

The question was not one she'd expected, and she burst out laughing. She might even have snorted. "What?"

"I was under the impression that you and Alistair were seeing each other."

"No," she clarified. "Alistair and I have known each other since we were children. We're very good friends." To further drive the point home, she added, "That's all. Nothing more."

"I'm relieved to hear that."

"You are?"

He smiled and the warmth reached his eyes. They were eyes she could get lost in. "Are you seeing anyone?"

She shook her head. "No, I'm unencumbered."

He laughed. "Unencumbered. I like that."

She held her breath, waiting.

But he glanced at his watch, breaking the spell, and frowned. "I have to get back to work."

Flustered, she said, "Of course."

He closed his eyes and took a breath. Then he cleared his throat, and Lenore realized he was nervous. That endeared him to her all the more.

"I was wondering," he said, "if an unencumbered Lenore would like to go for a walk or a picnic with an unencumbered me."

Her response was a generous smile, and she said, "Yes. I would like that very much."

His expression was beautiful for how pleased he looked.

Time was suspended for the briefest of moments, all that hope and good feeling lingering between them as fine as gossamer strands. Lenore could only look at him in wonder. Her heart beat so fast she could hear it in her ears.

The spell was broken by the back door opening and Hilda stepping inside, her handbag on one arm and a brown paper bag of groceries in the other.

"Oh good, you found her," Hilda said, setting everything down on the table.

Lenore looked to Hilda and back to John, and then her gaze swung back to Hilda.

"What?"

"I ran into Mr. Hadley on my way to town earlier. I told him you were all alone in the house."

"You did?" Lenore said, trying to catch up.

Hilda said to John, "Our Lenore is very intelligent, of that there is no doubt. But sometimes, she can't see the obvious right in front of her. It needs to be spelled out."

"Thanks for the advice," John said with a laugh.

Hilda's gaze swung between the two of them and she announced, "I think I'll sweep off the back porch."

When she was gone, John said, "As much as I hate to leave, I really must go."

Lenore nodded, understanding.

He reached for her hand and put his over hers, and she stared at it for a moment. His hand was large and held a reassuring warmth. It dwarfed hers and made her feel oddly feminine. She liked the way her hand felt in his.

"You're trembling," he said quietly.

She looked up at him quickly. "Am I?"

"I'll see you soon, Lenore."

He left by the back door and exchanged some words with Hilda that were indiscernible to Lenore, who walked around the kitchen in a daze. She heard Hilda laugh and wondered briefly what was so funny. It had been a strange morning with a sudden, dramatic change in events. She could hardly believe it.

Hilda stepped back into the kitchen with a smile on her face.

"So you were behind this?" Lenore said. She'd have preferred it if John had come here of his own free accord. But honestly, he didn't strike her as a man who did anything he didn't want to. After all, he hadn't ended up with Laura.

Hilda rolled her eyes and shook her head. "Stop trying to talk yourself out of this," she said.

"I'm not."

"You are! Now stop it. The way you two look at each other. And no progress. It was too painful."

"I don't know what you mean."

"Don't play dumb with me, Lenore."

Lenore opened her mouth to protest, but then thought better of it and closed it.

Hilda continued. "Those times he's been here for Sunday lunch, he can't take his eyes off of you. But he's just as bad as you are. How can someone so smart be so thick?" she asked, looking heavenward. "When I saw him this morning, I said hello, enquired after his health, and then told him that you were home and would be pleased if he stopped by to call on you."

"You didn't say that!"

"Of course I did. How else was I to get the two of you together?"

Lenore was about to protest, thinking the whole affair was unseemly, when Hilda cut her off. "As soon as I said it, he took off and left me standing there on the sidewalk."

Lenore smiled to herself.

Hilda laughed and began to go about the preparation of lunch. "I don't want you to spend the rest of your life in the kitchen with me doing menial work."

"It may be menial work, but I love doing it. I love taking care of people," Lenore said.

"I know that, Lenore. But you need a nice man, a home of your own, and lots of children. It's what you were born for."

In good humor, Lenore narrowed her eyes at the older woman. "And you think John Hadley is the right man for me?" she challenged.

Hilda looked at her. "John Hadley is the perfect man for you. Now, I don't want to talk about this anymore. My work here is done."

And that ended that discussion.

# Chapter Fifteen

## May 1932

Their wedding took place the following spring in the small white clapboard church in Lavender Bay. The sun shone bright in a cloudless blue sky.

After much debate with her mother, Lenore had chosen a simple dress of navy blue with a matching hat. Mrs. Wainwright had been disappointed. She would have loved for her daughter to enjoy a fabulous gown and headpiece and lengthy veil that would have the town talking, and perhaps a honeymoon trip to New York City, but she was smart enough to know that such extravagance would be in poor taste in the current economic climate, with so many people out of work.

That her daughter was so readily agreeable to a sensible dress had her thinking Lenore was spending too much time in the kitchen, and perhaps Hilda was not the best influence. Everyone had their place in society, and it couldn't be helped that the Wainwrights were at the top of the ladder. Lenore had said it was a fine dress and she'd be able to wear it again. This had left Mrs. Wainwright speechless. She couldn't imagine waltzing around the streets of Lavender Bay in her own ivory gown. That was safely packed away in a trunk in the attic. Upon seeing her mother's disappointment, Lenore had caved and said her mother could plan the menu and the reception, but only on one condition: it had to be at their house. Mrs. Wainwright decided she could live with that.

And now the Wainwrights and their guests filled the house on Bluebell Lane. Mrs. Wainwright had done the best she could, given the circumstances. There were no garlands of flowers adorning the doorways or ornate floral arrangements displayed in large crystal vases on ionic column pedestals, but there were vases full of daffodils, tulips, and hyacinths that had been picked from the garden.

Lenore had insisted that Hilda be there as a guest and not a servant, and had actually stomped her foot over it when her mother had started to protest. Mrs. Wainwright had to hire outside help for the day. Hilda stood in the front room, congratulating the newlywed couple. It was odd to see her all decked out in a plum dress and matching coat and hat.

John had worn a navy suit and tie and looked well. There was no doubt they made a handsome couple. Mrs. Wainwright wished they would have coordinated their colors and their outfits better beforehand. They both looked as if they were going off to the bank for a workday.

She liked John Hadley; she only wished he had a better profession. Like a businessman of some sort. In law enforcement, she could only imagine that he had to deal with a lot of unsavory sorts, and she hoped this wouldn't affect Lenore.

There was no luxurious buffet, no caviar or champagne, but she'd managed to put down a proper feast despite sugar and coffee being rationed. All the best linen had been pressed and the table covered. Both leaves had to be put in, and Hilda had polished the silver candelabra to an exquisite shine the other day. It stood in the center of the table, the thin white tapers lit, the flames dancing. And somehow, Hilda had managed to bake a beautiful wedding cake with real buttercream frosting.

Despite all the cutbacks, Mrs. Wainwright still held out hope for Laura. When Mr. Wainwright had questioned the expense of hiring waiters and cooks and even a chimney sweep, she'd shrugged and said simply that she was providing a lot of work for people, even if it was only for one day. He'd made no complaint after that.

People lined up around the dining room table, picking up her best silverware that was only brought out at Christmas and was now wrapped in a linen napkin, and her good china, a wedding gift from a favorite aunt. Instead of displaying the wedding gifts in the front parlor as had been done when she'd gotten married, they'd stored it all discreetly in a spare room upstairs. Lenore had liked the crystal and the china, but she'd been most enthusiastic about the Hotpoint Toaster Deluxe. Mrs. Wainwright had thought it was horrible looking. Someone else had given her a vacuum cleaner and Lenore had been excited about that, too, and Mrs. Wainwright wondered how Lenore could be a daughter of hers to be getting excited over appliances. The vacuum cleaner was already over at John's house, and thank God for small favors, Mrs. Wainwright thought more than once. She couldn't imagine having a monstrosity like that in her home. Her own display of gifts for her wedding back in 1905 had been overflowing with fine china, crystal, linens, and silverware. She still had every piece. Not an appliance in sight. What was the world coming to, she wondered more than once.

Mrs. Wainwright enjoyed the happy buzz that filled the place. Hopefully, children would soon follow. She liked the thought of being a grandmother. She knew that Mr. Wainwright was looking forward to that part, too, and he had only recently mentioned to her in private that he was thinking of not seeking re-election. She'd been disappointed, of course; she relished her role as first lady of Lavender Bay, but she'd noticed that her husband was more and more tired looking of late. The Depression was taking its toll, even on a small town like Lavender Bay. There was no escaping it. But she shoved those thoughts from her mind, determined to enjoy her daughter's happy day.

# CHAPTER SIXTEEN

Lenore couldn't stop staring at the gold band that now adorned her ring finger. She was a married woman, and to John Hadley! Their wedding day had been long, with the ceremony at ten in the morning and the reception in the afternoon at her parents' house. By the time the sun set, Lenore's feet were killing her. She couldn't wait to take off her shoes. What she wanted to do more than anything was to go to her new home with John and be alone with him. But guests, mostly cronies of her father, still lingered even though it was close to ten o'clock at night. They'd settled in the parlor and more coffee and cigars came out. The wives were in the dining room, seated in the chairs along the walls as tea and cakes and cookies were brought out from the kitchen. Lenore began to wilt. She didn't think she could do another round.

"Are you all right?" John said beside her.

"I am. It's been a marvelous day, but I'm ready to go," she said.

"Me too. I'd like to be alone with you," he whispered.

She blushed at that, feeling the welcome heat that rose up within her. She wanted to be alone with him, too.

Her mother approached and spoke to them quietly. "It's fine if you want to leave."

"Are you sure, Mother? We don't want to be rude," Lenore said.

"No, don't worry about that," her mother said, looking over her shoulder. "They've gotten comfortable and will probably be here all night."

Lenore hesitated.

Mrs. Wainwright smiled and patted her arm. "Come on, now, and say your goodbyes." She guided the new couple from room to room to bid their farewells, cutting short any lengthy goodbyes, and finally saw them to the front door. She handed Lenore a package wrapped in a linen napkin.

"It's two pieces of wedding cake. It'll be nice with a cup of tea later." She hugged them both and kissed her daughter on the cheek. "I'm very happy for you, Lenore."

"Thank you, Mother."

"Good night, Mrs. Wainwright, and thank you for a wonderful day," John said.

After much debate, Lenore and John had decided to hold off on purchasing a home, deciding that the small one-bedroom house he'd been renting on Lincoln Street would do for now. In the run-up to the wedding, Lenore had been adding her own touches to the place, putting her own stamp on things. There was a vase of flowers on a table in the parlor and a floral linen tablecloth covering the small table in the kitchen. When they returned from their honeymoon, Lenore would drive John's car over to her parents' house to collect all their wedding gifts. There was no money to take an extended trip, but they were leaving in the morning to spend one night in Buffalo and a second night in Niagara Falls before returning to Lavender Bay. She was excited about spending all this time alone with John.

When they reached the small front porch, John unlocked the door. As a policeman, he was always careful about locking things: his house, the car, the little shed in the backyard. When she told him they never locked their doors at home, he'd been appalled.

Without thinking, she went to step inside, but John held her back with one arm. "Mrs. Hadley, I intend to carry you over that threshold." Before she could say anything, he scooped her up and carried her through the front door, setting her down inside the small parlor.

Laughing, she kicked off her shoes and set them neatly against the wall. She stretched her toes, relieved to have those shoes off. They looked pretty but were very uncomfortable.

John turned on the lamp that hung over the kitchen table. It was now *their* kitchen table.

The kitchen was small, with a sink and a Hoosier cabinet. The table where they'd eat their meals was only big enough for two chairs, and that was fine with Lenore. The walls were a mint green, and the cast-iron radiator had been painted to match. The linoleum was old and pitted and scarred in places, but Lenore didn't care. It was their first home, and she adored it.

The glow from the lamp lit up her husband's features. As long as they lived, she would never get tired of referring to him as her husband. Her husband. Two simple words that brought so much joy. She smiled.

"Happy?" he asked.

She nodded. "Very."

"You're very beautiful, Lenore," he said quietly.

She blushed, unused to that specific compliment.

In two strides, he was at her side, wrapping an arm around her, lowering his face to hers. She slid her arm around his waist, eager to feel his touch. When he kissed her, all sorts of little sparks lit up her body. She pulled away to lay her cheek against his, loving the sandpapery feel of his stubble against her smooth skin.

She was anxious about their wedding night, and she wasn't. She was in possession of general knowledge but not specifics. It certainly wasn't the type of conversation you could have with anyone. Her mother would faint if she'd brought it up. Hilda would declare it not fit for consumption. She hadn't even talked about it with

John. She'd been raised too much of a lady to open that topic of discussion.

He started kissing her again. The pressure of his kisses increased, warm, needy, insistent. And Lenore's body responded in kind. He held her in his embrace, his big strong arms wrapped around her, pulling her close. Her curves fit perfectly against the hard, strong planes of his body. She listened to her body, knowing it needed something more. Taking him by the hand, she started to lead him toward the bedroom.

But John laughed and pulled her back to him. "Someone is eager."

Heat stained her cheeks, and she lowered her head, embarrassed. He must think she was a brazen hussy.

He reached out and lifted her chin with his finger, his eyes locking on hers. All humor was gone. He was all seriousness.

"We're not doing that here, Lenore. We're not going to be embarrassed or ashamed about anything that happens between us in the bedroom. Right?" Then with a wink, he added, "Or even what happens outside of the bedroom."

With a relieved smile, she nodded, her humiliation fading away.

He placed his hands on either side of her face and said gently, "Do you believe me when I tell you that our marriage bed will be wonderful and beautiful"—he grinned—"and a lot of fun?"

"Yes." She knew he would never lie about any of those things. Or about anything, for that matter.

He kissed her again quickly and pulled away, smiling. He slid his hand into hers. "Now, Mrs. Hadley, do with me what you will. Direct my path!"

She giggled and pulled him with her to the bedroom, which was located off the kitchen. John turned on the small lamp on the dresser, and it cast a pale golden light over the room. He removed his suitcoat and laid it over a chair in the corner. As he headed toward Lenore, smiling, he began to loosen his tie.

Lenore's breath hitched in her throat as he began to peel his clothes off. Slowly, she slipped her dress over her head.

Later, they lay side by side in the bed, and she realized she must have dozed off, because the pearly gray light of dawn filtered through the curtains.

"I'm hungry," she announced.

Laughter erupted from John, who rolled over and caressed her bare shoulder. He looked behind him at the bedside clock, which ticked along nicely. "It's only four in the morning."

"Did you want breakfast then?" she asked. Her stomach rumbled.

She went to flip the bedsheet back, but he laid his hand on her arm. "Wait a minute, Lenore."

She looked at him, expectant.

"Are you . . . all right?" he asked. There was some hesitation in his voice.

She kissed the tip of her finger and traced it over the scar that ran along the side of his face. He'd been a tender and considerate lover. It had hurt, but he'd promised her it would be better the next time. And she believed him.

"Am I all right? I'm perfect. I'm wonderful," she said, lifting her head up to plant a quick kiss on his lips. "But most of all, John, I'm hungry."

He laughed again and kissed her shoulder.

"How about some tea and wedding cake?" she asked. She'd cook breakfast later.

"Sounds perfect."

She pulled on her robe, used the bathroom quickly to wash her face, and went into the kitchen to turn on the kettle. She set the table properly and by the time John emerged from the bedroom, pulling his suspenders up over his sleeveless T-shirt, she had laid out the two slices of cake on plates and was in the process of making tea for them both.

"I could get used to this every day," he said, looking over the table. He leaned in and kissed her on the cheek.

"And I could get used to that every day," she said.

The wedding cake tasted better than she could have imagined. It was a simple yellow cake with strawberry-preserve filling and a buttercream frosting. They washed it down with their tea, and when they were finished, she carried the dishes to the sink and turned the faucet on. But John leaned over and turned off the tap.

"Come on back to bed with me," he said. "We don't have to get up for another few hours."

She didn't have to be convinced. She left the dirty dishes in the sink and the teapot on the table, and joined her husband back in the bedroom.

Their honeymoon flew by. John had rented them a room at the Lenox Hotel in Buffalo. They walked around the city and took in the sights, like the brand-new art deco city hall. After dinner, they went to the Moonglow, a nightclub on Michigan Street, and Lenore thought she'd never danced so much in her life. There was even a photographer who snapped their picture in a booth, which John paid for at the end of the evening. It was framed in a pale green paper holder that read *The Moonglow, Michigan Avenue, Buffalo, New York*.

The following morning, they made their way to Niagara Falls. She hadn't been there since she was a young girl, and it was as impressive as it had been back then. Appropriately, the American side of the falls was called the Bridal Veil. It was lovely. But when it was time to go, she was happy to head back to Lavender Bay and start her life as Mrs. John Hadley.

# Chapter Seventeen

When they returned from their honeymoon, John went back to work, and Lenore settled happily into her role as a housewife. It felt as if she'd been training for this her whole life. She loved everything domestic life entailed: cooking, baking, mending, sewing, knitting, and crocheting.

They weren't home long from Niagara Falls when she took the car over to her parents' home to collect her wedding presents. Although space was limited in her current home, she still wanted her things about her as she started her married life.

It was a beautiful sunny day, and the trees that lined the white picket fence out front were full of bright green leaves. It was odd to be arriving at her childhood home as a visitor. She brought the Model T to a halt next to the curb, the car shuddering as it stopped. John had taught her to drive during their courtship and now that they were married, he walked to work on days when the weather was nice and left her the car, although she often liked to walk as well. The car was large, noisy, and cumbersome. But because she had a couple of crates and trunks to bring back to her house, she had no choice but to take the car.

She went around back, to the kitchen door. The front door was primarily used for guests or company, and old habits died hard.

The trees in the orchard were full of leaves and pretty soon, there'd be plenty of fruit for pies and canning. The small vegetable garden near the back of the house had recently been turned over, ready for seeds. The back porch was empty.

Through the screen door, she spotted Hilda making pastry, likely for a pot pie for lunch.

*I should be doing that*, Lenore thought, opening the door and stepping into the kitchen. The room smelled of brewed coffee with a hint of woodsmoke, familiar scents to Lenore that would always remind her of home. Her old apron still hung on a hook behind the door.

Hilda's apron was covered in flour, and there was a smudge of flour on her cheek. Her eyes widened in pleasure when she caught sight of Lenore.

"Lenore! You're a sight for sore eyes. How's married life?" Hilda asked, setting the ball of pastry down and wiping her hands on her apron.

Lenore hugged her friend. "I'm happy."

"I'm glad to hear that."

With a nod toward the pastry, she asked, "Do you want me to finish that for you?"

Hilda scowled. "Not on your life."

"I wish you could have come with me." More than anything, Lenore missed Hilda's company. But on John's salary, they could not afford any help at present. Besides, there'd be nothing for Hilda to do. Lenore often finished her household tasks by late morning and felt idle for the rest of the day.

Hilda returned to the pastry and Lenore pulled a high stool next to the worktable and sat on it, crossing her leg and helping herself to a carrot. Next to the pile of carrots was a platter of leftover chicken.

"What's new here?" she asked, crunching on the end of her carrot.

Hilda looked heavenward and shook her head. "Your sister is going to be the death of your poor mother and father."

Lenore frowned. "Why? What has she done now?"

"It isn't what she's done, it's who she's doing it with." Hilda sighed.

"What do you mean? I thought she'd finally set her sights on Hollis Seaton." Lenore liked Hollis. He'd been Laura's guest at her wedding. He was her sister's age, a college graduate with a promising future. Both of her parents had approved of him heartily. He was polite and charming, and Lenore had thought they were a good match. Besides, he seemed to know how to handle Laura.

"He's gone." Hilda laid the pastry into the bottom of a deep pie dish, folding it over the sides.

"What do you mean, he's gone?"

"She has a new beau," Hilda said. Lenore did not miss the disapproval in her voice.

"And?"

"She thinks the sun rises and sets on him."

"But you and Mother and Dad don't?"

Hilda shook her head. "But you didn't hear it from me." If he was as undesirable as Hilda seemed to be suggesting, Lenore's parents, or at least her father, would mention something to her.

"What's wrong with him?"

"He reminds me too much of my first husband." From time to time down through the years, Hilda had spoken of her two husbands. The first one, according to her, had been a downright charmer. *He charmed my socks, and other things, right off*, she had said. Within a year, she was left with a baby boy and a disappearing husband. She'd later heard that he'd been killed, and she had shed no tears, for it had left her free to marry her next-door neighbor, a man twenty-five years older than she, a good man who was a positive influence on her son. She'd said those ten years she spent married to him were the happiest years of her life.

"And Laura can't see this?"

"Not through those rose-colored glasses of hers. She can't see what the rest of us see," Hilda said. "She only sees his film-star looks."

Laura was gullible. She'd been cosseted and shielded her whole life. They had done her no favors.

Lenore sighed. "Well, if we're lucky, she'll soon lose interest and move on to the next suitor." It was what she'd done in the past. Her attention span was short, and her head was always turned by the newest, shiniest object.

"I hope you're right." There was doubt in Hilda's voice as she stirred carrots, peas, and chicken in a bowl and poured the mixture into the pan. She moved over to the stove, where she began to make the sauce for the pot pie using a little bit of cream, some flour, and some leftover chicken stock from a canning jar. She mixed it all up with a wooden spoon, set the flame on low, and added salt and pepper.

"Where's Mother?"

"In the dining room, I suspect," Hilda replied. "Your father is due for lunch at his usual time."

"All right."

"You're here for your things," Hilda said, tilting a bit to look at Lenore over her shoulder.

"I am."

Hilda smiled. "Will you be staying for lunch?"

"I will if it's not too much trouble," Lenore said. She didn't want to create extra work for Hilda.

"There's more than plenty. When your mother said you were stopping by to pick up your things, I made extra."

Grinning, Lenore said, "You've twisted my arm."

Mrs. Wainwright was in the dining room, laying the table for luncheon. Gone were the fine linen and china and crystal and silverware and back were the everyday tablecloth, cutlery, plates, and glasses. One of the windows was open a few inches, and there was the sound of birds just outside. There was no sign of Laura, and Lenore wondered if she was upstairs or out.

When she entered the dining room, she noticed the frown on her mother's face as she laid the table for five. When she called out her greeting, the frown disappeared to be replaced by a generous smile. "Lenore, there you are."

Lenore hugged her mother, and her mother kissed her on the cheek.

"I set a place for you. You can join us for lunch, can't you?"

"I'd love to," Lenore said.

"Good, we'll need you to run interference," her mother said, her expression souring. She finished laying the plates at each chair.

"Mother, what do you mean by that?" Lenore set the glass pitcher of water in the middle of the table.

"Laura has invited her beau for lunch," her mother explained, looking grim.

"And?"

Mrs. Wainwright's shoulders stiffened. "To put it quite frankly, your father and I do not approve of him."

"Whyever not?" She couldn't imagine her parents being so upset over someone. And although Hilda had forewarned her, she wanted to hear it from her mother herself.

"I'll say nothing. You tell me what you think when you meet him," Mrs. Wainwright said evasively. "I don't want to color your perception."

"All right."

"She had that lovely beau Hollis Seaton. He was a good and kind man with a wonderful future, and he treated Laura like a queen."

"Let me guess, she became bored with him," Lenore said, suddenly feeling tired of the continuing drama with her younger sister. For the first time, she was grateful she no longer lived in this house. As sad as that made her feel. Suddenly she regretted saying she'd stay for lunch, wishing for the peace that was to be found in the happy home that belonged to her and John.

"Lunch won't be ready for another hour," her mother informed her.

"No problem. I'll start loading up the boxes and trunks into the car."

She spent the next hour lugging boxes and trunks down the stairs with the help of Laura, who griped the entire time about why she had to do the heavy lifting. By the time lunch was ready, they had some of the crates loaded, leaving the rest on the front porch. There was only so much room in the car, and she'd have to make several trips.

After washing her hands, Lenore stepped back into the dining room. Her father arrived shortly after and couldn't hide his delight in seeing her.

"Well, well, this is a pleasant surprise! How's the newlywed?"

"I'm well, Dad," she replied, leaning in to kiss him on the cheek.

"That John Hadley is a fine man," he said.

"He is that indeed, Dad."

"And you're staying for lunch?" he asked.

"I am. Mother and Hilda twisted my arm."

"Good for them. Now I won't have to."

As they took their places around the dining room table, Laura entered, pulling her newest suitor behind her, who'd just arrived. Immediately, Lenore was mesmerized, and instantly understood Laura's attraction to him.

Tall and broad-shouldered, he had a mop of glorious, thick, wavy black hair with a beautiful shine, and a pair of intense blue eyes. There was a cleft in his chin, and his teeth were straight. If she didn't know any better, she'd say he was some film star from Hollywood who'd ended up by mistake in Lavender Bay.

He said his hellos to Mr. and Mrs. Wainwright, who were polite but remained aloof, causing Lenore to do a double-take. There was nothing her parents liked better than entertaining. All were welcome.

Laura introduced her suitor to Lenore, clinging to him as she did so as if he might get away. She looked up at him, her face full of adoration.

"Lenore, this is Horace Howard. Horace, this is my older sister, Mrs. Lenore Hadley," she said.

Horace took Lenore's hand and raised it to his lips to plant a kiss on it, his eyes glued to hers, which she found unnerving.

He took his seat between Laura and her mother, just like John had done when he arrived that first day. When they were all seated, Mrs. Wainwright looked pointedly at Lenore before returning her attention to her place setting.

Hilda appeared with the wonderful-smelling chicken pot pie, a towel in her hands to protect them from the heat of the dish. She stepped into the room and set the pie within reach of Mrs. Wainwright, giving a side-eye to Laura's beau.

"Thank you, Hilda," Mrs. Wainwright said.

"It smells delicious, Hilda," Mr. Wainwright remarked from the other end of the table.

Hilda left and returned with a platter of leftover chicken and a serving fork, and set them in the middle of the table.

"You're not from around here, are you, Mr. Howard?" Lenore asked. She would certainly have remembered someone like him walking around Lavender Bay.

"No, ma'am. I'm from a little town in Pennsylvania, outside of Erie. Called McHill." Lenore did not recognize it. "And please, call me Horace. When I hear 'Mr. Howard,' I'm always expecting to find my father right behind me." He sat straighter, his shoulders back and his chin up.

While he spoke, Laura went about filling his plate with slices of leftover chicken, while Horace sat there with his hands folded in front of him, his fingers steepled. Her mother glanced quickly at that and then continued to scoop portions of pot pie onto everyone's plates. Mr. Wainwright sighed and took the plate that was handed to him, steam rising off the flaky crust.

It was a little strange to see Laura make a fuss over one of her suitors. She'd never done that before. At the Wainwright table, everyone helped themselves, although occasionally, when the mayor came home from work and was especially stressed or tired, his wife would fuss over him and take his plate and fill it with the right amount of the things he liked.

What happened next was even stranger. Once Horace's plate was filled, Laura began to cut up his meat into bite-sized pieces, humming as she did this. Lenore raised an eyebrow but said nothing.

When Laura was finished, she set the plate down in front of Horace. He rewarded her with a smile as brilliant as a flash cube, leaned close to her, and said, "Thanks, doll."

Laura beamed.

Lenore could practically see her mother grinding her teeth. This wouldn't do at all. Could Laura not see how strange it was?

"What is it you do for a living, Horace?" Lenore ventured, trying to quell the image of her sister cutting a grown man's meat for him.

"Now that's an interesting question, Mrs. Hadley. I *live*, that's what I do," he said proudly. The early afternoon sun slanted in the front windows, illuminating Horace's face, giving him an almost celestial appearance.

She was sure her parents must be delighted with that answer. "We all live, Horace." Lenore took a forkful of pot pie and slid it into her mouth, moving it around as it was hot.

"Ah, but some people hardly live at all," he countered. He was talking in circles, which Lenore found annoying, but Laura seemed to hang on his every word and hardly even looked at her own plate of food.

"What is it you do to earn money?" Lenore ventured. Normally, her mother would be appalled at this topic of conversation, but there were no looks from her. Lenore suspected her parents might have been trying to get to the bottom of that as well, without success.

"I go wherever the wind takes me; work tends to find me."

"Are you working right now?"

He narrowed his eyes at her, not liking her questions. "Not at the moment, but I've got irons in the fire from Buffalo to Toronto," he said with a gleam in his eye.

"That sounds promising," she said. "Will you be leaving Lavender Bay soon?" She practically had her fingers crossed in her lap.

"That had been the plan"—Laura's smile disappeared immediately but Horace patted her arm—"but plans change all the time. And this little lady would like me to stay, I think."

"I would, I would," Laura squealed, her blond hair bouncing around her face. "Don't leave, Horace. We've been having a lot of fun."

Lenore looked from one to the other, wondering what constituted fun in their books, blanching at the thought that they might be having too much of it.

Lunch proceeded in this fashion, Horace holding court to the point where Lenore wondered if he just liked to hear the sound of his own voice. And with Laura hanging on every word. Her parents were unnaturally quiet, as if they were simply trying to get through the meal. If Horace Howard copped on that Mr. and Mrs. Wainwright weren't big fans of his, he didn't let on, or he didn't care. But the silences between the topics of conversation were growing lengthier and tense, and Lenore was almost sorry she'd stopped by to pick up her wedding gifts.

It got weirder with dessert. Laura took forkfuls of apple pie from the plate and fed them to Horace.

Lenore scowled. "Are you unable to feed yourself, Horace?"

He snorted. "Of course I'm able to feed myself, but I like it better when Laura feeds me, don't I, honey?"

"Uh-huh," Laura said with a smile.

"Did your mother feed your father?" Lenore asked, wondering what his home life had been like.

His expression darkened. "If she'd taken better care of my father, he might not have run off when I was ten."

There was no more conversation after that, and Laura and Horace said their goodbyes after they finished their tea. Horace was effusive in his praise of the meal, thanking both Mr. and Mrs. Wainwright before they left.

Lenore watched them through the front window with an equal sense of curiosity and concern. Laura hung on Horace's arm as he escorted her to a newer Ford Model A in dark blue. Laughter bubbled up from her sister and floated through the open window. Laura was practically giddy with happiness. She kept looking up at Horace as if she couldn't believe her luck.

"If he doesn't work, I can't understand how he affords the brand-new car and taking her out every day," Lenore said, thinking out loud.

"We have wondered that more than once," Mr. Wainwright said. "While most men are away from home during the day, working, I might add, Horace is here every day, squiring Laura all over town. We all know the economy is in the dustbin, but I don't think I've ever seen the man in the same outfit twice. And it's a good question: how does he afford the brand-new car?"

Mrs. Wainwright sat at the foot of the table in her chair with the embroidered pillow behind her back, shaking her head with dismay.

Lenore didn't know what to say to make her mother and father feel better. She was at a loss for words.

She attempted to cheer them up. "You know how she is. Soon, she'll lose interest and someone more interesting or more fun will show up, and Horace will be yesterday's news."

"That's what we keep hoping, but every day, he shows up, honking that horn to let everyone on the street know of his arrival." Lenore's father wore a pinched, unhappy expression.

She felt guilty for being away, for being in love, and not being here to help her parents out. She must make Laura see sense.

"We shouldn't have burdened you with this, Lenore. You're newly married, with a husband and a home, and you shouldn't be worrying about this." Mrs. Wainwright sipped from her teacup.

"Nonsense. I'm glad you told me," Lenore said. "I'm going to try to talk some sense into Laura, but I need to think it over first."

"Of course," her mother said.

"But will she listen?" her father asked, his voice rising slightly. "She's always been high-strung. I don't want to see her get into any kind of trouble over this man." His complexion had gone ashen. They all knew what he referred to. A young woman having a baby out of wedlock was a one-way ticket to ruin and destitution. It irritated Lenore to no end that any time there was such a scandal, it was the woman who had to pay the price and the man got off scot-free. The right to vote had been granted to women twelve years earlier, but there were still strides to be made.

She stood, anxious to get home and think about this dilemma with her sister and how to fix it. After several trips to her new home, she loaded the remainder of the boxes with the help of her mother.

Before she left, she hugged her mother goodbye and whispered in her ear, "Don't worry, Mother, it'll be all right."

"I hope so. Give John our best. And will you come over for Sunday dinner?"

"We'd love to," Lenore said. Though she'd probably stop over again to visit before that.

As she drove home, she bit her lip, trying to think of what she'd say to her sister. She had to tread very carefully. If she went about it the wrong way and said something to make Laura feel insulted or offended or, worse, cornered, then it could blow up in their faces. The last thing they needed was for Laura to do something impulsive.

# CHAPTER EIGHTEEN

At home, Lenore parked in front of the house and unloaded each crate and trunk, half carrying them, half dragging them into the house, careful of the bumps and cracks in the sidewalk, not wanting to break anything.

Once she had the last box in the house, she closed the door behind her and piled everything in their small parlor. She had no idea where she was going to put it all and sadly, she realized, some of the gifts would have to remain packed away until they moved into a home of their own.

John wouldn't be home until six. She couldn't wait to see him. Sometimes, the afternoon could be long and lonely, but she kept herself busy. On the sunny days, she went for a walk around Lavender Bay, stopping to talk to friends and neighbors. If the weather was unpleasant, she stayed indoors, either crocheting or sewing.

But her favorite part of the day was when John came home from work. She liked to hear all about his day. He'd claim that it was kind of boring, but she was proud of him: keeping Lavender Bay safe for everyone. He had a very important job and she'd decided from the day they were married that she would create a safe and comfortable haven for him in their home, no matter where they lived.

That evening, as she continued to worry over her sister, John was late getting home. She'd turned off the stew on the stove and kept the lid on to keep it warm. When he walked through the door, he slid his arm around her waist and pulled her to him, kissing her on the lips. "Well, Mrs. Hadley, how was your day?"

She nodded and said, "Good. I've brought over the wedding gifts."

He looked around at all the boxes, crates, and trunks. "It looks like they'll need their own house."

"I'll make it work," she said. *Somehow.*

"I've no doubt about that," he said with a glance toward the stove. "What's for dinner?"

"Lamb stew."

"Let me wash up and I'll be right out."

As he washed up in the bathroom, Lenore ladled stew into two deep plates, making sure to give John extra pieces of lamb. She set the dishes down at the place settings on the table. As she carried over two small plates, each with a slice of bread, John entered the tiny kitchen. He'd removed his jacket and vest, and his bright red suspenders kept his pants up. He'd rolled the sleeves of his shirt up to the middle of his forearms. The smell of Lux soap enveloped him.

Impulsively, she threw her arms around him and kissed him. He responded by returning the kiss.

"What's this for?" he asked with a grin.

"Happy to see you, that's all," she said.

"Keep that up and I'll start coming home for lunch, too."

She knew he was only teasing. He took a packed lunch to work every day, too busy to come home, as much as he wanted to.

When they pulled apart, he pulled her chair out for her before sitting down himself.

"Smells good," he said, picking up his fork and spearing a piece of lamb.

Lenore stared at her plate, realizing she wasn't as hungry as she should be. She'd eaten a big lunch at her parents' house, and that thought led to Laura and Horace. Her thoughts spiraled, and she became oblivious to her stew.

"Lenore?"

The sound of John's voice brought her to the present.

"I'm sorry, did you say something?"

"I asked why you're not eating." He smiled indulgently at her.

"I started to think about something and got lost in thought," she admitted.

"Want to tell me about it?"

She shook her head, taking an interest in her plate of food. She would not be the kind of wife who burdened her husband with petty problems as soon as he walked through the door. Her mother had advised her against that, and Lenore thought it was good advice.

She pasted on a bright smile. "Nothing worth mentioning. Anything interesting happen at work today?"

He looked up from his plate. "I did my best. Found one missing bike, not stolen as originally thought. Broke up a fight between some hobos in the railyard. As soon as the next freight train pulled in, I made sure they were on it and moving on from Lavender Bay.

"Hilda isn't still feeding those drifters out the back door at your parents' house, is she?"

"I'm sure she is," Lenore said. "For the most part, they're harmless. But she's careful."

"Tell her to make sure someone is always in the house with her when she does," he said. It sounded ominous, but she knew Hilda could handle herself. In a recent fracas, she'd gone after them with a cast-iron frying pan, unafraid.

He chewed thoughtfully and when he was finished, he said, "Lenore, promise me you won't feed strangers from this house."

"John?"

"I can't be at work worrying about you at home and whether you're safe or not."

"I don't think there's anything to worry about."

He pressed. "We're not on a main street. It's more isolated here." That much was true. At one time, the small cottages on Lincoln had been laborers' houses, and these days they were mostly occupied by unmarried working men like Alistair Young, who lived at the end of the street. For the most part, Lenore was alone on the street during the day, except for Old Man Forrester, who lived at the corner of Lincoln and Orchard. But he was cranky and miserable. She'd said hello a couple times in passing, but he'd just harrumphed and grunted.

She reached over and laid her hand on her husband's arm, touched by his concern. "I'll do as you say. I even keep the doors locked when you're not here."

"Good." John looked over at the stove. "Is there any more stew?"

She laughed, stood, took his plate, and filled it up again. When she set it down in front of him, she said, "Save some room for the apple pie I made."

He reached up to her standing beside him, laying his broad hand on the small of her back and rubbing it. "Lenore Hadley, I am one lucky man."

She kissed his forehead and sat back down, thinking, *And I am one lucky woman.*

Later, after dinner, they sat in the front room with the radio on low. Occasionally an item of interest would come on and John would lower his paper to listen. The Democratic Convention was in a couple of weeks, and it would be curious to see who would be nominated to challenge Herbert Hoover. Lenore liked Franklin Roosevelt.

Lenore sat on the lumpy sofa that came with the place, trying to read the current edition of *Ladies' Home Journal*. But her attention kept drifting to her sister.

John spoke, startling her. "Since we've sat down, you've been on the same page of the magazine. And I know you're a faster reader than that, Lenore."

She laid the magazine down in her lap and sighed. John folded the newspaper and laid it aside.

"Come on, something's been bothering you since I came home." He grinned and said, "I try very hard not to leave my socks on the floor."

She burst out laughing and relaxed a bit.

He waved her over and she stood, walked over to him, and gave him her hand, which he used to pull her into his lap. Reluctantly, she relayed the story about her sister and Horace Howard, almost hoping that as she spoke it out loud, it might sound ridiculous and not a cause for worry. But then she remembered the look on her parents' faces and decided that there was definitely something to worry about.

John listened to her story and her concerns, and she relayed her parents' anxiety about the situation as well. As she spoke, he pulled a small leather notebook and stubby pencil from the pocket of his shirt and began scribbling.

When she finished, she asked, "Do you think I'm being overanxious about it?"

He looked up at her. "No, I do not. Trust your gut, Lenore. When I was training on the Chicago Police Department, the officer I trained under told me never to discount your intuition."

She nodded, feeling better for unloading her burden.

"Your sister may be under his spell."

"But how do I break it?" she asked.

"You might not be able to," he said.

Her shoulders sagged. "I was going to talk to her about him."

"Wait on that. And proceed with caution. Nine times out of ten that sends them running into their suitor's arms."

She took his advice under consideration, trying to formulate another plan.

"Don't do anything yet," John advised. "What did you say his name was again?" He licked his finger and flipped back to a previous page.

"Horace Howard."

"From McHill, Pennsylvania?" he asked, staring at the notebook.

She didn't know what John could do or would do, if anything. Grateful and feeling slightly better, she kissed him and then stood, smiling. "Now how about a cup of tea and a piece of pie?"

# Chapter Nineteen

Two nights later, over a dinner of baked potato and cube steaks with green beans, John said, "I have some news about Horace Howard." He picked up his glass and took a sip of water.

Lenore's head snapped up. "You do?"

He nodded, slathering butter over his baked potato, followed by a liberal sprinkle of salt. With his fork, he picked up a piece of cube steak and used his knife to shove some potato onto the fork before putting it into his mouth.

Lenore practically held her breath, her dinner forgotten.

"I called my counterpart in McHill, Pennsylvania. It's a pretty small town, not more than six, seven hundred people."

"That's smaller than Lavender Bay." Lenore reached for the pepper and sprinkled a small amount over her food.

"Yes. Anyway, Chief Maldridge over in McHill knows this Horace Howard."

Lenore's heart sank. If the law enforcement professionals knew who he was, it couldn't be good.

"Has he been arrested?" she asked. Her stomach went sour, and she laid her arm across her belly.

John tilted his head, cutting his steak. "Not yet. Maldridge said Howard is too slick to get caught. That he had him fingered for a couple of petty crimes in the area but could never prove it. Howard could always provide an alibi."

"Let me guess. A woman was always able to provide an alibi," she said. Why did women fall for men that were no good, if not completely dangerous?

John nodded, popping cube steak into his mouth. "They also had him fingered for a moonshine operation, but he left town and by the way Maldridge made it sound, they were glad to see the back of him and didn't pursue it."

"Figures he'd land in Lavender Bay. Lucky us."

"He said to keep an eye on him."

Lenore volunteered, "I can keep an eye on him."

John set his fork down. "Absolutely not. This man might be dangerous for all we know."

"More reason for me to follow him."

John looked alarmed. "No, Lenore. Leave him to me." His tone brooked no argument.

He laid his fork and knife on his empty plate and let out a sigh. "Maldridge said one more thing as well."

Lenore waited, holding her breath. Her dinner was only half eaten.

John looked at her. "Horace Howard left behind a young woman in the family way."

Lenore felt herself blanch. She didn't realize she was shaking until John reached over and placed his hand on hers. "Promise me you won't worry about this," he said. His forehead was creased, and the last thing she wanted was for him to be worried about her.

"I'll try my best, but she is my sister," Lenore explained.

"Fair enough." He pushed his plate away. "I think one chief of police in the family is enough."

"That's for sure." She stood, picked up the plates, and put the kettle on the stove. There was one slice of apple pie left, and she laid it in front of John. "I'm sorry, I have no cream."

"Don't worry about it. It's fine as it is. Doesn't need any dressing up." He picked up his dessert fork and cut off a bite.

As Lenore washed the supper dishes, she thought long and hard about what John had told her about Horace Howard and what she would do with that information. Eventually, she came to the conclusion that she needed to tell her sister, as unpleasant as it was going to be. No one liked to hear bad things about someone they thought they were in love with. And she suspected Laura wouldn't take this news easily. But tell her she must, and she prayed her younger sister would see some sense.

It was mid-morning when Lenore arrived at her parents' house. Breakfast had been cleared away. Her father was at work at the town hall, and her mother was at her philanthropy meeting, which was held every Wednesday. Quietly, she peeked in the kitchen and found Hilda in a chair against the wall, her head lolling, snoring lightly. Hilda napped like this every morning after the breakfast dishes were done. She pretended she didn't do this, and Lenore used to pretend she didn't notice.

She made her way upstairs. The door of her old bedroom was open, and she peeked in. It was still done up in pale shades of yellow, with daisy-print wallpaper. It was simple, the furniture unfussy, and she'd decorated it herself. It was hard to believe that that had been her bedroom for the first twenty-five years of her life. But that was all in the past now.

Laura's bedroom was across from her old room. Lenore rapped softly on the door.

"Come in," came the invitation.

If Laura was surprised to see her sister, she didn't show it. She was sprawled out on her stomach on her bed, legs in the air, her chin resting on her upraised hand. The current edition of *Photoplay* was laid out in front of her.

"Hello, Lenore," she said evenly, never lifting her gaze from the pages of the magazine.

Laura's room couldn't have been more different from Lenore's. It was all pink and white, and had always reminded Lenore of some intricate confectionary. It was also heavily scented with perfume, bordering on the overpowering.

"And to what do I owe the pleasure of this visit?" Laura asked, flipping the page of her magazine.

Lenore winced at the tone. It was true they weren't particularly close; they were too different to have one of those sisterly bonds she'd witnessed among her own friends. But still, Laura was her sister and she cared for her and her welfare. And at present, Horace Howard was a threat to her well-being. She foresaw no end of grief as far as that man was concerned.

"I stopped by to see how you're doing," Lenore said. She went to the window seat with its view of the back garden and the orchard. She pushed a few embroidered pillows out of the way and sat down and crossed her legs.

Laura sat up and swung her legs over the side of the bed, narrowing her eyes at Lenore.

"Why?"

Lenore laughed but it sounded artificial. "Can't I stop by and see my sister?"

"You never did before, so I don't know why you'd start now," Laura said. Her beautiful blond hair had been cut short, parted on the side, and crimped to within an inch of its life.

"Laura!" Lenore didn't remember her sister as being so bitter or cynical.

"What?" she asked coyly. "Let me guess, you want to talk to me about Horace." She tilted her head to the side and pursed her lips.

"Now that you mention it," Lenore said gently. She folded her hands in her lap. Behind her, a bird hit the window, momentarily startling her.

Laura performed an exaggerated eye roll. "Mother and Dad have already talked to me about him."

"Have they? What did they say?" Lenore asked. Best to proceed as slowly and cautiously as possible. The slightest thing misconstrued could set her sister off.

"They think I can do better. They'd like me to go back to Hollis," Laura said sourly.

"And how do you feel about that?"

"I disagree with them, of course."

"Why? What is it about Horace Howard that makes him special?"

Lenore's expression transformed from jaded to dreamy, and she released an appreciative sigh. "He's unlike anyone I've ever met."

*I'll say.* Lenore waited for her sister to say more.

The sun, high in the eastern sky, slanted in at an angle through the window, brushing the room with a morning glow.

"He's very exciting. For the first time in my life, I feel alive!"

All sorts of alarm bells went off in Lenore's head, but she proceeded with great care. "Certainly, you can understand Mother and Dad's concerns?"

"You're not going to lecture me on him, too, are you?" Laura flopped back on the bed.

Lenore continued to talk. As far as she was concerned, they weren't finished with this conversation. "John has looked into his background—"

Laura bounced back up to a seated position, her eyes ablaze. "He did *what*?"

Lenore held up her hand. "We were all concerned."

"Let me guess what he found out." Laura held up her hand and began to tick things off on her fingers. "He had a couple of scrapes with the law in McHill. And by scrapes, I mean they tried to blame him for things he didn't do. And then there was the girl who complained that he got her in the family way. Huh," she scoffed. "Tough to prove that one. I heard that the child is as redheaded as they come."

Lenore sat there, dumbfounded, her mouth hanging open. Her sister had all this information at hand and she was still enamored with Horace? All of this had put no doubts or cast any suspicion in her mind?

"How did you know all of this?" she asked, but she already knew the answer.

"Horace told me everything," Laura said. "We're a modern couple, there are no secrets between us."

Horace Howard wasn't only slick and clever. He was downright dangerous. He'd told Laura the worst about himself, and she still was in love with him. If Lenore was worried about her sister before, she was even more anxious over her now.

"Does none of this bother you? Aren't you the least bit concerned?" she asked.

Laura shrugged and pretended to inspect her nails. "I believe him. He's a victim of circumstance. The things he's been accused of are horrible. I feel sorry for him."

That was the worst thing Laura could say. Many a woman married a man she felt sorry for. For any number of reasons. They thought they could help him or save him. Or just love him enough to change him. But a leopard never changed its spots. That was a sad fact of life.

"Are you going to marry him?" Lenore asked. She had to know. Most of all, she needed to prepare her mother and father.

Laura shrugged again. "He hasn't asked. But if he does, my answer will be yes."

There was no sense in trying to talk her out of it. Laura had already made up her mind. To speak out against the idea would only make her younger sister dig in her heels.

Lenore stood up and rearranged the cushions as they were. Before she left, she stopped at the door and said, "I'd like you to come by my house sometime and have tea with me. Just the two of us."

Laura snorted. "Why? So you can talk me out of Horace?"

Lenore shook her head. That boat had already sailed. "No, because you're my sister and now that we're grown adults, I'd like us to be friends."

Her sister couldn't hide her surprise. "Okay," she said quietly.

The most important thing was to keep the lines of communication open. She had a feeling Laura was going to need someone to talk to. And Lenore decided it would be her. It was evident that someday her sister was going to need her.

The conversation with Laura had been illuminating, and it made Lenore realize yet again how much she appreciated the man she'd married.

# CHAPTER TWENTY

## 1933

By the following summer, Lenore had discovered that she was pregnant. She and John were over the moon to be starting their family.

"This is the one time I'd like to bend the rules," her father said, full of glee when they relayed their good fortune at Sunday dinner. "Because if this doesn't call for celebratory champagne, I don't know what does."

"Horace could get us some champagne," Laura said excitedly.

They all stopped talking and stared at her. What she suggested was illegal.

"As much as I don't agree with Prohibition," John said, "I've been sworn to uphold the law." Lenore knew he took his job very seriously.

Laura exhaled loudly as if she were bored. Lenore ignored her. She was not going to let her sister rain on her parade.

"And as mayor, I'm also forced to set an example," Mr. Wainwright said. "But there is talk that the law will be repealed."

"And when it is, we'll celebrate this baby with a proper bottle of champagne," John said, squeezing Lenore's hand under the table.

The rest of Sunday luncheon focused on the baby, Mrs. Wainwright saying the family needed a boy, and Mr. Wainwright saying he'd been happy with his girls and wouldn't mind another one. It was a pleasurable afternoon, made more so by the absence of Horace, who Laura said had some business to attend to. Whatever he was up to, Lenore was glad he wasn't there. As outgoing and charming as he was, his and Laura's relationship tended to cast a pall over things. Her mother would be tense, and her father would remain mute for the entire meal. It was wonderful to see them as their old selves.

When they parted, Hilda gave them plates of leftover chicken for John's lunch and half a peach pie for the two of them to enjoy later that evening.

John tucked everything on the floor in the back seat of the car. "Would you like to go for a drive?" he asked Lenore.

It was a glorious September day. The sun tinged everything in gold. There was warmth in the air, but the intense summer heat had dissipated, and Lenore couldn't remember a time when she'd been happier.

John helped her into the passenger seat, saying, "Careful, now."

Lenore laughed as she got herself situated. "I'm not made of spun glass, you know."

He bent at the waist, eye level with her. "No, you're not. But you're carrying our child, and that makes you more precious than spun glass."

"Oh, you," she teased, reaching over and tousling his hair. And as she did that, she had a premonition of doing the same thing to a small boy. A warmth filled her.

Smiling, he rearranged his hair and took long strides around the front of the automobile before hopping in next to her. He reached over, took her hand, and brought it to his lips.

"You've made me very happy, Lenore," he said. "The best decision I've ever made in my life was marrying you."

She blushed. John was easy to love but wasn't prone to flowery verbal declarations. It simply wasn't his style. She didn't mind. They were well suited to each other.

He checked over his shoulder and pulled away from the curb. "There's something I want to show you," he said.

He whistled as they drove through Lavender Bay, past the courthouse and municipal buildings on Maple, crossing over Main Street until it became Cedar Street, heading west and then turning north on Pearl Street, which ran parallel to Lake Erie.

Lenore enjoyed the view as John slowed down. He knew she liked the beach. She could hear the surf, and she closed her eyes, her body beginning to relax.

Pearl Street was occupied by grand and stately homes with their backs to the shore. She thought it must be heaven to sit out there and watch the sun set in the evenings. She bet you could open your windows and listen to the surf all night long in the summertime.

John pulled up to the curb in front of one of these houses. She assumed he was pulling over so they could enjoy the view. But he got out and dashed around to her side to help her out.

"What are we doing?" she asked with a laugh as she took his hand and stepped down onto the pavement.

He grinned at her, and she thought, *You're up to something, John Hadley.*

The air was still, and the late afternoon sun was still warm.

They walked arm in arm across the street and stepped up onto the sidewalk in front of 19 Pearl Street, a big old rambling house whose front windows faced east. It was a two-story house with a third-floor attic. In front, there was a large veranda and above that on the second floor, a small balcony. On the left side of the house was a stone-and-brick chimney and at the far end, the southwest end, both floors had a bay window. Lenore thought it was beautiful.

John stood next to her and studied the house. Lenore's gaze swung back and forth between her husband and the house, finally settling on her husband. He stood with one leg bent at the knee and his hand cupping his lower face, his forefinger sliding across his cheek absent-mindedly as if contemplating something. He wore a bemused expression.

"Do you want to tell me what's going on and why you keep staring at this house?" She looked up and down the street. At the end of the block, a girl and boy played hopscotch on a driveway. "Someone might call the police on us."

John laughed. "I am the police." He stepped closer to her until his side was almost touching hers. "What do you think of this house?"

Lenore's heart skipped a beat. "This house here? In front of us? I think it's quite grand."

"I do, too. I thought it would be perfect for our growing family," he said.

"What?" Her smile stretched and widened until her cheeks hurt. "What are you saying, John Hadley?"

"This house is for sale," he said. "And I think we should buy it."

It was a monstrosity of a house, bigger than the one she'd grown up in. She swallowed hard. "Can we afford it?"

"We can. We can use that money my aunt left me in her will years ago for a hefty down payment, then our mortgage payments would be doable on my salary."

"Are you sure?" she asked. John was usually so sensible and practical that she couldn't help but wonder if his idea to buy this house was an aberration.

"You're not convinced, are you."

"I'd say I was concerned," she said, studying the house. It was a fine home, certainly large enough to house lots of children. She'd decided already that she'd like seven or eight. When she'd relayed that information to John, he'd let out a low whistle and said he'd be busy the next decade giving her all those children.

*But my goodness*, she thought, *he certainly is easy to be married to.*

"There's no for-sale sign," she said.

"No, it's a private sale. It's about to go on the market."

"What happened to the family that lived here?" She was curious about their story. Being the mayor's daughter, she knew almost everyone in Lavender Bay. And she even knew some of the residents on Pearl Street, but her mind drew a blank when it came to this particular house.

"The children grew up and moved away and now the owner, a widow named Iola Anderson, is moving to New Jersey to live with her daughter."

She'd heard of Iola Anderson but had never met her. She wasn't one for socialization, and all her children had moved out of the area, either through marriage or employment. At the time, when it was spoken of, Lenore had felt sorry for the woman. To be all alone in a house this large. And now, at her age, to have to move to another state because she could no longer live alone. Lenore sighed and wondered if that would happen to them someday. Would their children leave them and wander off to far-flung places? She looked at her husband, thinking, *As long as John is there, I'll be fine.*

"You're absolutely sure?" she asked again.

"I've done the sums," he said. "Would you feel better going over them yourself?"

"No, of course not, I know you can add and subtract," she teased. "It was one of the things that attracted me to you."

"I'm absolutely sure about it, Lenore. Besides, we need a bigger house for all our wedding gifts," he said.

"That is certainly true."

❧

Within a month, they'd moved into the house at 19 Pearl Street. Although the biggest bedroom was the one with the balcony that faced the street, Lenore opted for the one in the back of the house that faced the lake. She kept the window open at night as long as she could, until one night at the end of October when John got out of the bed, shivering, to close it.

Climbing back under the covers, he said, "It's frosty out there tonight."

When she protested, he teased, "Lenore, you can open the window in the spring."

"Oh, all right," she said. With the pregnancy, her body had become like a furnace, and she was always hot at night.

"I can see my breath," John grumbled good-naturedly.

"Hold me and you'll warm up in no time," she suggested groggily.

"I think I will do just that," he said, pulling her closer to him.

While John was at work during the day, Lenore kept busy getting the house organized. Sometimes, she liked to walk from room to room, looking around at every detail, still not quite believing that this wonderful house was theirs. The rooms were big and spacious, with ornate woodwork. But her favorite feature of the house was the large stained-glass window on the staircase landing. The window was wide and long with a large, ornate pineapple in the center of it. The colors were vibrant gold, brown, and green, with a dark green border around the edge of it.

But she did get down to work, cleaning and scrubbing and painting. Hilda said she was "nesting." And to Lenore it didn't sound like a bad thing. The first thing she did was wash and paint the built-in cabinets in the dining room. They had glass-fronted doors, and she couldn't wait to display some of her wedding gifts. She made curtains for their bedroom and the baby's room. She scoured the sinks in the upstairs bathroom and the kitchen. Every day, she did something. And she was happy to be doing it. It was a grand house, and she imagined it filled with children running up and down the stairs and later, she and John growing old and sitting together out on the back porch.

Life was wonderful, and she was happy.

# CHAPTER TWENTY-ONE

Lenore stood back from the table and thought, *It's perfect. Everything is perfect.* She'd ironed her favorite linen tablecloth, the one with the red primroses and green ribboning, and set out the silverware and the glassware. She laid her hand over her blooming belly and absentmindedly rubbed it. Only a couple more months now. Her attention shifted from the table to the kitchen window, where a mixture of sleet and snow was hitting the glass sideways. November had been a terrible month, weatherwise, damp and rainy, but over the last few days, the temperature had gotten colder. Out the back window, the lake was turbulent, almost black in color. The spume from the waves was heavy and brownish white.

With a quick glance at the clock, she knew John would soon be home from work. Dinner was almost ready. The kitchen smelled wonderfully of roast beef and onions. She was hungry, but then she was always hungry. As she pulled the black enamel pan out of the oven, she heard her husband come through the front door.

He stood in the entrance to the kitchen, watching her. She went to him, kissing him on the lips.

"Dinner's ready, if you want to wash up." She brushed a light dusting of snow off the shoulders of his wool coat. "It's roast beef and mashed potatoes tonight."

"I'll eat quickly as I have to go back to work. I came home to tell you that."

"Why?" she asked.

"I can't tell you the specifics, but we're expecting some trouble tonight," he said.

"Oh, you're not alone, are you?" she asked, worried.

"No, everyone is coming in tonight," he said.

"It must be big," she said. Her anxiety increased. For the most part, being a policeman's wife caused her no worry. Lavender Bay was not a criminal hotspot, and it was mostly petty crime. From time to time, she wondered if John missed the excitement of Chicago. But she never asked, too afraid of the answer.

"I'll be late, so don't wait up," he told her.

He ate his dinner quickly, refusing a second helping, which was unlike him. As he ate, he alternated between glancing at the clock and checking his wristwatch. When Lenore asked him if he was all right, he quickly flashed her a reassuring smile, but it didn't reach his eyes. Once his plate was empty, he stood and headed off to the bedroom to change his shirt. She tidied up and made him two sandwiches wrapped in waxed paper for him to take with him. He was taking longer than usual, and she went upstairs to check on him. Through the open bedroom door, she spotted him, standing in front of his bureau, checking his gun for bullets. She froze. Although he carried a gun, he'd never had to use it. Immediately, she prayed that tonight would be no different.

Holstering the gun, he noticed her standing in the doorway. In a few quick strides, he was at her side, pulling her into his embrace. "Don't worry about that. Just a precaution. I had to blow the dust out of it, as I never use it." He laughed, but it didn't sound funny.

She leaned against him, and he kissed her forehead. "Don't worry, my love. This is Lavender Bay, not Chicago." She was glad of that.

He pulled away and placed his broad hand over the expanse of her belly. "How's Junior?"

She smiled. "Kicking up a storm today."

"That's my boy."

"What will you do if it's a girl?"

"Nothing, I'll love her just as much."

"Thank goodness for that," she teased.

His face became somber again. "Did you want to go to your parents' house for the evening?"

That was when she knew he was worried about whatever was going to happen that evening. He'd worked late before, but had never suggested she go to her parents' house.

"No, I'll be fine. I've got some sewing and crocheting to keep me occupied."

"I won't wake you when I come home."

"No, please wake me," she said. "Just so I know you got home safe."

"Okay, Lenore."

He kissed her again and headed out of the bedroom. She followed him down the staircase, her hand sliding along the banister on her way down.

She glanced out the window, dismayed that the snow and sleet continued. John pulled on his coat and put his hat on his head.

Before he left, he kissed her. "I'll see you soon. I love you."

"I love you, too."

But he was already out the door and closing it behind him.

# Chapter Twenty-Two

The radio played in the background while Lenore did some sewing, sitting in a chair in the parlor. Her current project was a skirt for the kitchen sink, and she was working on the rod pocket at the top of it. After a while, she set it aside, stood, and rubbed her hand along her aching lower back. A cup of tea was called for but on her way to the kitchen, she peered out every downstairs window to see if she could see anything going on. But all was dark and quiet.

She made herself a cup of tea and a small plate of saltine crackers and took them back to the parlor, trying to get comfortable in the chair. She ate a few crackers and set the plate and half-empty teacup on the end table. With a sigh, she picked up a magazine and flipped through it, not really seeing the pages. Finally, she laid that aside, too, and stood and began to pace back and forth to the front door, peering out the window, searching for any sign of headlights. Shortly after ten, she looked out a back window and thought she saw lights in the distance, further down the beach, but then there was nothing. Only darkness.

Despite the fear and worry that had consumed her all evening, by eleven, she began to get drowsy, and started nodding off in her chair. At each little sound, her head snapped up, and she half expected to see John walking through the front door. There was a crick in her neck from dozing in an uncomfortable position. She stretched and yawned. Placing her hands on the arms of the chair, she pushed herself up and went around the downstairs, checking all the locks on the windows and doors, just like John did every night before they went upstairs to bed. In the past, she'd thought John had been too overprotective but now that she was alone in the house and it was getting late, she could see the sense in making sure she was safe and secure. It dawned on her that she'd never spent a night alone. When she lived at home, sometimes her parents went away for a short trip, but Laura and Hilda were always in the house with her.

A few minutes before midnight, she made herself another cup of tea, deciding if John wasn't home in half an hour, she'd go up to bed, but she'd leave a lamp on downstairs for him. He could tell her all about what had happened tomorrow morning over breakfast. While she drank her tea, she picked up the magazine again and by twelve thirty, she'd dozed off and the magazine had slid out of her hand and lay on the floor at her feet.

A banging on the front door, punctuated by the doorbell buzzing, woke her from her sleep, and it took her a moment to realize where she was and why she wasn't upstairs in her bed. Hastily, she stood up and went to answer it, surprised to see her father's face through the glass pane. And he wasn't alone.

Why was her father there in the middle of the night? She hoped nothing had happened to her mother or her sister. Or Hilda. She undid the locks and threw the door open. A swirl of snow blew in and she shivered, pulling her shawl tighter around her shoulders.

"Dad? Is everything all right?" she asked. Her heart had jumped to her throat.

The other man was one of John's deputies, and to see the two of them standing there on her front porch in the middle of the night made no sense at all. She looked back and forth from one to the other.

They stepped in, silent, wearing grave expressions. They removed their hats. The only sound was the *tick-tock* of the mantel clock. In the golden-hued light from the lamp, she saw that her father was pasty-looking and that John's deputy, a young guy not much older than Lenore, was shaking and did not make eye contact with her. What had John said about him? *He shows promise.* For the life of her, she couldn't remember his name.

A sinking realization began to take hold of Lenore, rearing up within her and making its way to her brain. A knowing, before anything was said, that something terrible had happened.

And that little voice inside of her told her this was about John.

"Dad?" she said, her voice full of anguish.

Mr. Wainwright cleared his throat. The deputy next to him started crying, silent sobs. Lenore's eyes widened. "Dad?"

Her father's voice shook when he spoke, his eyes two pools of sorrow. "John is dead."

"What?" That comment made zero sense to Lenore. That was impossible. She'd just sent him off earlier with two roast beef sandwiches, wrapped in wax paper.

Her father stepped closer, his own eyes welling up. "There was an incident on the beach, and John's been killed."

"Killed," she echoed. This couldn't be true. Her legs started to shake, and she reached behind her, trying to grab onto the little end table but knocking it over in the process. She was falling into what felt like a terrible void beneath her, a void that was about to swallow her up, but her father and the deputy immediately caught an arm each, righting her and guiding her to the chair she'd been sitting in all night. The deputy had snot on the end of his nose, and she thought she should offer him a handkerchief. John had half a drawer of them, neatly ironed, upstairs behind his undershirts.

"But Dad, why are you here?" she asked. The things you thought of when you were in over your head, swimming and drowning in grief.

"They called me." He nodded toward the deputy beside him. "Matthew came to the house."

*That was his name!* Matthew Nash. He had a wife and a baby.

She was trying to make sense of all this, but nothing was slotting into place. John couldn't be dead. That was impossible. He was only thirty-five. That was way too young to die. Thanksgiving was coming up, and she'd been excited to plan her first holiday in their new home. John would get the turkey and she would make pies . . .

"I want to see him," she announced.

Her father scowled. "That's not a good idea."

"Dad, please. It's the only way I'm going to believe what you're saying."

Her father relented; he'd always had a soft spot for his oldest daughter.

"I will take you to see him," he said. He nodded to the deputy. Lenore told him where he could find her coat, and he held it for her as she slipped her arms into the sleeves. She remembered her pocketbook and as they stepped off the wide porch steps, she turned back.

"I forgot to lock the door," she said, going through the motions.

On the way to the town's municipal buildings in the deputy's car, they told her what had happened. The police department had gotten wind of some bootleg liquor coming across the lake late at night in small boats from Canada. John and his deputies had been waiting, and things had gone horribly wrong.

"Was he shot?" Lenore asked, remembering him checking his gun for bullets.

"No, no shots were fired," the deputy said, finally speaking.

"Then how was he killed?" Had he drowned? Had he fallen and hit his head? A thousand scenarios played out in her mind.

"He was stabbed."

"Stabbed?" she repeated, unsure that she had heard correctly.

There were no more questions to ask. They'd come to her later when she was alone. She sat silently for the rest of the short ride.

When they pulled up in front of the municipal building, her father looked over at her in the back seat. "Lenore, you don't need to do this."

She nodded. "I need to see him." She was determined in her resolve. He was her husband. He was a good man.

The least she could do would be to see him, so new and fresh in death.

The only wobble she had was when she spotted their car parked a short distance from the deputy's. The car John had driven away from her that night. She took her father's arm for support and made her way inside.

To see her dead husband.

Later, the memory of the drive to her parents' house would fail her. Numbness and shock lanced through her after seeing John, chalky white and lifeless in death. As they approached, every room of the house was lit up as if they were expected. And if they were expected, then they *knew*. That John was dead and no longer walked this earth. No longer breathed the air that she breathed.

Her father helped her from the automobile.

"Careful now, love, you've had a shock," he said gently.

Is that what John's death was? A shock? She could think of so many better words. *Abomination. Tragedy.*

As they stepped up onto the porch, the door was thrown open and her mother pulled her into her embrace.

"Lenore!" she sobbed.

It was then that Lenore broke down, safe against the bosom of her mother, enveloped in her perfume—something light, but for the life of Lenore she couldn't think of the name of it.

Her mother and sister got on each side of her, propping her up and directing her inside to the nearest chair. Hilda hovered, eyes red-rimmed, and like Lenore, not knowing what to say or think.

"What happened?" Mrs. Wainwright demanded. She pulled up a chair next to Lenore. "Is it true?"

Lenore nodded. The truth was irrefutable. John was definitely dead. She'd seen his lifeless body laid out on a table in the police chief's office until the coroner arrived. Despite the scarlet bloodstain that crept around to the front of his shirt, he'd looked as if he were asleep, and his hands were still warm. Not far from where he lay, the small black-and-white engagement picture of her that she had gifted him shortly before they were married sat next to the cup of pencils on his desk. He would never set eyes on it again.

Her father paced the floor, the boards creaking beneath his weight. All the lamps and lights were turned on, giving the room an artificial brightness that offered no comfort.

Something had gone horribly wrong that night. How did John end up dead in a sleepy community like Lavender Bay? How, how, *how*? These questions played round and round in her head like a merry-go-round.

Hilda laid her hand on Lenore's shoulder and Lenore held it for a moment, tears falling, grateful for the comfort of a friend.

"I'll make some tea," Hilda said, choking the words out.

"That would be appreciated," Mrs. Wainwright said, looking as if she'd aged twenty years since the last time Lenore saw her. When had that been? Tuesday? Wednesday? Chronologically, it was days ago. But it felt like a lifetime. A different life.

Laura sat on the other side of Lenore.

Mr. Wainwright continued to pace, leaning forward, his hands clasped behind his back, as if he held the weight of the world on his shoulders. He looked deep in the throes of conflicted emotions.

"Dad?" Lenore asked.

"Tell us what you know," Mrs. Wainwright encouraged. "Lenore has the right to know."

Mr. Wainwright stopped pacing and stood directly in front of them. "Yes. Lenore has the right to know what happened to her husband." He looked at each of them individually, his gaze finally resting on Laura, who shrank back.

"What I'm about to tell you is so unbelievable I can barely grasp it myself," he said. He shook with anger.

The ensuing silence was interrupted by the arrival of Hilda and the rattling of teacups as she carried the tray in with shaky hands.

Without looking at her, Mrs. Wainwright said, "Hilda, just set it anywhere."

With half a nod, Hilda did, and went to leave.

"Hilda, please don't go," Lenore said, reaching out for her. "Please sit down."

Unsure, Hilda looked to Mrs. Wainwright, who nodded, and she pulled a chair over and sat on the other side of Mrs. Wainwright.

"Put us out of our misery and tell us what happened," Mrs. Wainwright said.

"John had gotten wind of the transport of alcohol and firearms coming across the lake from Canada," Mr. Wainwright said. "They wanted to bypass Buffalo because the authorities up there are always on the lookout for things like that, so they chose Lavender Bay."

Lenore waited, wanting to hear the details of how her husband's life ended. Especially the why of it.

"When they landed in small boats down at the base of the cliffs, John and his deputies were waiting for them. They took them by surprise. And initially, there was no violence. Even with all those guns coming across the water, all those guns at their disposal, not one shot was fired." He huffed and paced again.

The four of them hung on his every word.

"But there's always someone for whom escape is necessary, no matter the cost."

He let that sink in, coughed, and cleared his throat as if trying to get his emotions under control. He pulled a handkerchief from his breast pocket and blew his nose loudly. He finished by wiping the tip of his nose several times before shoving the hankie back into a pocket.

"The attack came from behind, and John was stabbed in the back." He paused, coughed again, and when he spoke his voice shook. "He never saw it coming."

"That's awful," Laura said vehemently. She grabbed Lenore's hand and held it.

He leveled his gaze at her. "It's more than awful." He straightened up as questions came all at once.

"Did they catch him?"

"Do they know who did it?"

"Why? Why kill John?"

It was a cacophony of voices, impossible to distinguish one from the other. The only one who remained silent was Lenore. The details made no difference to her, for the ending was always the same: John was gone.

"Oh, they've caught him all right," Mr. Wainwright said with an angry laugh. "And there's a load of witnesses. I'm sure some of his co-conspirators are ratting on him right now to save their own necks!"

"Have you identified the man who did it?" Mrs. Wainwright asked.

"Yes, we have."

"Stop it and tell us!"

He wagged a finger at Laura. "It was your Horace Howard."

Laura gasped, dropped Lenore's hand, and jumped off her chair as if it were on fire. "That's a lie! That's a lie!"

"I'm afraid not, young lady. Your *charming* beau has murdered your sister's husband."

Lenore groaned and slumped in the chair.

"That's a lie. You're making it up," Laura cried, tears in her eyes. "You don't like him, and you want to blame him for John's death. All because you don't want him around. He would never do anything like this!"

Mr. Wainwright was angry now. "Wouldn't he? Well, he has. He'll get the chair for it, and even that is too good for that man!" His face was beet red, and spittle had gathered in the corner of his mouth. Raising his voice until Lenore thought the roof would blow off, he yelled, "And when his time comes, I'm going to pull in every favor that's owed to me to be the one to pull that lever!"

"You are so cruel!" Laura screamed, and ran from the house, leaving the front door wide open. A cold draft of air blew into the house.

Mrs. Wainwright looked after her, half got out of her chair, and sat back down and mumbled, "Maybe we should go after her."

"No," said Mr. Wainwright with finality. "She brought this down on our family by her own selfishness and foolishness. Let her go."

# Chapter Twenty-Three

After the funeral, there was a luncheon at the home of Mr. and Mrs. Wainwright. The house was packed. After the church service, where Laura had seated herself in the last pew, she had retreated to her bedroom and wasn't seen again for the remainder of the day. Lenore didn't have the energy to deal with her at that moment. People she knew, and some she didn't, came up to her to offer their condolences as she sat on a chair in the corner of the parlor. Her parents had taken over and were running things, and for that she was grateful. It was only when Alistair approached her that she stood, and he took her into his arms, offering words of comfort.

After the last guest had left and all the furniture had been put back and the tables cleared of cups and saucers,

Hilda retired to her quarters, and Lenore's parents sat down with her in the parlor.

"Your mother and I want to talk with you," her father said soberly.

She looked from one to the other. They'd been worried about her. And they had their own grief to deal with as well; they'd been very fond of John. More than once, she'd heard her father say that he couldn't have asked for a better son-in-law if he'd picked him out himself.

"We're concerned about you and the baby." Her mother reached over and took Lenore's hand in hers. "This has been an awful tragedy."

"And you're left in that big house alone," her father said. "We're worried about that."

"John installed locks on all the doors," Lenore said flatly.

Mr. and Mrs. Wainwright exchanged a glance.

Lenore's father pulled his chair closer to her. "Pet," he said, calling her by the childhood endearment he hadn't used in years, "Mother and I would like you and the baby to come and live here with us."

"Here?" Lenore repeated.

"It is your home, Lenore, no less than it was before you got married," her mother said softly.

"We'll send Laura away to live with your mother's sister for a bit," her father said.

"I don't want to kick Laura out of her home."

Mrs. Wainwright looked down at her hands, clasped tightly in her lap. "She needs to get away for a while."

"Why? Because she's guilt-ridden?" Mr. Wainwright asked, his temper flaring.

"Please," his wife begged. "I can't have this conversation again."

Mr. Wainwright's mustache twitched. Lenore had no interest in any further conversation about Laura.

"The house you and John bought is too big for only two people," her father said. "What are you going to do, all by yourself in that house?"

"Come home and live with us," her mother piped in. "We'd love to have you, and we can help with the baby."

"We're looking forward to the arrival of the baby. It will be a happy time." This from her father. Lenore looked at him. Was this thought supposed to cheer her up? She didn't want to do anything without John being there. Not even have this baby. If only there were a way for her to stay pregnant and walk around with that little bit of John still inside of her, she would. But whether she liked it or not, this baby was coming.

She folded her hands in her lap and looked down at them. "I really do appreciate your offer, but I want to stay in my home. In *our* home."

"But it's too much work," Mrs. Wainwright protested.

"No," Lenore said firmly. "I'll stay put." Her vulnerability might cause her to make a decision she would later regret. But this one thing she was sure of. She wasn't moving away from Pearl Street. She couldn't. It was the last place she'd seen John alive.

Her father reached over and patted her hand, smiling benevolently. "That's fine, Lenore. We can revisit this subject another time, when you're feeling up to it."

She didn't press the matter, though she knew very well that she would never feel up to it and she would never leave that house. It had been their home, hers and John's, and although they only lived in it for a short period of time, she'd been outrageously happy there. That was gone now. But she still had the house and all the hopes and dreams they'd shared about it.

Lenore sat, unmoving, for the longest time, seeing but unaware of the changing shadows on the wall in front of her. She knew not the day, the time, or the hour. She couldn't remember when the last time was that she washed her hair or brushed her teeth. She'd left John frozen in time on that last night he was alive, and she'd gone on ahead of him, without him. A fact she didn't like and could do nothing to change.

Finally, when she decided it was time to move from the chair, she stood, wobbly, unsure, and made her way to the bed. It was getting darker. Might as well go to bed for the night. Unconsciously, she rubbed her large belly.

She took a shirt of John's off the chair where he'd left it and pressed it close to her face. It smelled of him. She was afraid if she smelled it too much, it would lose its scent. She mustn't forget what he smelled like. Already the sound and timbre of his voice was fading, and this was disturbing to her. How could someone who'd been so very alive be suddenly dead? Buried beneath six feet of clay, sand, and dirt. It felt like an abominable sin to her.

Clinging to the shirt, she crawled into bed, hugging it. When the tears came, she turned her head away from it, not wanting to soak the fabric, and drenched the pillow instead.

# CHAPTER TWENTY-FOUR

Lenore drifted in and out of a deep sleep. In the distance, she could hear knocking. It brought her to the surface, and she looked around, wondering if John had already left for work. Had she forgotten to get his breakfast for him? Why hadn't he woken her?

But then she opened her eyes and remembered.

The banging continued, and she frowned, realizing someone was at the front door. Slowly, she pulled herself out of the bed, reached for her bathrobe, and stood, tugging it on. She slipped her feet into her slippers and left the room, heading down the long upstairs hall and then down the staircase, holding on to the banister. Her bump had grown, and she could barely see her feet beneath it.

The house was quiet, dark, and empty. Sad. It amazed her how the personality of the place had changed so dramatically since John had died. It was as if the house was as bereft as she was.

Although she wanted no company, she'd have to answer the door if only to get them to stop knocking. Whoever it was, she would send them away. Yesterday, the pastor of their church stopped and droned on and on about John being in a better place. Lenore wanted to cry out that he'd been in a great place with her, here in this house, waiting for their baby. She could think of no better place for her husband.

She spied Hilda through the glass. She unlocked the locks one at a time, thinking of John's penchant for them and how they had not saved him or helped in the end. Slowly, she opened the door, trying to think of an excuse to give Hilda, but her mind was blank.

Hilda carried a wicker basket over her left arm, and a suitcase stood next to her on her right side. She took hold of the edge of the door with her right hand, sliding her foot inside, and pushed it open.

"There you are," she said. "I thought I was going to have to break the door down."

"I was sleeping."

"I figured. It's almost noon."

"Is it?" Lenore glanced outside. The day was dull and wintry, the houses stark against all that snow, everything cast in a bright white light.

A blast of arctic air followed Hilda inside and Lenore shivered, pulling her bathrobe closed at the neck. *If your neck was covered, you'd feel warmer.* She didn't know where that thought came from and in the context of everything else, it made no sense.

Hilda was already on her way toward the back of the house, talking. Lenore stared at the suitcase, wondering what it was for. She hoped Hilda wasn't there to convince her to move back to her mother and father's house.

She followed her through the house to the kitchen.

"It's cold in here, Lenore," Hilda said. "You need to stay warm for yourself and the baby."

She set the wicker basket down on the table. It was still covered in the tablecloth that had been there the day John had his last meal. There was a small circular gravy stain where his knife had fallen off his plate. She had a hard time looking at that. It brought tears to her eyes every single time.

Hilda set the suitcase on the floor next to John's chair. She turned to Lenore, hands on her hips, and her expression immediately softened. She stepped forward, her smile gentle, and placed her hands on Lenore's shoulders. "Your parents have sent me over here to look after you." When Lenore went to protest, Hilda cut her off. "Just until you get back on your feet. And then I'll return to your parents' house," she reassured her. "And I'll have to get back soon. My replacement is questionable, and I don't know what state she'll have my kitchen in by the time I return."

This brought a small smile to Lenore's face, but it disappeared just as quickly.

"Now, let me get the heat on here," Hilda said. "Which bedroom could I use?"

Lenore shrugged, not caring. "Whichever one you want. There's a bunch of bedrooms upstairs." She choked on the last words, thinking how she and John had planned to fill those rooms with children.

Hilda studied her face. "When was the last time you ate anything?"

Lenore looked off to the side, thinking. "I-I-I don't know. What day is it?"

"Wednesday."

She lowered her head, shaking it. "I don't know, Hilda. I can't remember."

"It's as I thought. I'll make you something to eat. Something light."

"I don't think I can."

"You can and you will."

"I don't have anything."

Hilda held up the wicker basket. "I come bearing gifts." She moved the basket to the counter while Lenore remained standing in the center of the kitchen, unsure of what to do, thinking she might go back to bed. What else was there for her to do?

But Hilda made the decision for her, taking her by the shoulders and propelling her to the table and pulling out a chair for her. Once seated, Lenore slumped forward, leaning her head on her hands.

*I only need to get through the next minute, and then the minute after that. That's all. Nothing more than that.*

She hadn't realized how cold she was until the house started heating up. Hilda had made her something simple to eat: one poached egg on buttered toast with a sprinkle of salt and pepper, and a hot cup of tea with sugar. She set it down in front of her.

"I know you have no appetite, but you've got a baby to feed," Hilda said. She left Lenore alone to eat and went around the downstairs, opening drapes. When Lenore heard the back drapes sliding along the rod, she closed her eyes and stopped eating. The morning after John's death, she'd closed those drapes, closed them on the view of that back porch overlooking the lake, where John liked to sit out on the warmer evenings. He hadn't had enough time to sit out there and enjoy it.

She finished her breakfast, mopping up yolk with the last of the toast, realizing she had been hungry.

Hilda reappeared. "I've laid out clean clothes for you. There's a sinkful of hot water to wash your face and brush your teeth upstairs." She paused. "Maybe in a day or two when you're up to it, you can get into the bathtub."

Lenore nodded. She headed upstairs to wash her face, brush her teeth, and get changed. She'd always been good about following instructions. Those three little tasks required a lot of energy, and she wanted to go back to bed. But Hilda intervened and brought her back downstairs, sitting her at the table and giving her a few potatoes to peel.

"What would you like for your dinner? I've brought some ham and beef."

"Whatever you want, Hilda."

"Ham it is then."

It was a bitter cold and blustery day in January when John Henry Hadley, Jr. arrived first thing in the morning. Outside, the wind howled. Once she was presentable and the midwife had left and everything had been cleaned up, Lenore sat up in bed and held her newborn son, marveling at the miracle of him and examining each one of his fingers.

He was absolutely perfect.

She held him close and cried over him. Cried at the unfairness of it all, that John never got to see his son. She cried for all the children they wouldn't have. She cried over all their lost plans. All their hopes and dreams had gone up in smoke that fateful night on the beach.

When she was all cried out, she made a promise to her son: That she would pull herself up out of her well of grief and be devoted to him. That he would be her reason for living, her reason to carry on. There could be no better reason. She dried her eyes on a handkerchief and then got lost in admiring her newborn baby boy.

Her parents were her first visitors. They gushed over the newborn, insisting on holding him and passing him back and forth between them. It was good to see them happy. They had taken John's death hard, and this baby certainly was a harbinger of joy.

"Since you're being stubborn and refusing to move home," her mother said, sitting in a chair across from the bed, smiling as she held her grandson, "Hilda will stay here with you."

Lenore protested, "I can't afford Hilda." She had gone over her budget time and again. John's modest life insurance policy and pension might be enough to support her as long as she was careful. But hiring help was out of the question.

"We will continue to pay Hilda's salary." Her father sat in another chair next to her mother, waiting patiently for his turn to hold his grandson.

"I can't ask you to do that," Lenore said, shocked. She reached behind her to readjust the pillow she was leaning against.

"You didn't ask," Mr. Wainwright replied. "We offered."

"Oh, Dad."

"And since you won't take any money from us, we'll have to force Hilda on you," he teased.

"But what about Hilda? Maybe we should ask her first," Lenore said. As much as she loved Hilda, she also knew that she was a creature of habit. And being in her sixties, she might want to retire and live a life of ease. She'd been taking care of people her whole life. Maybe it was time for her to put her feet up.

"We've already talked to her about it. She was delighted as you might expect," Mr. Wainwright said. "I think she'd rather be here with you and the baby."

"But what about your own house?" Lenore asked. Hilda hadn't been too keen on her replacement.

"Edith is no Hilda, I'll grant you that, but she will learn in time," her mother said.

It wasn't hard for Lenore to accept this. Hilda had been good company these past few weeks. She was there if Lenore wanted conversation, and the distraction of the mundane tasks Hilda had set in front of her, like cooking, baking, and sewing, had kept her going.

# Chapter Twenty-Five

## 1934

Lenore set out for the post office on Main Street as she had a few letters to post and an advertisement to tack up on the notice board. She'd decided to sell her sewing machine. She hated to part with it, but she needed the money.

She'd left the baby at home with Hilda. At almost six months, his first tooth was poking through the bottom front gum, and he'd been fussy since yesterday. He'd also been drooling a lot because of it. Hilda had told her to take her time, to take a stroll and get some fresh air.

She walked down Pearl, turned onto Main Street, and headed southeast toward the post office at the far end of the block. It was a long walk, but Lenore didn't mind. It was nice to get out and about on such a beautiful, sunny summer day. The trees that lined the boulevard were in full foliage, providing shade for relief. Everything appeared shiny and bright, something she'd forgotten, another thing that had been buried beneath a weight of grief.

The post office appeared grander on the outside than the inside. Outside, it was made of blue stone, with an arched entranceway and above that, a simple decorative balcony. Inside, there was woodwork everywhere, from the doors to the façade to the service counters. The scuffed cream-colored walls were in need of a fresh coat of paint. More than once, Lenore had wondered how marks ended up at the top of the walls near the ceiling. The other walls were covered in life-sized murals depicting the history of the town.

Currently there were only two positions occupied by long-time employees of the post office. The postmistress was a Fern Mulvihill, spinster, who'd been there since before Lenore was born, and Abner Williams, who'd lost a leg in the Great War. It was her father that had secured him the position at the post office so he'd have a way to provide for his family.

There was a large corkboard on the back wall where the town's residents posted their notices. As the line was long for the counter, Lenore figured she might as well post her advertisement.

Ahead of her was a woman her own age who stood at the small wooden desk propped up against the wall, stubby pencil in hand, staring at the blank index card in front of her. After a moment, the woman bent her head, scribbled something on the card, and posted it to the corkboard with a thumbtack.

She turned around and almost bumped into Lenore. The other woman smiled, nodded, and stepped around her.

Lenore opened her pocketbook and pulled out her own index card. The previous night, she'd sat at the kitchen table, writing neatly on the card. This was the third one. She'd made mistakes on the first two and had ripped them into pieces and thrown them in the trash can.

Before she tacked it up, she scanned the other advertisements.

"Sugar," she muttered. Someone else had posted their sewing machine for sale. There couldn't be that many people in Lavender Bay who needed a sewing machine. There was no sense in putting hers up. She'd wait until the other one went down. She slipped the card back into her pocketbook. Her eyes landed on the index card that the young woman had put up.

*Seeking room and board. Teacher. References provided. Reasonable rate. Please reply to Post Office Box 36.*

A thought occurred to Lenore, and she turned on her heel and exited the building, forgetting all about the letters she had to mail.

She stood outside in the hot afternoon sun, looking up and down the street. Further along Main Street, she spotted her: the young woman who'd left the card up on the corkboard looking for room and board. She broke into a trot, trying to catch up with her.

It took three blocks before she was able to call out, "Miss!" and several shouts before the woman finally turned around. Lenore waved the card and slowed down as she caught up with the woman. She held her side as a stitch had started and she needed to catch her breath.

"Was it me you were calling out to?" the woman asked. Still breathless, Lenore nodded.

The woman smiled. Her face was narrow, and her nose was long. Her brown hair was pulled sharply back into a bun too severe for her face. It aged her. But she had a lovely smile, and her hazel eyes were bright and inquisitive.

Lenore held out her hand and introduced herself. "I'm Lenore Hadley."

The other woman shook Lenore's hand. Her grip was firm and warm. "Harriet Bauer, pleased to make your acquaintance."

"I hope you don't think me rude, but I couldn't help but notice your card on the corkboard," Lenore said.

"Of course not," Harriet said amiably. "You were right behind me in line."

A short laugh escaped Lenore. "Yes, I was, wasn't I." She felt tongue-tied but forged on and blurted, "I may have a room for you if you're interested."

Harriet's smile faltered a bit, and she took half a step back.

Lenore rushed to reassure her. "I can assure you that this is on the up and up."

"Do you run a boarding house?"

"Honestly, no, but I'm thinking of starting one," Lenore said. Granted, it was a half lie. Inspiration hadn't hit her until she saw Harriet's notice posted on the corkboard. But she'd been thinking about it as she chased Harriet down the street.

"I appreciate your honesty," Harriet said.

"Anyway, I have a room to let if you're interested."

"When would it be available?"

"Immediately." There were five bedrooms upstairs, and only two were currently occupied.

"May I see it first?" Harriet said.

"Of course."

"When would be a good time?"

Lenore thought for a moment. She didn't want to appear too eager and lose the possibility of some income. "Tomorrow afternoon, would that suit?"

Harriet nodded. "Two in the afternoon?"

Johnny would be napping, and Lenore said hastily, "Four would be better."

Harriet smiled. "Four it is then. Oh, wait, what's the address?"

"Nineteen Pearl Street."

"I'll see you tomorrow, Mrs. Hadley."

"Good day, Miss Bauer."

Lenore turned and walked in the opposite direction, toward home. As she went, she thought taking in boarders would be a good way to earn extra money. She'd see how it went with Harriet before she advertised for any more lodgers. She had all those bedrooms upstairs, plus, if she ever cleared out the attic and put in a proper window to replace the current one, which had a hole in it, there'd be that room as well. She did the sums in her head. She'd never get rich, but it would keep her head above water.

The closer she got to home, the more her mood lifted. Yes, a lodger would be a good idea. And she'd start with Harriet Bauer. She quickened her pace, anxious to get home and get the upstairs bedrooms ready.

Hilda stood in the middle of the kitchen, her hands on her hips, and frowned. "A lodger? You're going to invite a complete stranger into the house? To live here?" Behind her, the ironing board was set up, with Lenore's other dress laid out on it.

"Yes." Lenore laid her handbag down on the kitchen chair. She pulled an apron off the hook on the back of the kitchen door, pulled it down over her head, and reached behind her to tie the strings at her back.

"Do you really need to do this?" Hilda pressed. She returned her attention to the ironing, sprinkling a little bit of water from a glass bottle onto the garment.

"I do. I need the extra money," Lenore replied.

"I know things are tight, but it's that way for everyone," Hilda said. Lenore needed no reminders that they were still in the middle of an economic crisis. It was people like her who fell through the cracks, and she was determined that wouldn't happen to them.

Hilda was still speaking. "I can pay for the groceries."

Lenore tilted her head. "You're already buying extras."

Hilda went to protest but Lenore cut her off. "Hilda, I know you're buying extra food with your own money. How do I know this? Because I know the cost of groceries, and we always seem to have more than enough food."

"It's important to eat," Hilda said, shrugging.

"Yes, it is. But it's not your job to pay for the groceries. That's my job."

There was a grim set to the older woman's mouth as if she realized this was an argument she wasn't going to win. "See how it goes. Make sure you get references. And a deposit in case she damages the furniture or does a runner."

Lenore thought about Harriet and her initial impression. "She doesn't strike me as that type."

"Promise me you'll do all those things if only to put my mind at ease."

Lenore held up her hand like a Boy Scout about to take the oath. "I promise."

She tucked Hilda's concern to the back of her mind, but she was determined to do this. Because she had no choice.

# CHAPTER TWENTY-SIX

Harriet Bauer arrived promptly at four in the afternoon the following day. Lenore spied her through the window wearing a green, yellow, and white checked dress of a lightweight material. The fabric looked breathable, which was needed in this heat.

The baby was up, and Lenore cradled him against her. He'd slept better the previous night and had a good afternoon nap now that the bottom tooth had finally broken through. She shifted Johnny to her other arm so she could open the door.

"Harriet, come in please," she said.

Harriet stepped in and nodded toward the baby, smiling. "Beautiful baby, is he yours?"

Lenore found that question funny, as if she'd found this baby on the street or something, but she suppressed the urge to laugh.

"Yes, this is my son, Johnny."

"I love babies," Harriet said. "And children in general. I teach third grade over at Ben Franklin Elementary."

"A teacher! How wonderful."

Harriet followed Lenore into the parlor, where Hilda went from one houseplant to another, watering can in hand. She eyed Harriet.

"Hello, there," Harriet said to Hilda.

"Hello."

Lenore went to introduce Hilda but hesitated. She didn't want to say she was the help. She was, but to her, Hilda was more than that.

"This is my friend Hilda Wolf, who lives here," Lenore said.

Hilda scowled. "I'm the help."

"Come on, you're more than that," Lenore said.

Harriet piped in. "She's either a helpful friend or friendly help." Both women looked at her and smiled.

Holding the watering can at her side, Hilda said, "I'll bring some tea in."

"Thank you, Hilda."

"Did you want me to take Johnny?"

Lenore shook her head. "No, he'll be fine."

Holding her free arm out, she directed Harriet to the front parlor, with its view of the street. There was still the lingering scent of Murphy Oil Soap, as she and Hilda had tackled the woodwork downstairs over the last two days. She'd always loved its fresh scent.

"It's a nice place you have here," Harriet said, scanning the room and taking everything in. She sat in one of the two chairs across from the sofa, and Lenore realized that if she was serious about getting lodgers in, she'd have to get more furniture.

Lenore took one of the chairs and settled Johnny on her lap. He clung to his cloth rabbit, chewing on its ear.

"It's a spacious home," Harriet pronounced.

Lenore looked around almost as if seeing it for the first time. She supposed it really was too much house for three people, and that dream from not so long ago about filling it with children made her heart ache.

"Yes, I suppose it is."

"May I ask if there's a Mr. Hadley?" Harriet said, leaning forward slightly on her chair as if they were going to exchange some sort of confidence.

Lenore was blunt. "No, I'm a widow."

Harriet leaned back, her expression sober. "My condolences."

Lenore gave a slight nod and then changed the subject, not wanting to get caught in a downward spiral.

"You are looking for room and board?"

"I am. As I've said, I teach at Ben Franklin Elementary school. I've come with no notice as I'm replacing a teacher who's out with scarlet fever."

"I've heard that," Lenore said. It was known around town that the previous third grade teacher had ended up with some complications from scarlet fever. It was unfortunate. "And where are you living now?"

"Willow Street."

Lenore knew where Willow Street was, but she didn't know anyone who lived over there.

"And why do you need accommodation?" Lenore asked.

"I'm staying with my mother's second cousin." Harriet pursed her lips and lowered her voice. "It's not working out." She lowered her head.

"Where are you from?" Lenore asked, changing the subject deftly to avoid further embarrassment.

"Originally, I'm from Binghamton," she said.

"You've come a long way for a teaching job," Lenore said. Johnny clutched his fist, looked at Lenore and laughed. His new tooth made an appearance, and she kissed her baby on the forehead.

"The principal is a friend of my mother's second cousin, and she needed to fill the vacancy immediately."

"Of course."

Hilda entered with a tray bearing two teacups, the tea already poured.

"I'm sorry, I have no cake or pie," Lenore said, handing a cup of tea to Harriet.

"I don't eat between meals," Harriet said, accepting it.

"Would you like milk or sugar?"

"No, thank you. I drink it black."

"Very well." Most people had learned to drink their tea and coffee black.

Hilda retreated to the kitchen.

"Do you have other lodgers at present?" Harriet enquired, sipping her tea delicately before setting it down on the lace doily on the coffee table that was situated between them.

"No, but I'm hoping to bring in a few more," she said.

Harriet perked up and said, "I'd be your first lodger then?"

"Yes." Lenore realized she should have considered what kind of questions to ask potential lodgers. "And you have references?"

"Of course," Harriet pulled several envelopes out of her pocketbook and handed them to Lenore, who pulled the letters out and scanned them briefly, noting such words as "respectable," "fastidious," and "clean."

Harriet sat with her back straight and hands folded in her lap. She waited for Lenore to finish reading her letters of reference.

"I can take you upstairs and show you the rooms that I have available," Lenore said. "And as you're the first one, you could pick."

"That would be nice."

Hilda appeared from the kitchen and held out her hands for the baby, a broad smile on her face. "I'll mind Johnny, Lenore. You go upstairs with Harriet."

"How old is the baby?" Harriet asked as she followed Lenore up the staircase.

"Six months," she answered, hardly believing that her baby was that old already. She doubted she'd have any more children, and she wished the time would slow down a bit. And of course, she felt with each passing day, she was getting farther and farther away from John.

Upstairs, she showed Harriet the three available bedrooms. When she'd told Hilda her plan to take in boarders, Hilda had promptly moved from the bedroom she was occupying to the smallest bedroom, despite Lenore's protests.

She started with the largest room, which had its own balcony and looked out over Pearl Street.

The room was spacious, with a double bed and a small sofa situated in front of an unused fireplace. The faded floral wallpaper looked nice and welcoming in the daylight.

"Oh, this room is lovely," Harriet said. "I suppose it would be your most expensive room due to its size and the fact that there's a fireplace."

Although Lenore had not thought about charging more for the bigger bedrooms, she didn't hesitate with her answer. "Yes, it is." And before Harriet could inquire about the price, she moved on to the other two rooms. Both contained a single bed with a dresser, chair, desk, and small table. In each room there was a washstand in the corner with a ceramic pitcher and basin.

"Both these rooms are lovely," Harriet said. "May I inquire as to the price?"

Lenore told her the price, explaining that breakfast and dinner were included, along with lunch on the weekends.

With an approving nod, Harriet said, "That's reasonable."

Lenore hoped she hadn't underpriced herself.

"I'd like to take one of the smaller rooms," Harriet decided.

"Your pick," Lenore said.

Harriet chose the smallest room after Hilda's. It had a nice view of the lake and in the evening, the sun coming in from the west brightened the room.

They went downstairs and made arrangements, and Harriet asked if it would be all right if she moved in the following day. Lenore agreed.

After Harriet had left, Lenore found Hilda out on the back porch with the baby in her lap. She was pointing at the seagulls.

"Hilda, we have our first lodger!"

"That Harriet is a good egg. I can tell," Hilda said, pointing at another bird for Johnny.

Initially, it was odd having a stranger living in the house, but they soon settled into a routine. Harriet came home from school in the late afternoon, preferring to stay behind at the schoolhouse to correct papers and plan her lessons for the following day. She said she liked the peace and quiet of the classroom at the end of the day. Lenore wondered if she found Johnny too noisy to concentrate. In the evenings, she joined them for supper and passed the time with them in the front parlor, listening to the radio or chatting or sometimes playing cards. It wasn't long before it felt like Harriet had always lived there.

Not everyone was pleased with Lenore's decision to take in lodgers. Her parents were aghast.

With her hand splayed against her throat, her mother asked, "Is it that bad that you've had to take in strangers under your roof?"

Lenore was not about to divulge her financial situation to anyone, not even her parents. She suspected that Hilda knew the truth, but she preferred to keep her business private.

"Why didn't you come to us? We would have helped you," her father said. But she couldn't ask him. He hadn't won re-election in the last mayoral race. The mayor's daughter being involved with a man who went to the electric chair cast a pall on their family, and it was reflected in the vote. And though her father had been scrupulous about his money, she could hardly ask him for assistance. The whole affair had taken its toll: Mr. and Mrs. Wainwright had aged significantly in a short period of time. She supposed they all had.

"It's not your job to support me," she pointed out. And it wasn't, no matter how much they wanted to. She was a grown woman with a child and a house, and it was up to her to provide for them. She was sorry she hadn't gone to college now, but she preferred to stay home with Johnny, and how would that have worked out? And this had been her and John's dream house, and she didn't care what she had to do; she wasn't letting it go. She'd do whatever it took to keep it. His last home was here and therefore, it would always be hers as long as she was alive. The memory of him was the strongest here for her.

Her mother went to say something, but Lenore spoke before she could get her thought out.

"How's Laura?" she asked. Although she hadn't seen her sister, she always inquired about her. The chasm between them was deep, and Lenore hadn't any idea how to bridge that gap, or whether she even wanted to.

Her father nodded and said, "All right."

"She'd like to meet the baby," her mother said.

"Oh," Lenore said. She supposed her sister should meet Johnny. After all, why should an innocent baby be deprived of the affections of his aunt?

But she wasn't ready for any kind of teary reunion with Laura. And that's what it would be: tears and drama. She didn't think she could stomach that.

# Chapter Twenty-Seven

## 1935

One year later, Harriet Bauer was still boarding at the house. Out for summer vacation for school, she'd only just returned from Binghamton, where she'd spent a month visiting her family. There had been other lodgers, but none with the permanence of Harriet. There was the woman who'd come to Lavender Bay to work in the hospital. But after eight months and a terrible case of homesickness, she'd returned to her parents in Elmira. There were two women who'd taken secretarial work at the Gibson's Grape Jelly factory and were having difficulty finding rental accommodation in Lavender Bay. They stayed with Lenore for two months. Lenore hoped to fill all the rooms. She'd put an ad in the *Lavender Bay Chronicle* but so far there had been no response. But she was hopeful.

One day she was out back in the small yard bordered by a white picket fence. She was hanging laundry, her favorite task as it allowed her to stare at the lake. And that was a sight she never grew tired of.

Johnny toddled around the backyard, stopping to inspect everything. He hadn't been walking long and when he did, he held up his arms to keep his balance. Currently, he was inspecting a buttercup, squatting down, his bum padded by his cloth diaper.

"Mama?"

Lenore pegged the corner of a bedsheet to the line with a wooden peg. She looked over at him and smiled, her heart ready to burst at the sight of him, such a pretty baby with his blond hair and blue eyes.

"Fower?" he asked, pointing to the buttercup.

"That's right, Johnny. That's a flower."

She heard the rattling sound of an automobile out front, followed by the long honk of a horn. Johnny looked in the direction of the noise and pointed.

"Car," she told him.

Keeping one eye on Johnny, who went to inspect a dandelion, Lenore pulled the next item of laundry out of the basket to hang it on the line.

"Mrs. Hadley!" a voice called out as a woman came around the side of the house.

Peeking between two flapping bedsheets, Lenore spotted an unfamiliar woman, about fifty. She was what one would call handsome, with sharp cheekbones, a high forehead, and crimped black hair with silver strands. She wore a smart dress and polished shoes.

Uncertain, Johnny ran toward his mother, arms up, hands fisted. Lenore picked him up and held him close.

"Mrs. Hadley, I apologize for the intrusion. My name is Ellen Whitmer. I understand you run a boarding house."

"That's right."

Johnny had wrapped one arm around Lenore's neck, and the other held tight onto a buttercup.

"I'm looking for a room for my father. He rents a cottage in town, but the landlord is moving in himself."

That was happening more frequently with the difficult economic situation; landlords had to give up their more expensive homes and take up residence in their rental properties. It was a shame, really.

"You see, I live out of town. I've lived in Boston for over thirty years and well, it would make life a lot easier if Dad would come back with me, but he refuses. Lavender Bay is his home, he tells me." Lenore did not miss the exasperation in the other woman's voice. "Anyway, Fern Mulvihill at the post office said you were the only boarding house in town."

"That's correct."

"Do you have any rooms to let?" The lines of the woman's face deepened, and she wrung her hands.

"I have two, actually. Breakfast and supper are included."

The woman nodded, her posture relaxing.

"Would you like to see them?"

"I would, if it wouldn't be too much trouble."

"Follow me." Lenore carried Johnny on her hip into the house, entering from the back porch through the library.

"You have a lovely spot here, Mrs. Hadley," Ellen Whitmer said as she looked around.

Lenore thought so, too. "Thank you."

Hilda must have witnessed the interaction out the kitchen window, for she was waiting with open arms to take Johnny. The little boy went easily to her, and they disappeared into the kitchen after Lenore introduced Mrs. Whitmer to Hilda.

As they walked up the staircase, Mrs. Whitmer commented on the large stained-glass window on the staircase landing.

"That is beautiful. Of course, pineapples are the symbol for hospitality."

Lenore looked over her shoulder. "That's right."

As they stood at the top of the landing, Lenore said, "I have a large and a small room available, but let me show you the bathroom first. It's just at the end of the hall here, and it's shared by everyone."

That didn't seem to be a problem. "He doesn't need much. Just a porch to sit on, and its lovely that you have one in the front and the back."

"Your father doesn't mind children, does he?" Lenore said. It should be clear from the get-go that this might be a boarding house, but it was also Johnny's home.

"No. After all, he had me, didn't he." She laughed nervously.

Mrs. Whitmer viewed the larger room with a fireplace and the balcony that overlooked the street. Lenore was hopeful she'd take this one because it meant extra money.

"This room is lovely, but he doesn't need anything this grand."

Disappointed, Lenore showed her the smaller room.

Mrs. Whitmer stepped inside and did a three-sixty, taking a good look, inspecting the bed and the dresser and finally looking out the window that overlooked the street. "He'll be glad it looks out on the street as opposed to the beach." With a twitter, she said, "He's kind of nosy."

He sounded delightful.

They went downstairs and sat at the dining room table, where Lenore handed Mrs. Whitmer a sheet of paper listing the rules and regulations of the boarding house. Lenore could barely contain her surprise when Mrs. Whitmer paid for six months' rent in advance. It was a nice chunk of money, but she'd be mindful of it.

When all business was transacted, Lenore walked Mrs. Whitmer to the front door. They agreed that her father could move in at the end of the week. Lenore waved her off and returned to the kitchen, where Hilda was cutting an apple into small pieces for Johnny. In each hand he held a chunk, and he chewed a third piece, drool running from his mouth. The buttercup sat on the table.

"Chew good, Johnny," Hilda said, keeping an eye on him.

"Good news, we've got a new boarder!" Lenore announced.

Hilda peppered her with questions. "Did she take the larger room? When is she moving in?"

"It's not for her. It's for her father. Apparently, the landlord is evicting him because he has to live there himself."

"Unfortunately, there's a lot of that going on. Sign of the times."

"She even paid for six months in advance."

Hilda broke into a smile. "That's wonderful."

Lenore agreed. "It certainly is!"

Unfortunately, the new lodger wasn't as wonderful as they'd hoped. Lenore recognized him as soon as his daughter propelled him through the door.

"Come on, Dad," she said sharply.

He was old Mr. Forrester from the corner of Lincoln, just a few houses down from where she and John had lived after they were married. In the beginning, Lenore used to wave to him, but he refused to wave back, usually muttering something unkind. It was rumored that he threw things at the children who cut across his lawn to get to the side street.

Lenore did not know if this was going to work out. Next to her, Hilda's eyes had gone wide.

"I wanna go home!" Mr. Forrester shouted.

"You can't, Dad. It's no longer home," Mrs. Whitmer said harshly. "Now come on."

Lenore and Hilda exchanged a glance.

Once she got him over the threshold, her features softened as if she'd crossed some kind of Rubicon. "It's all right, Dad, you're going to be happy here."

Lenore was doubtful.

Mrs. Whitmer introduced her father. "This is my father, Elmer Forrester."

Lenore put her hand out to greet him, but he slapped it away, reminding her of a dog that appeared friendly but snapped as soon as you got too close.

"Dad!" Mrs. Whitmer said.

Lenore and Hilda stepped back.

"Mrs. Whitmer, why don't you take your father upstairs and show him his new room," Lenore suggested, "and I'll get him a cup of tea."

The other woman brushed a few loose strands of hair back into place. She placed her hands on her father's shoulders and gave him a gentle push toward the staircase.

Lenore didn't even have the tea made when she heard Mrs. Whitmer coming down the stairs at a rapid clip. She popped her head into the kitchen. "He's all settled in. Now I must go as I have a train to catch."

And before Lenore could offer to walk her to the door, she disappeared, the sound of the front door slamming behind her punctuating her exit.

"Do you get the feeling he's being dumped here?" Hilda asked.

"I do, but if he turns into a problem, we'll have to get in touch with her and have her come collect him."

Hilda stood with her hands on her hips. "She'll never come back, and we won't be able to get rid of him with a shoehorn."

The tea went cold, and Mr. Forrester didn't make an appearance until dinner.

He sat down at the table, joining Lenore, Hilda, Johnny, and Harriet. His cardigan was misbuttoned, and he had gray, wiry hair sticking out from his ears and his eyebrows.

Harriet, who hadn't met him before, welcomed him.

He grumbled something in response. Harriet looked at Lenore, who could only shrug.

It was chicken stew with dumplings for dinner. Hilda was a magician in the kitchen with limited supplies.

"This is lovely, Hilda," Harriet said. "Very flavorful."

"Thank you, Harriet."

From his seat, Mr. Forrester barked, "What did you do, woman, run the chicken through the stew?"

Hilda pressed her lips together and did not reply.

Lenore was annoyed. She couldn't have this man running the show. "Mr. Forrester, we do not address the female population in this house as 'woman.' Her name is Hilda. That's Harriet. And I'm Mrs. Hadley. I'm sorry you find your dinner unsatisfactory. Perhaps you'd rather take your dinner elsewhere."

He muttered something unintelligible but bent his head and finished the food on his plate, surprising everyone by asking for a second helping. After dinner he pushed his chair back and stood, throwing his napkin down onto the seat of his chair and not bothering to stop it as it slid onto the floor. "Now, where's the newspaper?"

"I'm sorry, we don't have one. We only get the Sunday edition."

Mr. Forrester stared up at the ceiling and emitted an exasperated sigh.

Lenore immediately tried to smooth things over. "But starting tomorrow, I will make sure there is a daily newspaper."

"Can I sit on the porch, or is that only done on Sundays?" Mr. Forrester said.

"Of course you can sit on the porch," Lenore said easily. "I'll bring a chair out front for you. Or would you rather sit out back with the nice view of the lake?"

"Now why would I want to look at the lake?"

"Very well, let me get you a chair." Lenore carried a straight-backed chair out onto the front porch.

When she returned, Hilda muttered, "He's a real charmer."

This was met with a giggle from Harriet.

His daughter had paid well in advance, and no matter how unpleasant he was, Lenore thought, he was a lodger, and it was her job as the landlady to make him as comfortable as possible. After all, this was his home.

# CHAPTER TWENTY-EIGHT

The new lodger proved to be quite a challenge for all involved. The following week, Harriet came running down the stairs to the kitchen in the morning. She was still in her nightgown and bathrobe and her hair, normally secured into a tidy bun, flowed freely to her waist.

Hilda looked at the clock on the wall. "You're going to be late for school. Look at the time. Your breakfast is ready."

"I can't get into the bathroom! Mr. Forrester has been in it for the last half hour!" Harriet's voice was high and loud.

Lenore took over. "Harriet, sit down and eat your breakfast, and I'll go upstairs and make sure Mr. Forrester is all right."

With a purposeful stride, Lenore headed up the staircase and when she arrived at the bathroom door, she listened for a moment, hoping that the old man hadn't died or something awful like that. When no sound was evident, she rapped gently on the door.

"What?" came a loud voice from the other side of the door. The acoustics in the tiled bathroom made an echo.

"Are you all right, Mr. Forrester?"

"Of course I'm all right, why wouldn't I be?"

"You've been in there a long time."

"So what? I'm busy," he shouted through the door.

"I understand that," Lenore said gently, "But we have other people who need to use the bathroom."

"They'll just have to wait until I'm finished!"

"You've been in there for half an hour. It's time to let someone else use it," Lenore said.

"I said I'll come out when I'm ready."

Lenore's temper flared. "Mr. Forrester, I will give you five minutes to vacate the bathroom. And if you're not out, I will unlock this door and remove you myself!" For emphasis, she jingled the ring of keys she kept on her person.

In three minutes, there was a flush followed by the sound of running water, and then the door swung open abruptly, startling Lenore. Mr. Forrester buckled his belt as he emerged. He glowered at her as he passed. Harriet came up the stairs as the old man slammed the door to his bedroom.

Lenore stepped aside and announced, "It's free, Harriet."

# CHAPTER TWENTY-NINE

In the meantime, an arrangement had been made where Lenore's parents would collect Johnny every Saturday to spend time at their house with them and with Laura. Lenore encouraged it; Johnny should know his aunt. He would come home in the evening, talking all about "'Aura." There were signs of ice cream and sand about him; her sister must be taking him to the beach, which she thought was good.

One fall evening when her parents brought him home to her, they sat for a few minutes in the parlor to tell her about his day. The evenings were becoming short, with darkness descending around suppertime. Lenore turned on a lamp. Johnny was worn out from all the fresh air and activity, and he soon fell asleep in her lap.

Harriet bid hello to Mr. And Mrs. Wainwright, but disappeared after they refused her offer of tea.

"We have some news," Mrs. Wainwright said as Lenore cradled her sleeping toddler.

"Good news, I hope," she said.

"It is very good news," her father said with a raise of both eyebrows. "Laura is getting married."

Lenore sat back in her chair, shoulders slumped, her mouth open. She hadn't even known her sister was seeing anyone.

"His name is Edwin Knickerbocker," her mother said with a smile. That was good; it appeared they approved of him.

"He's a fine young man," her father said, putting in his vote of confidence. He leaned forward, clasping his hands.

"Does he know . . ." Lenore's voice trailed off.

"He does," her mother said simply.

Had they moved on? Had they put those horrible events of November 1933 out of their minds? She hadn't. She doubted she ever would.

"That's good. Everything is out in the open then," Lenore said. At least he wouldn't be blindsided by idle gossip. That wouldn't have been fair. She fiddled with the hem of Johnny's shirt, unable to meet her parents' gaze.

Her mother got to the point. "She'd like you to attend the wedding."

Lenore frowned and did not lift her eyes. "I don't know about that." She thought for a moment and stammered, "It's too soon."

"Lenore, it's been almost two years," her father said gently.

She shrugged. Did she want a relationship with her sister? At that moment, she didn't think so. Could you forgive someone yet not want anything to do with them?

Her father spoke softly, leaning back and to one side of his chair, elbow on the arm, fingers of one hand stroking his chin. "She is your sister, and there's no way of changing what has happened. You know my feelings on the subject, therefore I won't belabor it." He sighed. "But someday, your mother and I won't be here."

Lenore looked up at him. At one time, she'd taken for granted that her parents would always be there. It had been hard to imagine life without them. But now she knew differently, knew how fate could be cruel and how your life could change in an instant.

"After us, you and Laura will have known each other the longest. And your mother and I both know that you and she are as different as chalk and cheese. But you can't shut her out for the rest of your life. It will serve no purpose. Do no good."

Her father could be quite eloquent when the situation demanded it. It was what had earned him four consecutive terms as Lavender Bay's mayor. But his eloquence fell flat with Lenore.

Uncertainty gripped her. She didn't want to have to make that decision today. And probably not tomorrow either.

"Think about it," her mother said. "And maybe you'd allow us to take Johnny to the wedding?"

They looked at her, expectant. In turn, she stared at her beautiful little boy, the image of his father, sleeping contentedly in her lap. She did not want to pass her anger onto him. He was building a relationship with his aunt, and that was good.

"Of course," she said.

Her parents didn't stay long and as they were leaving, she stood, trying not to wake Johnny. Her parents kissed her cheek and her father whispered, "Think about what we've said. But we're pleased you'll allow Johnny to go to the wedding."

"Good night, Mother and Dad," she said. Balancing the heavy toddler in one arm, she locked the door behind them, watching as they got into their car and pulled away.

She carried Johnny upstairs and when she reached her bedroom, she didn't bother turning the light on. She smiled at his sleeping face, and gently laid him in his crib next to her bed, pulling off his shoes and socks, and placing a blanket over him.

She went downstairs to do some final cleaning up. On her way down, she noticed a sliver of light beneath the door to Harriet's room. The lodger liked to read before bed. Lenore used to like to read but these days, she could barely keep her eyes open once it got dark. She wondered if she'd always be this tired.

Downstairs, Hilda was in the kitchen, peeling a turnip she would then chop into small cubes and set in a pot of water for the following day. There were a couple of carrots on the drainboard, and Lenore hoped she'd leave them until the morning.

"Johnny had a good day then?" Hilda asked with a smile.

"He's tuckered out. Fell asleep in my arms."

"Good. Having him at your parents' house on Saturdays gives you a break, too."

The truth was, Lenore missed Johnny when he wasn't there. She didn't like him away from her and out of her sight, but she knew she couldn't become like that: nervous and anxious. That would be no way for him to grow up.

"Would you like some tea, Hilda? I'm making myself a cup." Lenore held the big kettle under the tap and filled it, setting it on the stove.

"No thank you. I'll be up and down to the bathroom all night long if I drink anything now," the older woman said.

"Fair enough."

Once the tea was made, Lenore sat across from Hilda. "Laura is getting married," she said, opening the conversation. "to someone named Knickerbocker."

Hilda nodded, not surprised. "I'd heard earlier in the week that she'd gotten engaged."

Lenore couldn't help but feel a little hurt. She thought she and Hilda shared everything.

Hilda caught her expression and smiled. "Lenore, that wasn't my news to share." She set the paring knife down on the table. "I won't come between you and your sister. Like your parents, I won't be caught in the middle."

"Do you think I should go to the wedding?" Lenore asked, sipping her tea.

Hilda shrugged. "It's not for me to say."

"But you have an opinion, I'm sure of it."

The older woman laughed, and her eyes lit up. "You know me too well, Lenore." She continued, "It requires a lot of energy and effort to stay mad at someone for *years*. Grudge-holding will wear you out over time."

Lenore was about to protest, to point out that if Laura had never brought Horace Howard into their lives, then her John would still be alive. Johnny would have his father and she would have her husband. But before she could say anything, Hilda said, "I know what you're going to say, and there's no doubting that what happened was a terrible tragedy. You'll grieve for your husband for the rest of your life, but do you also want to carry all that anger and rage around your neck like a millstone? It wasn't Laura who killed John. You need to separate her from the crime."

Lenore knew intellectually that what Hilda said made sense. She just hadn't arrived there yet on an emotional level. Between her parents and Hilda, they certainly had given her something to think about. But maybe not that night. She'd think about it another day.

Hilda cut the last bit of turnip into cubes and piled up the waxy scraps, putting them into a bucket to be taken out to the compost pile in the morning. She stood and put her hand on her lower back. "Well, that's it for me. I'm going up."

"All right, Hilda, have a good night's sleep."

"Are you coming up?"

"Not yet," Lenore said.

Hilda nodded. "Good night then."

"Good night."

She didn't linger too long in case Johnny woke up and started crying. Ten minutes later, she rinsed out her teacup and set it on the drainboard to dry. She made one last check of the windows and the doors, making sure everything was locked up for the night. She lingered at the back door that led out to the porch, opening it and peering out, hoping to get a glimpse of the lake but only seeing darkness. For a moment, she listened, letting the sound of the surf crashing onto the shore lull her, like it always did. Finally, she closed up the door, locked it, and checked it twice before turning off the lights and heading upstairs.

The day of Laura's wedding was a cool but sunny autumn day. The wedding was to be a small affair, starting with the ceremony at the church, then followed by a luncheon at the Wainwright residence, as Lenore's own wedding had been years earlier. The guest list was considerably smaller than Lenore's, comprised of only immediate family and close friends.

Lenore's parents came to pick up Johnny early in the morning, and as they were leaving, her mother eyed Lenore's apron over her everyday dress but said nothing. They did not ask her if she would be attending.

She kissed Johnny goodbye as her father carried him out. He was always excited to go off with his grandparents, knowing it was going to be a day of adventure.

Before Lenore closed the door behind them, her father said, "The ceremony starts at one sharp."

Muttering to herself, she headed back to the kitchen. There were dishes to be washed. In the kitchen, Hilda said to her, "I laid out the mauve dress on your bed. I pressed it last night."

Pursing her lips and putting her hands on her hips, Lenore said, "I still haven't made up my mind about whether I'm going or not."

Hilda stared at her. "She's your only sister. You'll regret it if you don't. She may have set fire to the bridge, but you can put it out."

Knowing Hilda was right but annoyed all the same, Lenore stamped her foot and marched out of the room with Hilda's laughter ringing in her ears.

# Chapter Thirty

Cars lined the street near the church. An unfamiliar car was parked directly out front, decorated with tissue-paper flowers and a sign reading *Just Married* in an uneven script. Tin cans hung from strings tied to the bumper. A dark cloud passed overhead, sending the sun into the shadows and threatening rain. Lenore parked at the end of the block and walked up to the church, the same church where she'd married John not that long ago.

With a mixture of fear and discomfort, she approached the path that led to the front entrance. As quietly as she could, she opened the door and slipped inside. The air was damp and smelled of candle wax. From the vestibule, she could see her father handing off Laura to Edwin Knickerbocker. Instead of an extravagant white gown, Laura wore an emerald-green suit with a large corsage pinned above her left breast. It shocked Lenore to see how mature she appeared. But then she hadn't seen her sister since John's death.

She slipped into the last pew, relieved when no one seemed to notice her. It was a small wedding. There weren't more than thirty people in the church, and most of them were congregated in the front pews. She could see her parents in the very first pew with Johnny. She didn't want him to notice her, or he'd turn disruptive and draw attention to her. It was Laura's day, and she wouldn't want to take anything away from her.

She moved further along the pew, toward the wall and one of the wooden columns, into the shadows, observing the ceremony. As Laura and Edwin faced each other, she studied Laura's choice for a husband and decided she liked the look of him. He had an honest face, and the way he looked at Laura—it was as if he'd saved up all the love he had in the world and offered it only to her.

Halfway through the ceremony, it dawned on Lenore that Hilda and her parents were right; she would have regretted it if she'd missed it. A lot of the blame for John's death had been placed on Laura's slim shoulders and maybe that was because of grief, but it was unfair. She swallowed hard. A terrible thing had broken up their family. Laura had never had Lenore's strength, but Lenore's strength had shattered with her husband's death.

Now it was time to reclaim that strength and put everything back together as best she could.

The ceremony was over, and the guests clapped as the newly married couple turned to face them. Arm in arm, they made their way down the middle aisle, all smiles.

As they approached, Lenore stepped out of the shadows to smile at her sister. Laura's eyes widened. "Lenore!"

She pulled gently away from Edwin and pulled Lenore into an embrace. "Thank you for coming," she said into her ear. When they pulled apart, they both had tears in their eyes. Lenore's throat tightened with emotion.

Laura reached for Edwin. "Edwin, this is my sister, Lenore."

He put out his hand and offered up a boyish smile. "Nice to meet you, Lenore." His handshake was firm. Masculine.

"Welcome to the family, Edwin," Lenore said with a smile.

Laura looked over her shoulder to see the rest of the guests gaining on them. Quickly, she said to Lenore, "Will I see you again?"

Lenore smiled and said, "Yes."

Laura's chin quivered and she lowered her head.

Edwin put a protective arm around her and said gently, "Come on, Laura, let's go."

When she looked up at him, she smiled, and took one last look at Lenore before departing, arm in arm with her new husband.

Despite everything, Lenore was happy for her.

# CHAPTER THIRTY-ONE

## 1936

Lenore, Hilda, and Harriet sat in the parlor one evening. With the end of summer, the nights had gone cooler. Mr. Forrester sat on the porch as he continued to do despite the longer evenings and the cooler weather. He would go out in his coat and scarf and not come in until evening tea was served at seven.

Lenore sat in her chair, crocheting a blanket for Johnny. He was out of the crib now, and sleeping in a small bed next to Lenore's. He'd need something for the winter. She'd taken several of John's old sweaters and unraveled all the yarn for the blanket. She supposed as Johnny got older, she'd repurpose the yarn again for a scarf or hat or mittens. Across from her, Hilda sat in the rocker near the fire. It was the first fire lit that fall. Lenore knew that Hilda's arthritis was flaring up with the chilly air.

And seated on the sofa was Harriet, reading an Agatha Christie novel she'd taken out from the library. Lenore kept her eye on Harriet. She was chattier and bubblier than usual that evening, and Lenore wondered what was up. Her lodger had bought a new dress, the first one since she'd arrived at the house. It had a modest neckline and a calf-length skirt with a flared hem. Its muted gold color suited Harriet's complexion. Lenore was glad the other woman had splurged on herself.

Lenore looked over at Harriet, who held her book up but had a broad smile on her face. She caught Hilda's eye and directed her attention to her lodger with an almost imperceptible nod. Briefly, she returned her attention to her crocheting, working on her stitches, looking up from time to time and always finding Harriet practically beaming.

Finally, she couldn't take it anymore, and she set the crochet down in her lap.

"Harriet, what is going on? You're all smiles this evening. I never thought Agatha Christie's novels were that funny."

Harriet lowered the book in front of her. "They're not."

Hilda chimed in. "You're all atwitter tonight, Harriet."

The woman appeared to be bursting. "I suppose I could tell you."

Lenore and Hilda leaned slightly forward.

"Alvin Cole, the haberdasher, asked me to go out tomorrow night."

Lenore clapped her hands, genuinely pleased. "Harriet, I'm delighted to hear that."

"I know his father," Hilda said. "They're good people."

This encouragement broadened Harriet's smile.

Although Harriet was not pretty in the conventional sense, Lenore thought there was something absolutely lovely about her. It was a shame some men couldn't see that, that they chose to focus solely on looks. In the years Harriet had lived there, Lenore could not recall another time that Harriet had been asked out. This bothered her and Hilda, and they'd discussed it at length many times during the day when Harriet was at school. But there'd been times when Harriet had entertained a crush on the opposite sex. Whether it was another teacher or someone from one of the clubs she belonged to, Harriet had a routine she adhered to that Lenore and Hilda were now familiar with. She talked non-stop about this person, how he said this or did that, and wasn't he just the best? This went on for a while and then suddenly, one day, they were never mentioned again, leaving Lenore and Hilda curious as to what had happened. Had Harriet dipped her toe in the water? Had she been rebuffed? Had the object of her affection made it plain that he was not interested? It was heartbreaking to witness. The constant disappointment. Because if there was one thing Lenore was sure of, it was that Harriet would make a good wife and mother. She had a gentle, caring way about her. Johnny loved her.

"That's wonderful news," Hilda said. She'd stopped rocking and put down the garment she was mending.

Harriet beamed, nodding her head.

"When is this happening?" Lenore asked, dying of curiosity.

"Tomorrow night at seven. He'll come over as soon as he closes up the shop." Harriet's voice was full of excitement.

"We must meet him," Hilda announced.

"What will you wear?" Lenore asked.

"I was going to wear this dress," Harriet said, indicating the new dress she currently wore.

Lenore and Hilda both spoke at once.

"That's perfect!" said Hilda.

"The color suits you," Lenore added.

Harriet talked excitedly about the date, and Lenore and Hilda soon got caught up in it, Lenore offering to lend her her tortoiseshell combs for her hair, and Hilda promising she'd iron her dress in the morning.

The opening of the front door and the appearance of Mr. Forrester shut down their happy conversation.

"What's the holdup with the tea, Hilda?" he barked.

"It's coming."

He settled into her rocker when she vacated it, inching it closer to the fire. *I'll have to get another rocker*, Lenore thought. Although he was a lodger and his needs came first, Hilda worked hard here at the house and didn't ask for much. Her comfort was just as important to Lenore as her boarders'.

At the end of the night, they all went upstairs, happy for Harriet and crossing their fingers, hoping this one might work out. Except for Mr. Forrester; he was oblivious to the developments and complained about the number of steps on the staircase.

The following evening, Harriet paced back and forth in the parlor, waiting for Alvin Cole to make an appearance.

The weather was cold and outside, the house was being pelted with rain and wind. As a result, Mr. Forrester had remained inside. He was dozing in the corner of the sofa, the newspaper crumpled up next to him.

It was a shame about the weather; it was a horrible night to go out on a date.

Johnny played on the parlor floor with some wooden blocks that had been a gift from Laura and Edwin.

"Harriet, you'll wear the floor out with all that pacing," Hilda said with a laugh.

Harriet stopped mid-stride. "I'm sorry."

"Don't be nervous, Harriet. Alvin said he'd be here at seven and he will be."

"You're right, of course. I've never been on a date before," Harriet admitted.

Lenore and Hilda exchanged a glance.

Harriet bit her lip and headed over to the front door, looking out, hoping for a glimpse of her suitor, then resumed her pacing.

But when the burr walnut mantel clock with its mother-of-pearl face showed fifteen minutes past seven, even Lenore began to wonder. Harriet had stopped pacing and slumped onto the sofa, shoulders sagging, and propped her elbow up on the arm and laid her cheek along her fist.

"He must have got delayed," Hilda said. But a scowl appeared across her features, and she looked at Lenore.

Harriet brightened, sat up straight and said, "Maybe I should go up to the haberdashery and see if he's all right."

Lenore did not miss the alarmed expression on Hilda's face.

"No, no need to do that, Harriet," Lenore said gently.

Johnny had taken his hand and knocked his blocks down, startling them. When he saw their reactions, he launched into a fit of laughter. Mr. Forrester let out a long, choked snore and they all stared at him for a moment, making sure he was still breathing.

"Why not?" Harriet asked. "He could be hurt or something."

It was Hilda who spoke up. "It wouldn't look right."

"What do you mean?" Harriet asked, her eyebrows knitting together. As intelligent as she was, she could be naïve to the ways of the world. And although she and Lenore were roughly the same age, sometimes, Lenore felt years older than the other woman.

With gentleness, she said, "Because you don't want it to appear that you're chasing him."

"Oh," Harriet said, as realization dawned on her.

"Besides, it's terrible out there."

"Give him some time," Hilda told her.

"I'm sure there's a valid reason," Lenore added. But as the clock headed toward eight, she began to doubt.

When it struck eight, she decided it was time to put Johnny to bed. She stood and instructed him to pick up his toys. He wailed, protested, and threw a block against the wall, startling Mr. Forrester from his nap.

"You rascal!" Mr. Forrester griped.

Lenore scolded Johnny, and in the end, he picked everything up, but with great theatrics.

Harriet also stood, shoulders drooping. "I might as well go up, too. There's no sense in waiting any longer."

"I'm sure he had a good reason," Lenore said, but realized it sounded lame, even to her.

"Yeah, right," Harriet said, heading toward the staircase.

"Good night, Harriet," Hilda said quietly, shaking her head.

Lenore and Hilda were just as disappointed as Harriet. *Sometimes, people can be so cruel,* Lenore thought as she carried Johnny upstairs.

# Chapter Thirty-Two

The following morning, Harriet went off to school after refusing any breakfast. Mr. Forrester offered to eat her share, and to keep the peace, Lenore gave it to him.

When the dishes were washed, dried, and put away, Hilda walked to town to do some shopping. She returned with bags full of groceries and set them down on the kitchen table. She paused, holding on to the edge of the table, trying to catch her breath.

Lenore directed her to a chair and made her sit down. "Hilda, how many times have I told you that when you have a big shop, I'll drive you. I don't like you walking all that distance with a heavy load."

"No, it's good for me, I need the fresh air," Hilda said, still gasping for breath.

Lenore was doubtful of that. She put the kettle on, made Hilda a cup of tea, and set it down in front of her. By then, Hilda was settled down.

"I went to the haberdashery this morning," Hilda said, taking a sip of her tea and closing her eyes in pleasure. "Nothing like a nice cup of tea."

"You didn't."

"Oh, I did. I wanted to know where that Alvin Cole was last night."

Lenore wasn't convinced that was the best approach. But curiosity got the better of her and she asked, "And? Where was he?"

Hilda harrumphed. "He said the weather was too bad. I asked him why he didn't have the decency to call and let Harriet know." She shook her head. "He looked dumbfounded as if the thought of a phone call hadn't crossed his mind."

"Oh no," Lenore said, folding her arms against her chest.

"So, I gave him a piece of my mind."

Lenore was pretty sure she did.

"I told him the Cole family *had* a reputation for being decent people, but nothing lasts forever. Then he was tripping all over himself, even offering me a fedora at one point free of charge. He said he'd be here tonight at seven to see Harriet."

Lenore leaned forward, resting her arms on the table. "What did you say?"

A look of triumph spread across the older woman's face. "I told him that if he showed up at this door tonight or ever, I'd chase him down the street with a cast-iron frying pan. And then I told him that Harriet was too good for him."

Truer words were never spoken.

The spark that had been Harriet disappeared for a few weeks after what became known between Lenore and Hilda as the Alvin Cole incident. Normally chatty, she'd become quiet, as if the fizz and bubbles had left, leaving behind something flat. They worried about her and did everything they could to engage her and to bring the old Harriet back to life.

# Chapter Thirty-Three

## 1937

By spring of the following year, Lenore had gained a third boarder. Over the winter, she'd had some people stay short term, but never for more than a couple of weeks, citing the room was too large for their needs. And too expensive. Lenore was hopeful for a permanent boarder and the steady income that would bring in.

Alma May Mandelson was a small woman on the later side of fifty with salt-and-pepper hair. She'd come from Allegany County to replace the town's librarian, who had retired. She claimed her current living situation was no longer tenable and said no more, and Lenore could only imagine what that meant. Mrs. Mandelson—a longtime widow with no children—liked the idea of having her own sitting area in the large bedroom that faced the street. She balked at paying more but Lenore held firm and, in the end, Alma relented and agreed to Lenore's terms.

But for someone who claimed to value her privacy and paid extra for the more spacious accommodation, she seemed to spend many evenings in the parlor with the rest of them.

Harriet sat at one end of the sofa and had just finished telling a story about one of her students that had them all laughing, except for Alma.

Alma pursed her lips. "Children should be seen and not heard."

"Even in school?" Lenore teased.

"I agree with you, Mrs. Mandelson," Mr. Forrester said gruffly. He looked pointedly at Johnny, who was banging a toy hammer against the leg of his mother's chair.

Alma ignored Lenore's quip but nodded at Mr. Forrester. Turning her attention to Harriet, she said, "It sounds like you don't have control of your classroom."

Harriet looked startled, as if that thought had never occurred to her. "I w-w-wouldn't say that."

"I would," Alma said with a harrumph.

"This new generation is too wishy-washy. They've no backbone." This from Mr. Forrester.

Harriet shrank back into the corner of the sofa.

Lenore gritted her teeth. Those were unkind things to say. She'd heard from one of Laura's neighbors, whose daughter was in Harriet's class, that the kids adored her. Johnny dropped the hammer and climbed into her lap, squirming and whining, trying to get comfortable. Lenore brushed his hair away from his forehead.

"Isn't it his bedtime?" Alma said, her frown deepening as she looked at the child.

Lenore wasn't going to take any interference from her lodger. She was beginning to suspect what had happened with the woman's previous living arrangement. It wasn't difficult to put it all together.

"Johnny has a set bedtime," she said.

"But I'm a paying lodger, and I'd like a break from children in the evenings," Alma said.

"Yes, you are a paying lodger with a private sitting room with no children in it," Lenore pointed out.

Alma pursed her lips and stood up, her back erect, and said, "Good night."

In unison, they said, "Good night, Alma."

She marched up the stairs, chin held high.

Within five minutes, Mr. Forrester stood, going up to his room as well.

As soon as they were both out of earshot, Lenore sighed. Harriet's shoulders relaxed and she let out a giggle.

"There's always someone who will find something to complain about." Hilda shook her head, her knitting needles flying in her hands.

Lenore didn't know if she was referring to Mr. Forrester or Mrs. Mandelson or both. She continued to cradle Johnny until he fell asleep. He was getting older and more often than not, he'd want to climb down and take off. She was trying to hold off those days a bit longer.

Carefully, she stood, not wanting to wake him. "I'll put him to bed."

Harriet said, "I should go up as well."

"Don't go up yet, Harriet. Stay here and talk," Hilda said.

"All right then." Harriet scooted over on the sofa to be nearer to Hilda.

As Lenore carried Johnny up the stairs, she smiled to herself. She knew that Hilda was fond of the young woman. At least someone was getting along with someone in the house.

When Mr. Forrester didn't show up for breakfast the following morning, Lenore was concerned. Harriet and Alma weren't down yet either, but that wasn't unusual for a Saturday. They didn't get up as early in the morning on the weekends.

"It's unlike him," Lenore fretted. "He never misses a meal." Breakfast was served between seven and eight, and he was always the first one down.

"I know," Hilda said with a sigh, "but the peace and quiet are heavenly."

Lenore laughed. "I'll run up and check on him."

She took the stairs two at a time. The hallway and bathroom were clear, and all was quiet upstairs. She knocked on the door to his room. "Mr. Forrester?"

One of the other doors opened and Harriet appeared. Lenore smiled a good-morning to her as the young woman walked past, toward the bathroom. Harriet yawned, smiled, and closed the bathroom door behind her.

Lenore knocked a bit more loudly this time, trying not to disturb Alma, who was not up yet. When there was no answer, she rapped harder. Nothing. Gently, she tried the doorknob, but it was locked. Concerned over the welfare of her boarder, she felt she had no choice but to pull the ring of keys from her apron pocket and unlock the door.

The first thing she noticed was that the room was stuffy, and then she scrunched up her nose. There was a smell of unwashed human wafting through the air. She knew Mr. Forrester played it fast and loose with personal hygiene, but she was going to have to have a talk with him.

"Mr. Forrester?" she called out. When there was no answer, she stepped further into the room and stopped abruptly in her tracks. The grumpy old man was on his back in his bed with the covers pulled up over his chest. His mouth hung open, and he stared straight at the ceiling, eyes wide and glassy. His skin appeared pale and waxy.

Lenore ran to the bed. "Oh no." She shook him several times, but he would not rouse.

Harriet appeared in the doorway, her hair in its neat little bun. "Lenore, is he—" Her hands flew to her face.

Lenore looked over her shoulder. "Harriet, run down and get Hilda. Tell her it's an emergency."

Soon, Harriet returned with Hilda in tow. Hilda stepped forward. "Well, that's a first for the boarding house."

"Is he dead?" Harriet asked, swallowing hard.

"Yes."

Alma appeared in the room, tying a sash around her housecoat. "What is all the commotion? It's Saturday morning. Am I not entitled to some peace and quiet on my day off?"

She spied the late Mr. Forrester in his bed, and her eyes bulged and she let out a scream.

"Mrs. Mandelson!" Lenore said sharply. Now was not the time for hysteria.

"Haven't you seen a dead body before?" Hilda asked.

"Not in my own house. My husband had the decency to pass away in the hospital!" Alma said, trembling.

Harriet put her arm around Alma and gently steered her away. "Come on, we've had quite a shock. Let me take you downstairs and make your breakfast for you. There's that wonderful strawberry jam that Lenore made over the summer . . ." Her voice trailed off as she led the librarian out of the room.

"What do we do?" Lenore asked. She had no experience with this kind of thing.

Hilda was so calm; Lenore was grateful. "We call the doctor first," she said. She looked over Mr. Forrester and added, "And then we'll take it from there."

Lavender Bay's only physician, Dr. Charles Worthington, arrived quickly and pronounced Mr. Forrester dead. Lenore contacted Mrs. Whitmer, who didn't seem too upset by her father's passing, and Lenore realized that it must have come as a relief. She knew when the day came when her own parents passed away, she would feel a lot of things, but relief wouldn't be one of them.

The doctor made the arrangements for the body to be removed and once Mr. Forrester was gone, Lenore and Hilda packed up his belongings and stored them up in the attic until his daughter could collect them. Then, donning headscarves and large aprons that covered their clothes, they tackled Mr. Forrester's room. Harriet offered to mind Johnny downstairs to keep him out of their way.

The first thing they did was to open the windows and strip the bed. With a bucket of hot water and some Murphy Oil Soap, they washed down all the woodwork and the furniture. They vacuumed the carpet, and Lenore wiped down the curtains with a damp cloth. She covered a broom with a rag and tackled the cobwebs. When she was finished, she handed the broom to Hilda, who beat the mattress. The two of them flipped it over and put fresh, clean bed linen on it.

By lunchtime, they were finished. They stood back, hands on their hips, and looked around. That was much better. Smelled better, too. Hard to believe that it had been recently occupied by a deceased person.

Later that day, after all the commotion had subsided, Lenore was still quite shaken and decided some fresh air was called for. She took Johnny and set out on foot for her parents' house. Laura, due with her second child, would be there with baby Edna. She was happy that there were babies in the family again. She missed those days.

Although the day was cool, there was warmth in the sun's rays, and she'd picked up a second-hand Radio Flyer wagon, which Johnny currently sat in, pointing at all the things they passed as they made their way from Pearl Street to Bluebell Lane. As it was a dry day, she took the long way, heading south on Pearl until she hit Primrose Street. At the corner of Adams and Primrose, they stopped at the house belonging to the Williams family, whose father, Abner, worked in the post office alongside Fern Mulvihill. They had a golden retriever, Lady, who bounded toward them at the sight of the wagon coming around the corner.

As the excited dog whined and pranced around the wagon, Johnny laughed and clapped his hands.

Mrs. Williams emerged from her house, wondering what the commotion was, a frown on her face. She wore a pinafore apron over her dress. The frown was replaced with a smile as she recognized Lenore, and she threw her hand up in a wave. She made her way down the front steps of her home and joined Lenore on the sidewalk.

"Mrs. Hadley, how are you?" she asked. The other woman was in her mid-forties, a handsome woman with square shoulders, high cheekbones, and gray eyes.

"I'm well, thank you," Lenore responded. It was nice to get out of the house and talk to other people for a change. "How are you and your family?"

Mrs. Williams nodded and smiled. "We're all well, thanks be to God." She gestured toward Johnny. "He's growing fast. He's the image of his father, isn't he?"

Lenore smiled. She loved when people told her Johnny looked like John. "He is growing fast. I don't know where the time goes."

"There's an old Irish proverb: 'The days are long, but the years are short.'"

"Well, that certainly is true!"

Mrs. Williams' smile disappeared as she said, "I heard about your boarder, dying like that in the middle of the night."

Her tone made it sound like it was an inconvenience, and although Mr. Forrester had been crochety, Lenore was pretty sure he hadn't died on purpose to discommode her. "It was unfortunate."

"It seems a lot went on last night in Lavender Bay. Did you hear about Alistair Young?"

Lenore braced herself for bad news. She held her breath.

"His house burnt down last night."

Lenore's eyes widened. "That's awful! Is he all right?"

"He's fine, but he's lost everything!" Mrs. Williams said. "He only has the clothes on his back."

"Where is he staying?"

"Nowhere at the moment. The school has allowed him to set up a cot in the gymnasium at night until he finds other accommodation."

"How awful," Lenore said, oblivious to Lady slobbering on Johnny with her wet, sloppy kisses. Johnny giggled in response. Her thoughts were firmly on her friend Alistair, and she was determined to help him any way she could.

After stopping at her parents' house, she returned home and left Johnny with Hilda, then drove the car over to McKinley High School, where Alistair taught English. School had already let out for the day, and she didn't have a lot of time as she had to get home and help Hilda get the supper on.

The corridors smelled of beeswax and sawdust. She moved along the dimly lit hallway, thinking she hadn't been there since she graduated, class of 1924, all those years ago. Before everything. Memories came slamming back. It had been a much simpler time.

There was no one about, and the sound of her heels striking the floorboards echoed along the corridor. She hoped it might alert Alistair to her impending arrival. When she reached the closed gymnasium doors, she hesitated, unsure of what to do. Did she just walk in, or did she knock? She stepped forward, hesitated again, and stepped back, biting her lip. Finally, she knocked. And when there was no answer, she rapped sharply on the door, this time louder. When there was still no answer, she opened the door slightly and popped her head in. Alistair was striding toward her, the top buttons of his shirt undone. His long, thin, angular features almost looked delicate, and there was evidence of worry lines on his forehead and dark purple circles beneath his eyes.

"Lenore!" he said. "What brings you here?"

She reached for his hands, holding them in hers. "I've come by to see how my friend is doing. I've heard about the fire."

Alistair rubbed the back of his neck and said evenly, as if they were talking about a spate of bad weather, "Yes, that was most unfortunate."

"And you're staying here?" Behind a medical screen with dark blue curtains was a single cot with an Army blanket and a small wooden table with books piled on top of it.

"I am. Temporarily."

"Where will you go?" she asked.

"I'm not sure. My home is gone, and I can't afford to rebuild. I'm staying here while I consider my options, though I must confess, they are limited."

"That's what I wanted to talk to you about."

He waited, expectant.

"Why didn't you come to me?"

Alistair looked around the gym, anywhere but at her. A slight pinkish tinge colored his cheeks. "I couldn't impose on you like that, Lenore."

"That's nonsense, Alistair."

She looked around his temporary living arrangement in a large gymnasium that smelled like sweaty socks, body odor, and floor wax. This wasn't good enough for her friend. "It just so happens that I have a room for you to stay in." To save him from any further embarrassment, she added quickly, "Just until you get back on your feet." When he didn't say anything, she added, "You'd have your own room and breakfast and dinner every day." It occurred to her that he had no kitchen to cook a meal. "How are you eating?"

"Some of the other teachers have offered to bring in food for me. Sandwiches and a plate of dinner ..." He rubbed the back of his neck again, embarrassed.

"Well, I have my car out front. We can pack up your belongings and you can be in your own room tonight."

"That is a wonderful offer, Lenore, and I appreciate it, but I'm afraid I wouldn't be able to pay you much."

Now it was Lenore's turn to go scarlet. "I should have made myself clear: I don't expect you to let a room from me. I'm offering you a place to stay for however long you need." And to clarify, she added, "Free of charge."

"I can't impose on you like that—"

She reached out and laid her hand on his arm. "Yes, you can." This was a nice man who'd been a dear friend since childhood. Looking around at his sparse living conditions in the cavernous gym, she thought the sooner she got him out of here the better. "Now, do you have a lot to pack up?"

He shook his head. "No, only my books over there. I've lost everything."

"Don't worry, we'll source some clothing for you."

They were able to get his belongings to her car in a single trip. Before they left, he put the cot and table away, shut off the lights, and locked the doors of the building.

"This is very unorthodox, Mrs. Hadley," Mrs. Mandelson said when she was introduced to Alistair later that evening at the dinner table.

They were all gathered in the dining room, around the large, rectangular walnut table. Lenore sat at the head with Johnny to her right and Hilda to her left. Harriet sat next to Johnny, and Mrs. Mandelson had taken the seat next to Hilda. After Lenore introduced Alistair to everyone, he took the seat next to Harriet.

"What do you mean by that?" Lenore asked, although she knew full well.

"This, this, this," Mrs. Mandelson sputtered, her face turning beet red as she waved her fork around, with a piece of roast chicken speared to it. "Usually, boarding houses are either all females or all males." Presumably she had been willing to overlook the late Mr. Forrester's maleness because he was old.

How quickly things had changed in twenty-four hours.

"I understand that, Mrs. Mandelson," Lenore said. "But we have someone in need." She didn't want to belabor the fact that her friend was now homeless.

Harriet passed the bowl of mashed potatoes to Alistair, who thanked her.

There was a grim set to the librarian's lips. "It's not right," she said with a knowing look over to Harriet, and then to Alistair. "They're young and . . . healthy . . . and it's an opportunity to get into mischief."

Both Alistair and Harriet stared straight ahead, their faces scarlet, their forks frozen mid-air.

"I trust them," Lenore said pointedly, indicating the conversation was over.

Mrs. Mandelson emitted such a heavy sigh they probably heard it across the water in Canada. "I guess I'll assume the role of chaperone."

Hilda rolled her eyes, and Lenore wanted to laugh, but it was important to keep the peace among her lodgers. She trusted both Harriet and Alistair without a doubt and besides, he would not be residing there long term. It was only temporary.

# Chapter Thirty-Four

## September 1939

Everyone was gathered around the radio in the corner of the parlor. Lenore and Alistair had turned the sofa around and pulled over some chairs. Britain had declared war on Germany, and they all feared what that might mean for the United States.

Not much had changed since Alistair joined them, except that what had started out as a temporary situation was now permanent, and he was now a paying lodger. Lenore suspected that his decision to stay had something to do with Harriet. Or everything. Even Hilda commented on it from time to time. But neither went down the road of speculation or conjecture, not wanting to jinx it.

The money helped immensely. The bills were paid, and in return, Lenore made sure her lodgers had good food for breakfast and dinner and a clean, comfortable home.

Johnny, now five, had started school in September. He was gone all day and Lenore missed him terribly.

"Will the United States be drawn into it?" Harriet asked. They all leaned forward in their chairs. Lenore reached out and turned the volume up slightly on the radio.

"Don't be a fool," Mrs. Mandelson said. "After the last war, they'll never want to go through that again."

Alistair rubbed his chin, appearing thoughtful. "I don't know. Maybe not right away, but I fear it may be inevitable."

Mrs. Mandelson scoffed at the idea and narrowed her eyes at Harriet. "Isn't the name 'Bauer' of German origin?"

"It is."

"Isn't your surname German?" Hilda asked the librarian.

Mrs. Mandelson scowled. "That's my late husband's last name. I was a Smith before I got married." She lifted her chin slightly.

Lenore was just about to guide the conversation onto another topic when Alistair spoke up.

"Harriet, didn't you tell me that the Bauers have been in this country for over a hundred years?"

Harriet smiled warmly at Alistair. "That's right. I did. And my mother's people were of French origin."

With this information, Mrs. Mandelson gave a little sniff.

"We're all Americans here in this house," Hilda said with a tone of finality that would allow no argument. Mrs. Mandelson went to say something, but Hilda fixed a withering stare on the librarian, who thought better of it and closed her mouth.

They sat, quiet and tense, listening to the news, but as soon as Lenore turned the radio off, everyone spoke at once, speculating on Britain and France's chances against the Reich, and *when*—not if—the US would join the war.

Secretly, Lenore had to agree with Mrs. Mandelson. She hoped they'd never go to war. She was too young to remember the Great War, other than the sorrow surrounding her uncle's death, which coated her impressions of that time period in a film of sadness. But they were still in the midst of the Depression. How long would they have to scrimp and make do with things? How long were they expected to operate under crisis conditions? Were there any good times in their future?

Sensing Lenore's discomfort, Hilda said, "Let's talk about something else."

They all looked at Lenore, and it was Harriet who spoke first. She reached for a magazine off the table, flipping quickly through the pages. "I was thinking of cutting my hair and going for a style like this." She passed the magazine to her left, to Hilda, who studied it and said, "It's a very smart style."

Mrs. Mandelson looked at it and nodded slightly. "I suppose it would suit you."

When it landed in Lenore's lap, she said, "That's lovely."

Harriet had beautiful hair, long and thick, although it was rare to see it styled any other way than in a bun at the nape of her neck.

When the magazine landed in Alistair's lap, he didn't bother looking at the style, tossing the magazine onto the coffee table. "I think it would be a shame for you to cut your lovely hair."

Harriet looked at him, her lips parting slightly. The air became awkward, and soon the conversation turned back to the topic of war.

The bleakness of the two colliding situations, economic depression and war, made Lenore weary, and she stood and announced she was going to bed. She'd already taken Johnny up earlier, before they sat down to listen to the radio.

Hilda eyed her sharply. "Do you feel all right?"

Lenore waved away her concern. "I feel fine." She said her good-nights.

"But what about tea?" Mrs. Mandelson asked.

Lenore hesitated in the doorway, thinking she could do that one task before she headed up.

Hilda spoke up. "I'll make the tea. Go on up, Lenore."

"I can make the tea," Harriet volunteered, jumping up.

Hilda smiled a thanks at her.

"I'll help you, Harriet," Alistair said, and he followed her off to the kitchen.

As Lenore headed up the staircase, her hand skimming the banister, she heard Mrs. Mandelson say to Hilda, "Do you think it's safe to leave those two alone in the kitchen?"

"Did you want tea or not, Mrs. Mandelson?" was the reply from Hilda.

# CHAPTER THIRTY-FIVE

## 1941

With America's entry into the war after the bombing of Pearl Harbor in December, there was a rush of men to join the armed forces. All of the sudden, every able-bodied male was leaving for boot camp and shipping off to Europe or the Pacific. One day Lavender Bay was full of hale and hearty young men, and the next day it wasn't. Or that's what it seemed to Lenore. Laura's husband, Edwin, had already left, leaving her on her own with their two young daughters, Edna and Edith. Laura was in such a state over the affair that she moved back to live with their parents, with the intention of staying until her husband returned from the war. Lenore was over there as much as possible to offer handholding, comfort, and help with the girls.

An unexpected snowstorm had prevented Harriet from traveling home to spend the holiday with her family, and had also left Mrs. Mandelson stranded, unable to get to her sister's house in Ohio.

After Christmas dinner at the house on Pearl Street, Lenore and Hilda and the tenants all gathered in the parlor to exchange gifts. Lenore had been busy crocheting all year. There were afghans for Hilda and Mrs. Mandelson, and scarves and mittens for Harriet and Alistair. They were all pleased with their gifts.

A smiling Harriet handed Lenore a gift wrapped in Christmas paper. "We all chipped in and got you a little present."

Lenore looked around at them. Even Mrs. Mandelson was smiling. "You didn't have to do that. I wasn't expecting anything."

"That's the problem," Hilda quipped.

She carefully unwrapped the gift, sliding her nail beneath the taped parts. She'd save the wrapping paper for next year. Inside the package was a wooden board, and Lenore had no idea what it was or what she was expected to use it for. But she flipped it over and let out a squeal of delight. It had a fine sheen and had been engraved with large black script. *Mrs. Hadley's Boarding House.*

"This is wonderful. I absolutely love it," she said. She looked at each of them again. "I shall treasure this for as long as I live."

"If you'd like, I could hang it for you tomorrow," Alistair said.

"That would be great. Outside next to the front door?" You couldn't temper her smile; it was one of the most thoughtful gifts she'd ever received. She stood and carefully set it on the table next to her.

"Now," she said. "I think it's time for Christmas pudding."

1942

One good thing the war had done was end the Depression. Factories boomed, getting ready for increased production for anything military related. And although food was rationed once again for the war effort, people were practiced at making do with what they had, and they survived.

March was blustery that year. It seemed as if it would never stop raining. The rain poured down on the roof, and Lenore placed metal buckets around the attic floor beneath the leaks.

One evening, the occupants of the boarding house were gathered around the dining room table, enjoying a game of Monopoly. Lenore thought it was great fun. Hilda didn't play, but she sat with them and joined in the conversation. Harriet regaled them with tales of her class, and Johnny entertained them with his own idea of how he'd fight the Nazis. Lenore gave silent thanks that Johnny was a long way from turning eighteen.

Harriet turned to Alistair, seated next to her, and said, "You're awfully quiet tonight."

He looked at Harriet and smiled, his expression filled with tenderness. He picked up the dice, as it was his turn, and rolled them around in his hand. He looked around the table at everyone.

"Come on, Alistair, roll the dice," Johnny said.

"In good time, Johnny," he said, still palming the dice and rolling them around in his hand. His gaze bounced around again to everyone. Lenore thought he was acting strange. He cleared his throat. "I guess now is as good a time as any."

"Good time for what?" Mrs. Mandelson asked.

Harriet looked at him, expectant, her smile bright.

"I want to do my part for my country. I've joined the Army. I leave next month."

Harriet's expression crumpled. "No, Alistair!"

There was a slight lift of Mrs. Mandelson's eyebrows.

"Oh, Alistair," Lenore said, leaning back in her chair. Men like him weren't built for war. He was a teacher of English, a lover of poetry, and now to go off to the battlefield . . . the idea made her queasy.

Harriet covered her face with her hands and lowered her head.

Alistair spoke in low tones as if Harriet were the only person in the room. "I must do this. It's important."

She didn't say anything, but she did nod.

"Harriet, would you like to make the tea?" Hilda suggested kindly.

"I would, thank you." Harriet slipped out of the room.

Getting up just as quick, Alistair said, "I'll help."

"Well, it's the right thing to do," Mrs. Mandelson declared.

"I agree," Hilda said. "But it's hard to see them go off."

A heavy pall descended on the table, and Lenore looked at the abandoned board game, the pair of dice sitting in front of Alistair's empty seat.

"Can I have cake?" Johnny asked, looking every bit like a mini John.

"Yes, of course." Lenore smiled at him.

"Can I take Alistair's turn?" he asked.

Hilda leaned forward. "Go ahead, he won't mind."

Johnny picked up the dice and tossed them across the board. Then he stood from his chair, leaned over the table, and moved Alistair's piece around the board. "Ha, go to jail!" and he moved the piece to the corner.

The boy rolled for Harriet next, but after a few turns lost interest and sat back in his chair, folding his arms across his chest and swinging his legs.

Hilda smiled and winked at him.

"Hilda, did I show you my muscles?" he said, stretching out his arm and showing her his bicep. Johnny did this all day long when he was home. Hilda humored him. They all did.

Hilda widened her eyes in mock surprise. "Oh my, I guess you're big and strong all right. But if you want to keep that muscle, you'll have to keep eating your vegetables."

Johnny hated vegetables and was quite vocal about it. Every night at dinner was a challenge.

Muttering under his breath, he played with the little dog token from the game. Hilda laughed.

"How long does it take to make tea and slice cake?" Mrs. Mandelson asked, glancing in the general direction of the kitchen.

"Let me see if they need any help." Lenore pushed back her chair and stood.

As she neared the kitchen, she halted in her tracks when she caught a moment transpiring between Alistair and Harriet. As Harriet cried, her shoulders shaking, Alistair held her face tenderly in his hands, speaking softly to her. Not wanting to invade their privacy, Lenore pivoted quietly and reentered the dining room.

"It'll be a few more minutes." She cast a knowing glance at Hilda, who gave a slight nod.

Mrs. Mandelson leaned back and folded her hands in her lap.

They sat idly, making conversation. The topic swung from the weather to rations and back to the weather.

Alistair and Harriet entered the room, with Harriet's arm looped through his, both of them beaming. There wasn't a teacup or a slice of cake in sight.

"We have an announcement to make," Alistair said. He looked down at Harriet next to him, who gave him an encouraging nod. "Harriet and I are getting married before I ship off."

Immediately, Lenore jumped up and clapped her hands. Hilda, all smiles, got up as fast as she could with her arthritis. Even Mrs. Mandelson smiled.

"That is the best news I've heard in a long time!" Lenore said, hugging them.

"Definitely, I'm so happy for you both," Hilda agreed.

Alistair looked at Harriet. "We'll have to make arrangements quickly."

Harriet was so overcome with joy that she could only nod.

"We can have the reception here!" Lenore said. The thought of planning such a happy event lifted all weariness and sadness from her.

"I'll make the wedding cake," said Hilda, just as excited as Lenore. Harriet was like a daughter to her.

"You're too wonderful," Harriet gushed. Beside her, Alistair beamed.

"It's not every day you have a wedding," Lenore said. Her mind swirled with ideas. She had all her fine china, crystal, and silver out there, and it would be perfect for the affair. The everyday ware just wouldn't do.

As they talked about the wedding and everyone got caught up in the joyful air that had filled the house, Johnny sat at the table, waiting for the game to resume. He rolled his eyes and put in his own two cents' worth: "Weddings. Yuck."

And they all laughed.

# Chapter Thirty-Six

Alistair and Harriet were married on a sunny April day. The daffodils, hyacinths, and tulips had started to open and bloom. The air, though cool, smelled like spring and hope. Harriet looked lovely in the ivory-colored wedding dress she'd borrowed from another teacher at the school where she worked, who'd been married in it the year before. Lenore and Hilda thought it was wonderful to see a bride in white again after a decade of dark-colored, sensible, to-the-knee wedding dresses.

The house on Pearl Street, crowded with wedding guests, was filled with a festive air like it had never been before. People walked around the dining room table, filling their plates. Johnny chased Laura's oldest daughter, Edna, through the house. The young girl giggled with delight. Lenore pulled him aside and asked him to slow down before they started knocking over guests.

Lenore wore the same mauve dress she'd worn to Laura's wedding years ago, and Hilda was in the plum dress she'd worn for Lenore's wedding. Mrs. Mandelson donned her Sunday best: a shirtwaist dress of navy blue.

Late in the afternoon, as the guests began to thin, Lenore stepped out onto the porch to get a breath of fresh air. In her hand was a plate of wedding cake. Johnny had Edna by the hand and was walking down Pearl Street. He knew the rules: look both ways before crossing, don't go to the beach without an adult, and keep an eye on his cousin.

Alistair was seated on the railing in the far corner of the porch but stood when she appeared. "Lenore."

"Alistair! I didn't know you were out here. Is everything all right?" She forked off a small piece of cake and slipped it into her mouth. Hilda had outdone herself again.

He broke into a smile and declared, "Everything is perfect. I can't thank you enough for hosting our wedding here. You have no idea how much it means to Harriet and me."

She swallowed the mouthful of cake and wiped a stray crumb from the corner of her mouth. "You don't have to thank me. Hilda and I were only too happy to do it. It's not often we get to celebrate something wonderful."

"That's true." His smile disappeared, and his features distorted with a heaviness she wished she could relieve him of. He would soon be shipping out to boot camp at Fort Benning in Georgia. After that, he'd be heading to Europe. "Who knows what unpleasantness the future holds for all of us."

"No one knows," she said gently. Not wanting to drag the wonderful day down, she forced a cheery smile. "But we'll handle whatever is thrown at us."

He nodded. "I know I don't have to ask, but please look after Harriet for me until I get home."

"Of course. Hilda and I will take good care of her."

His smile was one of relief. "Thank you."

"And you make sure to take care of yourself over there," Lenore said. "Keep your head down."

He laughed but his smile disappeared quickly.

"Are you nervous about it?" she asked.

"Not really. I'm more nervous about leaving Harriet," he admitted. Appearing thoughtful, he added, "It's unpleasant but something that needs to be done. Best to get over there and get on with it."

It was a good attitude to have, she thought. She'd worry about him, though.

The front door burst open, and Harriet appeared, looking lovelier than Lenore had ever seen her before.

"Alistair, there you are!"

The gloom that had enveloped him immediately dissipated at the sight of his bride, and he broke into a generous smile. "I'm right here."

In three strides he was at her side, escorting her back into the house, his hand on the small of her back.

Lenore smiled, happy for them.

# CHAPTER THIRTY-SEVEN

## CHRISTMAS 1950

Lenore looked around the dining room table, making sure she'd remembered everything. It was covered in her best Christmas tablecloth, an ivory affair with embroidered poinsettias at each corner. Ceramic angel candleholders held tall, thin red tapers. She would light them later. In the corner stood a record player in its own cream-colored case, playing Bing Crosby's "White Christmas." She never got tired of that song.

Johnny flew down the staircase, his footfall sounding like he had army boots on. How many times had she told him not to make such a racket? It was a losing battle.

Silverware in her hand, Lenore marched to the hall and put her finger up to her mouth to quiet him and then pointed to Hilda sleeping in a rocker next to the fireplace. That was her favorite place. The warmth of it eased her arthritis. The older woman could no longer do the things she used to do, and that was all right with Lenore. Hilda would always have a home with her.

"Where are you going?" Lenore asked her teenaged son.

"I'm going to the hill for some sledding," Johnny replied. He grabbed his coat, scarf, hat, and gloves off the coat stand and sat on its bench, pulling on his boots. There had been a foot of snow dumped overnight on Lavender Bay.

"But it's Christmas Day."

"You can't go sledding on Christmas Day?" He looked up at her, grinning. He was the image of his father, with the same light-brown hair, those sapphire eyes, the broad forehead and strong chin.

"Of course you can," she replied. "But we'll be having dinner at two."

He was now a senior over at McKinley High School, with plans to go to college next fall for a teaching degree. Lenore still had some money left over from the inheritance her parents had left her, to pay for it. A college education for her son—how she wished John could see all this. But there was a part of her that believed that on another plane of existence, John saw everything.

Johnny had turned out to be a good boy. Although he wasn't a straight-A student, he worked hard for his grades, and liked sports about as much as anyone his own age.

"All right then," she said with a sigh, knowing there was no way she'd deny him any fun, especially on Christmas Day. "But when you come back, bring in some more firewood from the shed."

"Will do, Mother," he said, jumping up and bouncing out the door.

Through the window, she watched him pick up his sled off the front porch and head off with it. Looking around, he trounced through the heavy snow, leaving big footprints all the way to the street, and then headed south in the direction of the hill.

Once he disappeared, Lenore resumed setting her table to the sounds of Christmas music and light snores from Hilda in the parlor. The delicious smell of roast turkey floated in from the kitchen.

It was going to be a large gathering: the three of them plus her current tenants, except for Miss March, who'd gone home to her family in Corning for Christmas. Alistair and Harriet were coming with the children. And Laura and Edwin would be there with the girls.

Lenore smiled as she set the silverware around the long table. She'd laid a linen napkin across each plate. Using the good crystal, silver, and china gave her joy. Earlier in her life, she'd not given one hoot about such things. But after almost twenty years of thrift and deprivation, she'd learned to enjoy and appreciate it. She'd already set out the butter and salt and pepper. The sugar and creamer and dessert plates would be brought out later.

Finished, she stood back and admired her work, pleased. Christmas dinner was a turkey *and* a ham with all the trimmings. There'd be mashed potatoes, roast potatoes, stuffing, green beans, carrots, creamed spinach, and cranberry sauce. No Hoover stew or watered-down soup anymore. Depression and war were behind them, luckily, and hopefully for good.

Hilda mumbled something in her sleep, her mouth moving but her eyes remaining closed. Lenore headed back into the kitchen to check the turkey. She opened the oven, pulled out the rack, and basted the turkey before closing it back up. There was plenty of time to cook everything else. She decided she'd go upstairs and bring down the gifts for the children and place them under the tree. Johnny had already opened up his gifts before breakfast. There'd been a new sweater, a new pair of pants, and a couple of new issues of his favorite comic books. In his stocking were the requisite orange and nuts. She'd given each of her lodgers a small box of candy and an afghan in their favorite colors, like she always did.

Missing from the dinner table would be her parents, who'd passed away in the previous five years, her mother of a heart attack and her father from emphysema. Their house had been sold and the proceeds split between Lenore and Laura. It would have been easy to splurge, but Lenore had taken her share and invested it into her house. Her business. There was a new roof, a new kitchen, and all the bedrooms had a bathroom added on. Being able to offer lodgers their own private bathroom allowed her to raise her prices. Currently, she had a nice set of boarders. She couldn't complain.

Later, about twenty minutes before dinner, she pulled the turkey out of the oven and set it on a hot plate to rest for a few minutes before she started carving it. Hilda shuffled into the kitchen, looking sleepy.

"What can I do?"

"You could check the potatoes."

Hilda took a fork and pierced one of the potatoes in the pot of boiling water. "They're done. If you drain them, I'll heat up the milk and add some butter."

As Lenore was draining the potatoes, she heard Johnny call out, "Mother, company's here."

And just in time, too.

She heard the front door open, and the volume of noise rose. They must all have arrived at once. The excited twitters from all the children filled the air, and she could hear Laura, Edwin, Alistair, and Harriet wishing Johnny a Merry Christmas.

"Go on out and see them," Hilda said, making a shooing motion. She'd poured some milk into a small saucepan and begun heating it up. Hot milk made the mashed potatoes starchier, she'd always claimed.

Lenore removed her apron and threw it on the back of a kitchen chair. Two of her boarders stood in the front hall with her guests. Everyone was in a jovial mood. Edna and Edith were herding Alistair's children into the parlor to look at the tree and more specifically, all the presents underneath it. Johnny was gathering everyone's coats and hanging them up on the coat stand. When he ran out of hooks, he laid them in a pile on the bench.

Lenore hugged everyone and told them to go in and make themselves comfortable in the parlor and that dinner would be served shortly. She instructed Johnny to give the adults a before-dinner cordial.

Hilda was pouring milk and butter into the pot of potatoes. "I'll mash those, Hilda. Go on in and sit down."

Harriet entered the kitchen.

Lenore turned to her and said, "Were the children excited this morning?"

"Harry was awake at five in the morning!" she exclaimed with a big smile on her face. Looking around the kitchen, she said, "What can I do to help?"

"I'm going to mash the potatoes. Can you start carrying all the dishes out?"

With a nod, Harriet picked up the bowls of creamed spinach and stuffing and carried them to the dining room. Laura's voice could be heard, directing everyone over to the table to sit down.

"Hilda, go on and sit down," Lenore said. "We're ready."

Hilda didn't argue. Slowly, she made her way out of the kitchen and headed toward the dining room.

Harriet continued to carry out bowls of food and Lenore followed her, carrying the platter of turkey. The platter of cold ham had already gone out.

When she set the turkey down at the head of the table where she sat, she looked around at all the people gathered. It warmed her heart. Her wish had come true. Her home was filled with family and children.

---

# CHAPTER THIRTY EIGHT

## 1997, CHICAGO

Johnny had a lovely place here, Lenore thought, not for the first time, as she stared out the window at the long and narrow backyard that sloped gently before breaking into a small copse of silver birch trees. She loved those trees. They were the first to lose their leaves in the autumn and the last to bud in the spring. Currently all the trees were bare, and everything was covered in white.

She'd moved to Chicago five years ago when she could no longer live alone. She hadn't wanted to leave her house on Pearl Street. In fact, she cried when she closed the door on it for the last time. Her niece Edna had promised to look after it. Hilda had been gone a long time. And although Alistair had died years ago, Harriet still lived in Lavender Bay, surrounded by children and grandchildren. They kept in touch through the odd phone call or letter.

Johnny entered the room, carrying her breakfast tray.

"Good morning, Mother," he said, setting the tray on the table in front of her and rubbing his hands together, something he did unconsciously. She wondered if he was aware of it.

She smiled at the sight of him, thinking that this was what her John would have looked like had he lived to an old age. Johnny had gone completely grey, but John would be forever young.

"Are you warm enough?" Johnny asked.

"I'm fine." She wore a thick housecoat over her nightgown, and a blanket she'd crocheted years ago covered her lap.

"Heading off to work?" she asked. He taught at the university level. Much to her disappointment, he'd never married and there had been no grandchildren for her.

"I am," he said. He was dressed for the day in a pair of jeans and a heavy turtleneck. His work uniform, as she liked to think of it. "Rose will be here in half an hour."

Lenore nodded, looking over the tray in front of her. It was the same breakfast she'd been eating for the last sixty years: a slice of toast, lightly buttered, and a small bowl of porridge with a glass of juice.

If it was Rose coming today then it was either Monday, Wednesday, or Friday. She wasn't quite sure. The desire to know was minimal, so she didn't bother asking.

"I dreamt of your father again last night," she said.

"How is he?" Johnny asked.

She held the spoon in her hand, almost forgotten. "He was just as I remember him." The last few weeks, she'd been dreaming a lot of John. It was such a great comfort.

"Tell him I said hi."

Lenore laughed. "I will."

"I'll be home for dinner, Mother," he said, leaning over and kissing her on the forehead.

"All right, John, go on, or you'll be late."

The sound of his laughter trailed behind him as he left. She listened as he thudded down the staircase, opened the front door and closed it behind him, then turned the key in the lock.

Bypassing the porridge, she picked up the toast and caught sight of her hand, studying it. The skin was almost translucent, with blue and purple veins threading just beneath the surface. *When did that happen? When did I get so old?*

She took a bite of toast. She hadn't told Johnny that the last couple of mornings, she'd woken to the sound of John calling her name. His voice had been as clear as a bell. How she had missed that voice!

After she ate half of the toast, she set it down on the plate, having had enough. Leaning back in the chair, she turned her head slightly to look out the window. Rose had affixed an acrylic bird feeder on the outside of it so Lenore could watch the birds, which she enjoyed immensely.

When she thought of the decades that had passed since John's death, it made her tremble. But there had been things she had to do. She'd had a child to raise, a house to keep, and people to look after. When she closed her eyes, she liked to think of the house on Pearl Street and all who had lived there with her. It was pleasant to go back in time; it was like flipping through the pages of a favorite book.

Her life hadn't turned out the way she expected, but it had been good.

A cardinal approached the feeder, its red vibrant against the stark snowscape.

"I'm ready, John," Lenore whispered.

After all, she'd kept him waiting long enough.

# PART THREE

## NADINE

# Chapter Thirty-Nine

Within a week of closing on the house on Pearl Street, Nadine had hired a contractor to do the renovation. He was due to start on Monday. But on Monday morning, he was a no-show. He called her at about half past nine.

"Are you running late?" she asked.

"No. I'm calling because there's a problem," he said.

"There is?"

"The check you gave me didn't clear." He sounded angry, and she couldn't blame him.

"What? Really? I'm so sorry," she said, her face reddening. "Let me call my bank and see what's going on." There was plenty of money in that account. She'd checked it only last week. "I'll call you back."

"Yeah, sure." She did not miss the dismissive tone in his voice. Embarrassed, she scrolled through her phone, searching out her banking app. She logged in, and her mouth fell open when she saw that the balance was only twenty dollars. *That can't be right.*

She scrolled back over the debits and deposits and saw that four days ago, the bulk of the money had been withdrawn. Her mouth went dry, and she swallowed hard. Her first call was to the bank, as she wondered if they'd been the victims of some sort of scam or identity theft.

But she was on hold so long that she hung up and called Richard at work.

"Richard Eberhardt."

"It's me," she said.

"What can I do for you, Nadine?" His tone was cool, and Nadine was suspicious.

"The money is gone from the bank account." She tried to keep the panic out of her voice, but she couldn't help it. It was a lot of money.

"It's not gone, Nadine, I withdrew it," he said evenly.

"What? Why?" she asked.

"Because you're not taking another cent from me. You want a divorce, fine, but I'm not funding your new life."

"Richard, I'm entitled to half of everything." She'd hoped things would be amicable or at least civil.

"We'll see about that."

"I told you I was taking money out for renovations," she said. "You said you were okay with it."

"On the advice of my attorney, I've put the money into a special bank account until the divorce is final."

Anger rose within her, and she was about to launch into a tirade, but she knew that's what he wanted. To hurt her. She wouldn't give him the satisfaction.

Coolly, she said, "Your behavior validates my decision to divorce." Before he could respond, she hung up.

She spent the next fifteen minutes going through the rest of their accounts to find that all the money had been cleared out. Gone. She had some money in her new bank account here in Lavender Bay, but there wasn't enough to do the extensive renovations she'd planned. She would have enough to live off of for a while, but her dream of opening an inn would have to be put on hold.

The realization that she limited money and no way to get any caused her to lean against the parlor wall and slide to the floor. She pulled her knees up to her chest and circled them with her arms. Money had never been an issue in her life. It had always been there. Now she had none, and she squeezed her eyes shut, every muscle in her body tensing.

How was she supposed to support herself if she couldn't get her inn off the ground? Those thoughts swirled around in her head and soon mixed with thoughts of her failed marriage, and she stared, not blinking, out the back window at the lake without seeing it.

Here she was, trying to rebuild her life, but it seemed almost as if it wasn't meant to be. There was no one she could go to for a loan for the renovations and besides that, she wouldn't. *Neither a borrower nor a lender be* had always been her motto. And granted, she expected to get a sizeable payout with the divorce settlement, but there were no guarantees for that either. No, she couldn't pin all her hopes and dreams on a maybe.

She laid her head on her knees and bawled. She never heard the front door opening.

"Nadine, what's wrong?"

She looked up to see Maureen standing over her, staring at her, her eyebrows drawn together.

Embarrassed at being caught in the middle of a meltdown, she jumped up and swiped the tears away from her eyes. "Nothing," she said hastily.

"Nothing?" Maureen questioned. "It doesn't look like nothing to me."

Nadine hung her head and started crying again. She buried her head in her hands and her shoulders shook.

Immediately, Maureen was at her side and put an arm around her. "Come on, it's not that bad."

Nadine lifted her head. "Oh, it's bad."

"Remember what Dad used to say? We're Cooks! We can stand the heat in the kitchen!"

Although she didn't feel like it, Nadine laughed. She'd forgotten that particular saying of their father's. She looked at Maureen and asked, "Why are you here?"

"Mom told me you closed on the house, and I wanted to see it and to congratulate you."

Left unsaid was the fact that she'd closed on the house over a week ago and that she hadn't yet called Maureen to invite her over to see it. She couldn't add shame to her list of negative emotions that day. She could be ashamed tomorrow; she had an opening in her calendar.

"But first tell me what's wrong," Maureen pressed. "Obviously something's upset you."

Nadine poured forth her whole story while Maureen listened attentively. When she was finished, her sister asked, "What's Plan B?"

"There isn't one," Nadine wailed.

"All right, let's think this through." Although Maureen wore an expensive blowout, there were dark circles beneath her eyes, and the fine lines on her face appeared more pronounced than usual. "Why don't you show me around and we can put our heads together and figure this out."

Nadine nodded, relieved to be doing something other than crying.

They started with the downstairs, looping from the large front hall through the dining room on the right and then to the kitchen.

"A back staircase, nice," Maureen commented as they walked from the kitchen through the back hall and to the library on the other side.

They finished their tour of the main floor in the front parlor.

Maureen looked around with an appreciative glance. "Nice big rooms with high ceilings, and those incredible views of the lake. It looks like all the original woodwork. That's amazing. You're not going to paint over it, are you?"

"No, I want to restore it," Nadine replied. The varnish had darkened and dulled over the years, and there were heavy-traffic areas like the staircase banister where it had gone sticky or cracked, looking like parched earth.

"It's a fine place, Nadine. It'll be a show home when you're finished with the reno—" Maureen stopped mid-sentence, remembering that the renovations were now on hold due to lack of finances.

Nadine had been so excited she'd told everyone. But now, she'd have to tell them—with her tail between her legs—that there would be no renovations in the immediate future. For the hundredth time, she wished for the divorce to go through.

"Come on, show me the upstairs," Maureen said.

As she followed Nadine up the staircase, she took in her surroundings. "Look at that beautiful stained-glass window on the landing." They paused on the landing so she could study it. "I bet it's original. But I see some idiot painted the frame brown and there's paint on the stained glass. There must be a half an inch of paint around the perimeter. That's an easy fix, Nadine. You'll need to scrape it off."

Nadine made a mental note of her suggestion.

They stopped at the top of the staircase. Maureen stared at the bare bulb hanging from the ceiling. "I've got just the thing for this."

"You do?"

"I'm an interior designer, remember?" Maureen cast her a sympathetic glance. "Look, I've got a garage full of paint, fabric, and wallpaper, and you're welcome to it."

Her sister's generosity overwhelmed her. "I don't know what to say."

Maureen waved her off. "You don't have to say anything. I'm your sister and I'm happy to help."

Nadine could only muster a thank-you, she was so overcome with emotion. But she was grateful. And admittedly, she felt a lot better. The feeling of despair was beginning to lift.

She showed Maureen the five bedrooms and opened a door on the second floor that revealed a staircase going up. "That's the attic up there. But we'll skip that. There appears to have been mice at one point." Nadine had gone up only one time, right after she closed on the house. It was a large room, also with a high ceiling and a couple of small windows. But there were little rodent skeletons scattered throughout, and she'd managed to walk through a cobweb, getting it in her mouth. She was in no hurry to return.

Maureen grimaced. "You'll have to clean that up before you open for business."

Nadine bristled. "Of course." She wouldn't leave little skeletons lying around; she wasn't stupid. But she decided not to get her feathers in a ruffle.

"What do you think?" she asked. As much as she hated to admit it, Maureen's opinion mattered to her.

They stood in the middle of the hall and Maureen glanced around, taking everything in.

"I think it's a wonderful, old house. It's great that all of the bedrooms have their own bathrooms. That saves you a lot of money in the long run. And they're in pretty good shape aside from a cracked tile here and there. They just need a good scrubbing."

It looked as if all the bathrooms were added at once. Each one was the same: white pedestal sink, white tub and toilet, and small, hexagonal black-and-white floor tiles.

"I need some advice on DIY," Nadine said. "Although renovations are on hold, I need to get the house up to livable conditions. I can't live with Mom forever."

Maureen smiled. "I'm sure Mom wouldn't mind."

Nadine supposed not. She and her mother had been getting along fine. It helped that Nadine was almost never there and when she was, she made herself useful by doing laundry, cooking, and cleaning.

"It's a shame about the inn," Maureen said with a sigh. "I thought it was a wonderful idea."

"You did?"

"Yes. Other than short-term rentals like Airbnb, Lavender Bay has no tourist accommodation that has character. There's the motel out on the highway, but people need to discover Lavender Bay. It has a lot to offer."

"Jeez, Maureen, maybe you should get a job with the chamber of commerce."

Maureen hesitated as if she wanted to say something but held back.

"What?" Nadine asked.

"Have you thought about Herman?"

Nadine frowned. "Herman? I think about him all the time."

With a laugh, Maureen said, "No, not that. About operating an inn with a dog on the premises."

That had been one of the first things she'd looked into, having a dog onsite. There had been no sense in filling out any forms or applying for licenses until she was sure that Herman could be at her side. Because she wasn't doing it without him.

She rattled off facts like bullet points. "If there are no more than eleven guests, then the department of health doesn't regulate it. As long as I serve breakfast only. Temporary occupancy. And as long as no one stays longer than one hundred and eighty days."

"You've done your homework." Maureen appeared impressed. "You know, you could even run a dog-friend-ly inn."

"Hmm." Did she want the beautiful house on Pearl Street overrun by dogs? She loved dogs, and Herman got on with everyone: humans and canines and cats. Although the latter were sometimes wary of him because of his exuberance.

"You might want to start thinking about it before you hang out your sign saying you're open for business," Maureen said.

Nadine pushed that thought aside for the moment and returned her attention to the renovation of the house. With a wave of her hand around the room, she asked, "Any suggestions?"

"Yes. Focus on one room at a time," Maureen said. "Pick the easiest room to redo yourself, and that will boost your confidence." She looked out the window, her eyes not seeing, as if lost in thought. Then she turned to Nadine. "Have you started all the paperwork, licenses and such for opening an inn?"

Nadine shook her head, hands in the back pockets of her jeans. "I have it all. I know what I have to do, but I can't move forward until the house is in better shape."

"True." Maureen headed toward the staircase. "Come on, let's see where we can start."

Nadine wondered at the use of "we" but said nothing. It may just have been an expression. But she followed her sister, eager to hear her ideas.

# Chapter Forty

Nadine arrived at her sister's house the following morning. The weather was still pleasant, and she'd forgotten how much she loved this time of year, when the weather was still warm and the leaves were starting to turn their beautiful fall colors of vibrant red, orange, and yellow.

Maureen and Allan and their kids lived in a renovated Victorian over on Daisy Lane, which ran off the other end of Pearl Street. There weren't many houses on Daisy Lane as it was a short street, and the houses that were there were large and stately, including her sister's home. You didn't know where to look first, between turrets and bay windows and a wraparound porch. It had to be about five thousand square feet. The house's color scheme of white, pale yellow, and moss green reminded

Nadine of a daisy, and she wondered if that had been intentional on her sister's part.

The house was as perfect as everything else in her sister's life.

At the end of a long driveway was a recently built garage, modeled in keeping with the aesthetics of the house. When the garage door lifted electronically, Nadine stood there in her sister's driveway, mouth agape. Maureen had not been exaggerating when she said she had supplies. Nadine's first thought was how they managed to get their cars in here during the winter. Metal shelves lined the sides and back walls. They were packed with bolts of fabric, rolls of leftover wallpaper, cans of paint, and all sorts of equipment from paint and wallpaper brushes to hammers and screwdrivers. In the corner, area rugs, rolled up and secured with rope, leaned against the wall. A long table housed all sorts of bric-a-brac, from light switches to outlet covers to a variety of lamps to framed pictures.

Maureen laughed when she saw the expression on her sister's face. "I collect things. It drives Allan nuts, but you never know when you're going to need it." As if adding emphasis, she said, "Like now."

After a thorough inspection of the house on Pearl Street, it had been determined that one of the upstairs bedrooms would be done first. The walls were in pretty good shape and between the two of them, they were able to pull up the old carpet, revealing the original hardwood floor underneath. The woodwork would be cleaned, and the walls and ceiling painted. That was something Nadine could do on her own.

"This is what I was thinking for that upstairs hall light. As opposed to the bare lightbulb," Maureen said. She held up a small crystal chandelier and actually, it was the perfect size.

"I can't accept that," Nadine said. "That must have cost a fortune."

Maureen laughed and held it out toward her. "Feel it."

Nadine fingered one of the crystal teardrops and frowned. "Is that plastic?"

"It sure is. I paid twenty dollars for it. This will do until you can get a proper one," she said, handing it over. "Cheap and cheerful."

"Thanks." Nadine set it down near the door of the garage to keep it separate. But soon that pile grew, with cans of paint and an area rug they determined would be perfect for the small bedroom.

After an hour, she had plenty of paint and a lovely fabric to make curtains for the room. Excitement coursed through her, and she was anxious to get started.

They loaded up the trunk of Nadine's car, and she turned and threw her arms around her sister.

"Thanks," she said. "I can't tell you how much I appreciate it."

"I'm glad I could help. Is it okay if I stop in from time to time?"

"Of course. Stop in any time," Nadine said. She'd like to have that kind of relationship with at least one of her sisters. With a wave and a toot of the horn, she reversed out of Maureen's driveway and headed home.

Nadine waited for Maureen to arrive. Her sister had called her the previous night and had somehow convinced her that she could gut the bedrooms herself which at the time, Nadine believed, but with the light of a new day, was now doubtful. Maureen was going to show her how to remove the plaster and lath in the bedrooms. All the paint and fabric she'd brought from her sister's garage now sat on floor in the dining room, and Nadine was anxious to use it.

While she waited for Maureen, she decided to clean the old paint off the stained-glass window on the staircase landing. Donning yellow rubber gloves, she filled a bucket with a mixture of vinegar and hot water and started on the window using a rag and a scraper.

The sound of the front door opening was followed by her sister's voice.

"Nadine?" The top of Maureen's head popped into view.

"Up here."

Maureen looked up and smiled. "Sorry I'm late. Got detained."

"No problem."

She came up the stairs, carrying a claw hammer in one hand and a crowbar in the other. She stopped in front of the window and inspected it. "That looks better already. It's beautiful. I can't imagine what you'd pay for something like that today."

Holding up the crowbar and claw hammer, Maureen asked, "Are you ready to get your hands dirty?"

"I am."

Nadine followed her sister up the rest of the staircase and they stood in the hall.

"You'll save yourself some money doing the gutting yourself. Last night, I called a guy I know who does drywall and who owes me a huge favor. He's going to put up new walls here for you once everything is gutted."

Nadine was overwhelmed by her sister's help. "Thanks so much, Maureen."

She followed Maureen into one of the bedrooms.

"Start with this room first," Maureen advised. "It's the smallest and hopefully, won't take too long."

They looked around. Suddenly, Nadine was unsure.

"I don't know if I can do this," she admitted.

"Of course you can! Didn't you reno the first house you lived in?"

"I did but I was also twenty years younger . . . and stupid."

Maureen grinned. "We were all stupid back then. Look, this is going to be a mess. Wear a mask, keep all the doors closed, and get a dumpster."

Nadine nodded.

Maureen looked her over. "Okay, you've got old clothes on, that's good. Do you have a mask?"

"Will a bandana do?" She pulled a red paisley bandana from her back pocket.

Maureen pulled a couple of masks from her pocket and handed one to Nadine. "Here, take one. I'll get you a box from the drugstore." She looked at her sister and added, "You don't want to be breathing in all that dust."

"No, I do not. But I can pick some up. No need for you to do that. You've done enough." She couldn't and wouldn't ask any more from her sister.

"Okay, this is lath and plaster. It's going to be messy when it comes down. But first, before you even do that, you need to remove the trim. And you're going to use the claw hammer and the crowbar to do that. And be very careful because you don't want to destroy the woodwork."

Inside the bedroom, Maureen crouched down and pulled a utility knife from her back pocket. She looked up at Nadine as she spoke. "Use the utility knife to loosen any caulk along the top of the baseboard. Then"—here she pulled out a putty knife from her pocket, leaving Nadine to wonder what else she had back there—"use the knife to pry the baseboard away from the wall to give you enough space to get the crowbar in there."

She demonstrated this, and she made it look easy. But Nadine guessed it probably wasn't.

"Now, because we don't have to worry about the walls because you're replacing them, we don't have to be extra careful with the crowbar." She inserted the bent claw end with the nail slot of the crowbar behind the top of the baseboard and loosened it, maintaining her crouch and crab-walking along the wall, until the entire section loosened enough for her to pull it off.

"Now you'll mark the baseboard on the back, or you won't remember what goes where." She pulled a black Sharpie from the pocket of her jacket and used her teeth to uncap it. She turned the baseboard over and wrote on the back of it. "Keep it simple. I just put 'LS' so you know it's on the same wall as the light switch." She pointed to the baseboard below the window. "Label that 'WW' for wall with the window."

Nadine nodded and Maureen said, "Or label it any way you see fit, so that you can remember it."

Under Maureen's instruction, Nadine worked on the rest of the trim in the room. It wasn't easy. Sometimes it was good and stuck, and she had to put some weight behind the crowbar, but in the end, she got it all removed. She and Maureen carried the pieces to one of the other bedrooms and laid them out along the floor. It was a good thing the house was empty or there'd be nowhere to put anything.

They returned to the bedroom and Maureen wielded the hammer and grinned. "Now for the fun part." She swung the hammer against the wall, landing right in the center of it, leaving a big hole. Chunks of plaster fell to the floor and a plume of dust rose from it.

"Oops, we forgot our masks," she said, setting the hammer down and adjusting the mask around her face. Nadine did the same.

Maureen handed her the hammer. "Your turn."

Nadine took the hammer and swung, making a smaller hole in the wall, resulting in the same thing: chunks of plaster falling to the floor and more dust. Turning around, Maureen closed the door and opened the windows in the room.

When a good portion of the wall was removed, they pulled out the remaining pieces with their hands, revealing the original lath behind the wall.

There was a growing pile of plaster on the floor and a fog of dust in the room.

"Now, we need to remove the lath from the studs. Use the crowbar to do this." Again, Maureen demonstrated.

"What about all those nails?" Nadine asked when all the lath was gone from the first wall, eyeing the nails sticking out of the studs. There were lots of them. Too many to count.

"If the nails don't come out with the lath, you'll have to remove them with the hammer. They all have to come out."

"Okay."

Maureen's beautiful hair was covered in fine white plaster dust. Nadine was pretty sure her own hair looked the same.

Her sister went to the master bedroom and opened the door that led out to the balcony overlooking Pearl Street. She left it open, and the air that rolled in was refreshing. She poked her head back into the room. "You know, you could get them to put the dumpster right below the balcony, that way you can toss everything in from here, rather than dragging it all the way down the stairs."

Nadine was amused at her sister's use of the word "toss," as if the old plaster didn't weigh a ton.

When they finished the second and third walls, she realized that quite a bit of time had passed. "Maureen, you don't have to stay. I can finish this up."

"I don't mind. Come on, we only have one more wall to do. Let's get it finished."

"Are you sure?"

"I am."

"Don't you have plans with Allan or the kids tonight?"

"Nothing that can't wait," Maureen said, and she turned her back to Nadine and swung the hammer into the fourth wall.

When they finished, Nadine knew she could do no more. Her sister offered to call a dumpster company on her behalf in the morning, and Nadine was so weary that she readily agreed.

As she locked the door behind them to head back to their mother's house, Maureen said, "It's a lot of work."

"I used muscles I didn't know I had." Nadine reached around and massaged the back of her neck. What she wanted was a long, hot bath.

Maureen laughed. "I know, right?"

They walked side by side down the wide steps of the front porch toward the driveway. Maureen had parked her car behind Nadine's.

"I can't thank you enough for all your help," Nadine said. She was overtired and when she got to that point, it wouldn't be much of a stretch for her to get all weepy.

"No problem. I'll help when I can." Maureen headed to her car, waved goodbye, got in and drove away.

Nadine stopped at the drugstore on the way home for Motrin and a box of masks. She drove home and parked on the street in front of her mother's house. Her plan was to get cleaned up and go to bed.

Herman stood near the front door, wagging his tail and whining when he spotted her.

"Hey, bud," she called out, happy to see him.

As soon as she went inside, Herman began yelping, leaning all his weight against her, his wagging tail hitting her thigh.

"I'm home now." She gave him a reassuring hug. The dog lifted his head and licked her nose.

"Thanks."

Her mother walked out of the kitchen. "He's been sitting there waiting for you for the past—" She stopped in her tracks when she eyed Nadine. "You're a mess!"

"I know," Nadine said, her voice weary. "I'm going up to soak in the tub."

Her mother nodded. "Did you want some dinner? I've got leftover goulash."

"No thanks, Mom. I'm too tired to eat."

As she walked up the stairs with Herman following close behind, her mother called up. "Aunt Gail called, she said for you to stop by the shop when you get a chance."

"Sure," Nadine said.

Once the tub was filled and the steam rose from the surface of the water, Nadine stepped out of her clothes and piled them near the door. Herman paced back and forth between the bedroom and the bathroom, but finally backed into the bathroom and settled on the mat, panting.

Nadine slid into the tub, lay back, closed her eyes, and groaned. Every muscle ached. She hung her arm over the side of the tub and smiled when Herman rose from his position so his head touched her hand. Despite her exhaustion, she obliged him and gave him a few pats, and he soon settled down. She closed her eyes, thinking she'd rest them for a few minutes.

When she woke, the water had gone cold and Herman had disappeared. She stepped out of the tub and released the drain, the water swirling down. She dried off quickly and made her way to the bedroom. Herman was conked out right in the middle of the bed.

She gathered her dirty clothes in her arms and went downstairs, throwing them into the washing machine. After pouring in detergent and fabric softener, she chose her settings, started the machine, and headed back up, stopping only once to say good night to her mother, who was watching a crime documentary.

Herman grunted and lifted his head slightly when Nadine nudged him over. She climbed beneath the covers and purposely avoided setting her alarm because after today, she felt she'd earned herself a sleep-in.

# CHAPTER FORTY-ONE

But as luck would have it, Nadine was wide awake by six in the morning. For more than twenty minutes, she repositioned: on her back, on her left side, then her right, trying to go back to sleep, remembering her promise to herself to sleep in. But she started thinking about the house and everything she wanted to do. There was so much she almost didn't know where to start. But she remembered Maureen's sage advice of taking one room at a time, and she decided she would tackle the next easiest room: another one of the bedrooms.

As her mother was still asleep, she decided to take Herman with her. After a quick breakfast, which she ate standing in front of the kitchen sink, she scribbled a hasty note and left it on the table.

It seemed the beautiful September weather had vanished overnight. The sky was gray and dull, and there was a mist rolling in off the lake.

She drove the short distance to her new home and let Herman out of the car, and together they trotted up the front steps.

It was a thrill that she owned a house of her own. That it was hers and hers alone. Thinking of it reminded her to get a will made once her divorce was final. Obviously, it would be left to Emma, and it made Nadine smile to think it would help her daughter to fulfill her dream of owning a house on the beach.

As soon as she arrived upstairs, she rolled up her sleeves and got to work. Ignoring the pile of debris on the floor, she moved on to the next bedroom. With the first swing of the hammer against the wall, the noise of the impact reverberated around the room, resulting in Herman giving his two cents' worth with a few barks from the safety of the doorway.

For the rest of the morning, she removed trim and pulled down walls, taking the debris from the room and piling it with the rest. Despite the rain, she opened the upstairs windows and the balcony door, stepping outside from time to time to lower her mask and take some deep breaths.

Her phone pinged in her back pocket, and she pulled it out and read two texts from Maureen:

*Dumpster will be delivered tomorrow morning between 9 and 12.*

And then the second message:

*Drywaller will be there to meet with you tomorrow at 5pm.*

Gutting every room upstairs had taken a lot longer than she thought it would. For some unknown reason, using some magical formula known only to her, she had estimated it would take her a week to gut the upstairs bedrooms and hallway.

It had taken her seventeen days.

She bundled up the lath and tied it with string. Using a shovel, she moved the plaster debris from the floors of the bedrooms into industrial-sized garbage bags. But she soon found out she was unable to lift any of the bags weighing more than twenty- or twenty-five pounds high enough to heave them over the balcony into the dumpster.

The drywaller, a man named Mike, had come out and given her a price. She'd have to dip into her savings, but she didn't care. There'd be brand-new walls at the end of it. As soon as she was finished gutting the upstairs, he would start, so she was anxious to get it done. From working morning to night, she managed to lose fifteen pounds.

Mike had also told her that his two college-aged boys were home for the weekend and were looking for some cash, and would be more than willing to clean up the upstairs under his supervision, including getting all the debris into the dumpster. Nadine jumped at the offer, thinking it would be money well spent.

Things were finally moving along.

# Chapter Forty-Two

It was Nadine's first free day in almost three weeks. She'd given Mike a key to the house so he and his sons could get in and clean up. She was looking forward to a day away from the house, and her first stop was going to be her aunt's antique shop in town. She left Herman with her mother and promised to be back soon.

Opting to take the shortest route, she turned south from Heather Lane and walked along Pearl Street, catching glimpses of the lake between the houses. Like the day, the lake was gray, and the foamy surf whipped up against the shore.

Prime Vintage, the only antique shop in Lavender Bay, was on the corner of Main and Pine, just down the block from Coffee Girl on the same side of the street.

Her aunt had been dabbling in antiques for as long as Nadine could remember. When Nadine and her sisters were young, Aunt Gail would drag them, along with her own two daughters, Esther and Suzanne, to flea markets and auctions.

A large sign hung from the corner of the building, displaying the name of the shop in Old English script. The entrance was flanked by large bay windows displaying fine china, vases, and various pieces of silverware. In the left window, behind all the items, was a large painting of a young blond child with a terrier at his side. The portrait must have come from a family that had been wealthy at one time. But the fact that it was currently for sale indicated that the descendants either needed money or weren't interested in their heritage.

Antique shops always aroused curiosity in Nadine. She often wondered about the people whose belongings had ended up in these shops. Had they cherished these items during their lifetimes? Did they pull out the good china only on Christmas and other special occasions as she did?

Brutus the dog was missing from his usual spot in front of the doorway. The day was likely too misty for him. He was used to the heat of the southeast of the country. She stepped into the shop. Paintings stood on the floor, leaning against the cream-colored walls. There were all kinds of furniture, from bedroom sets to dining room sets to all sizes and sorts of tables and desks. She eyed a vanity table with longing but decided it was definitely not in her budget. The store was well lit, as antique chandeliers of every sort hung from the ceiling, switched on at their full wattage. It gave the interior a warm glow.

Brutus lay on his back on a plush red velvet settee with ornate scrollwork. One tawny ear hung over the side of the settee, and he snored contentedly. She shook her head and laughed. Everyone in town knew Brutus and that he had the run of the place. He'd worked hard in his life down south, finding missing people and tracking down escaped felons, and therefore people cut him a lot of slack. He'd earned a life of ease.

She walked along the narrow aisle to the back of the shop, taking everything in. There were books piled on a winged armchair. Every available shelf and tabletop had some kind of figurine or knick-knack on it. As she made her way through, her hip caught a small accent table and it teetered, but she immediately righted it before it crashed into anything else.

At the back of the store was a glass counter and showcase displaying various pieces of jewelry and watches and even a couple of antique pistols, which she hoped weren't loaded.

Off the back of the store was a small room she knew to be Aunt Gail's office. The curtain dividing it from the sales floor was half open, revealing the turquoise walls behind it. The sound of her aunt laughing and giggling made her smile. She spoke, but her voice was muffled. And then more laughter.

Nadine called out as she approached the counter. "Aunt Gail?"

"I must go, ta-ta," she heard her aunt say into the phone.

Aunt Gail emerged and if you didn't know she was the older sister of Louise Cook, you'd never guess it, as the two were as different as day and night. Where Nadine's mother was trim with short silver hair, Gail Campbell was robust, with vibrant red hair and a flair for the extreme. Currently she sported a pair of glasses with multi-colored striped frames, bright red lipstick, and a heavy knit shawl that fell to her knees.

"Nadine!" She came out from behind the counter and immediately pulled her niece into a warm embrace, giving her a good hug. When she pulled away, she kept her arms outstretched, hands on Nadine's arms, and studied her. "You're looking well."

She dropped her smile and said, "Now, there are no secrets between your mother and me—in fact, I was speaking to her just now—and she told me about Richard. That dirty dog!"

"That's exactly what he is."

"I'm so sorry for your troubles, honey," she said. "But you did the right thing in coming home. Be with people who love you."

A smile broke out on Nadine's face. "That's the plan."

"And how's Emma getting on at college?"

Nadine nodded. "Good. She likes it. In fact, I think she likes it a little too much." The last conversation she'd had with her daughter was over the weekend and she couldn't talk long because she was on her way to a party.

"Good for her! You're only young once."

That wasn't the way Nadine felt. She hoped her daughter wasn't neglecting her studies while she was enjoying herself.

"I heard you bought the old Hadley place," Gail said.

"I did. It needs a lot of work, and Richard has tied up our money, but I'm managing."

"Your mother told me that, too." Aunt Gail shook her head and repeated, "That dirty dog."

They were interrupted by a shuffling Brutus, his eyes mournful, his ears dragging on the ground. He stopped and looked at Gail.

"Your lunch is ready, Brutus," she announced.

The old dog shuffled off behind the counter and disappeared into the back room. The air was soon punctuated by the sound of him gobbling up his food.

As if making an excuse for him, Gail said, "When he worked, he probably had to eat on the run. Always busy."

This was followed by a long burp from behind the curtain.

Her aunt shrugged, arms raised as if to say *What can you do?*

Nadine had to suppress a smile. The dog was a character, just like her aunt.

"Anyway, I've been meaning to stop over and see the place," Gail said.

"I'd love for you to come over."

"But I don't want to bother you. I'm sure you're busy."

"Never too busy for you. Please stop by any time," Nadine encouraged her. She shifted the conversation, asking about her cousins. "How are Esther and Suzanne?"

"They're fine. Looking forward to catching up with you."

"I'd love to see them."

"As soon as you get settled, we'll all get together. But there's a reason I asked you here. I want to show you something." She waved her hand. "Follow me."

Gail pushed the curtain aside and walked through the back room, with Nadine right behind her. An old roll-top desk stood in one corner, piled with ledgers and papers and cups full of pens, pencils, and markers. There was a calendar on the wall from the year 1982. Against the opposite wall were two beige metal filing cabinets topped with black wire baskets full of papers and receipts. Brutus sat at the only window in the room, a tall, narrow one, his chin resting on the sill. Gail led Nadine to a smaller storage room with a tiny bathroom off to the side. Every available space was stacked with boxes. A fire extinguisher stood sentry by the back door.

Gail pulled a set of keys from a pocket beneath her shawl and opened the back door onto a fenced-in space behind the store, part of it paved and part of it a small grassy area with a dog bowl full of water. At the far end of the yard was a steel-framed storage space as wide as the lot.

With the same set of keys, Gail unlocked the padlock that secured the small building. She pushed the door open and flipped on a light, illuminating the window-less space. It was packed with furniture.

"I had this put up three years ago because I'm running out of room, and I was tired of keeping everything in my garage at home."

"Where do you get all this stuff?" Nadine asked, looking around. Articles of furniture were stacked on top of one another, some piles as high as the ceiling. There was everything: bookshelves, tables and chairs of various sizes, bed frames and dressers and bureaus. There was an old television unit with a stereo compartment to the left of the screen and a radio unit to the right.

"Mostly estates or auctions. I've been around so long that people call me when there's estate pieces that need to be sold."

"Huh."

"Last year I purchased a lot of furniture from the old Glenville Arms. Have you ever been to Glenville?" she asked, her hand on a generous hip.

When Nadine shook her head no, Gail continued, "Anyway, the owner of the Glenville Arms died—that little inn had been around *forever*, run by four generations of the same family, and there was no one to take it over so everything was auctioned off."

She pushed furniture out of the way as she made her way through the crowded space. She stopped at a bunch of antique mahogany tables. "I got the little tables from their dining room with the matching chairs."

They were fine tables, small and square with space to seat four. The solid mahogany chairs had fabric seats and curved, scrolled legs. They were in pretty good shape.

"I was going to gift you a dining room table, but your mother tells me you plan to turn the place into an inn," she said.

"Yes, that's the plan."

"Then I'll give you these tables and chairs for your dining room. I assume you'll be giving your guests breakfast?"

As an innkeeper, the only meal she'd be serving would be breakfast. She looked over the furniture. The gift was too generous. "I can't accept these."

"You can and you will," Aunt Gail said firmly. "You probably don't need all twenty tables?"

"No, I only have four rooms for guests," Nadine explained.

"Then take five or six tables, and you can put two together to seat six or eight," her aunt suggested.

"Oh, I don't know . . ." It was a generous gift to be sure, and she did need furniture for her inn. Right now, she had none.

Gail turned and made her way through the slog of furniture, heading toward the door and leaving Nadine no choice but to follow. "That's settled then. I'll pick out the five that are in the best condition, and I'll have Marty drop them off."

"Who's Marty?"

"He's my delivery man. He's retired and he was looking for some part-time work."

"I'd appreciate that as I have no way to transport them."

Gail flipped off the light switch and the interior went dark. She closed the door behind them and locked the padlock. "In fact, if you ever need anything transported, picked up, or moved, let me know. Marty is reasonable."

"Thanks, Aunt Gail."

Rain began to fall as they stepped inside the back room of Prime Vintage.

"I can't thank you enough, Aunt Gail," Nadine said. She swallowed a lump in her throat, feeling overwhelmed by her family's generosity.

The older woman waved her away. "What good is family if they won't help you when you need it?"

They'd just stepped out into the main shop when the front door opened and a small, spry woman with salt-and-pepper hair stepped in, clinging to the shoulder strap of her purse. Her face transformed into a smile when she spotted Gail.

"Kay, how are you?" Gail said to the other woman. Brutus was back on the settee, sleeping, his jowls puffing out with each blast of a snore.

"Kay, this is my niece, Nadine Eberhardt. Louise's daughter." She turned to Nadine and said, "This is Kay Bright. She runs the Lavender Bay Historical Society."

They said hello and Gail interjected, "Nadine bought the old Hadley house."

"I heard that," Kay said, still clutching her purse. "I heard you're going to turn it into an inn."

Nadine took a deep breath. "Hopefully."

"No hoping about it. Get it done," Kay joked. "This town needs an inn."

"Would you have anything at the Historical Society about the Hadley place?" Nadine asked.

Kay's eyes traveled up and looked off to the left. She placed a forefinger to her chin. "Off the top of my head, I'd say no."

Nadine felt a stab of disappointment. Wouldn't it have been nice to have something historical to add to the house. Or see how it used to be.

"But I'll have a look around," Kay promised.

"Thanks, I appreciate that. It was nice meeting you and thanks, Aunt Gail, for everything," Nadine said, figuring she should leave the two women alone.

They said their goodbyes, and Nadine headed out. Brutus did not even bother to lift his head as she walked past.

A week later, Nadine received a piece of mail at her new house from the Lavender Bay Historical Society. She tore it open, and inside there was a notecard from Kay Bright:

"I found your house on the 1910 and 1920 censuses. Included are the photocopies."

Nadine pulled them out and unfolded them, her eyes scanning the papers.

The census record was laid out in a grid, and the headings across the top of the page included location, name, age, race, sex, marital status, and number of children. There were columns for nativity, citizenship, occupation, and education. When she found her house number, she almost shouted with glee.

There was the first family in residence at 19 Pearl Street. Surname: Anderson. Her eyes scanned down the list and then widened in surprise: the Andersons included a husband and wife, six children, the wife's brother, the husband's aunt, and a cousin.

She'd get a frame for the census and hang it right here in the front hall.

Nadine leaned against the wall, recalling Edna Knickerbocker's words: *It's a house that takes in strays.*

# Chapter Forty-Three

By the following spring, Nadine's divorce was final and she'd received her settlement money. All the upstairs bedrooms had been completed: painted; hardwood floors refinished; and decorated, with Maureen's help, in subdued tones and colors. A plumber was coming to make sure the bathrooms were all in proper working order, and the guy Nadine had originally hired to do the renovations was back, as she needed the entire kitchen overhauled and up to code for an inn. He was also going to renovate the third-floor attic and install larger windows. It was a huge space and although it couldn't be used for guest accommodations, she'd use it for her own room, freeing up the entire second floor for guests. She hoped she was that busy.

Many nights she lay awake, wondering if she'd get any guests at all. Nightmares of an empty inn haunted her.

When she confessed this to her mother, Louise's solution was simple: plan a grand opening and get the show on the road.

Following her mother's advice, she firmed up the completion date with the renovator, gave him an extra two weeks, and made an appointment with an attorney to make sure she had all her ducks in a row with licensing and permits.

One morning over breakfast, she discussed her grand opening plans with her mother, Maureen, and Angie. They'd all gathered for brunch on a Sunday. There were scrambled eggs and bacon, and rye toast with Gibson's grape jelly.

Nadine and Herman had been living at the house on Pearl Street since after Christmas. The holiday had gone well. Emma had chosen to spend Christmas in Lavender Bay with Nadine and the Cooks, and then flew out to see Richard in January.

"When's the grand opening?" Angie asked, picking up a strip of bacon from her plate and biting into it.

Nadine gave her the date.

Maureen spoke up. "That's perfect. Right in time for the Lavender Bay Parallel Parking Championship! You should notify the organizer and let them know you have rooms available if any of the out-of-towners need accommodation."

Nadine's head was swimming. "Wait. What? Parallel Parking Championship?"

Angie, Maureen, and their mother laughed.

Louise stood and brought the coffeepot over, pouring some in everyone's cup. "I know it sounds strange, but this is the twelfth year. People come from as far away as Buffalo, Cleveland, and northwest Pennsylvania."

Angie spoke up next. "It's only a one-day event. You have to parallel park, and the winner gets a trophy."

Maureen held up a finger. "But if you hit the curb, it's an automatic disqualification."

The questions came fast from Nadine, her brunch forgotten. "How did I not know about this? And people actually sign up to participate?" This was mind boggling, but she was willing to go with it.

"There were over one hundred entrants last year," Louise said, scratching her arm. "Lots of people from Lavender Bay participate. It's kind of fun."

"Get out." Nadine still wasn't sure whether they were teasing her or not.

"We're serious. Go online later and look it up." Angie smirked. "That jerk across the street, Java Joe, won it two years ago and still has the sign in his window."

Nadine had missed that on her visit to Java Joe's and decided as soon as she could, she'd be looking into this event.

"There's all sorts of festivals here," Louise said.

"Other than the usual ones like Thanksgiving, Christmas, Fourth of July, et cetera," Maureen added.

Angie held up her hand and lifted her fingers one by one, ticking off the list. "There's the Parallel Parking Championship we've already mentioned, there's Jacques Aubert Day"—Nadine had forgotten about the day celebrating the town's founder—"there's the Grape Festival in September, there's the Lavender Bay Beach Sports Tournament the first week in August . . ."

"Don't forget the Beach Barbecue Championship," Maureen said.

Their mother chimed in. "And the hot air balloon festival, that's always a lot of fun."

"Wow, this town has a lot of championships," Nadine noted.

"This town likes a winner," Angie said sarcastically.

Nadine's mind worked frantically over how she could maximize these opportunities for her own business.

"Back to the inn. I'd like to donate some loaves," Angie said.

"Loaves?" Nadine was clueless.

Louise laughed, Maureen giggled, and Angie, always short on patience, rolled her eyes.

"Loaves," Angie repeated with a sigh. "Banana loaf, blueberry loaf, orange cranberry loaf."

"I'll never eat all that," Nadine said.

Angie shook her head and looked at her mother and Maureen seated across the table from her. "What are we going to do with her?"

Louise laughed and shrugged. "Accept her as she is?"

This resulted in a hearty laugh from Maureen.

"The loaves are for your welcome hampers for the rooms. Mom told me all the wonderful things you're putting in them," Angie explained.

"Oh," Nadine said when it finally dawned on her. And then, "Of course. The guests will love that."

Louise grinned. "If someone handed me baked goods, I'd like it."

"That's so thoughtful, Angie. I really appreciate it," Nadine said.

"I'll provide loaves the first week and if they're a hit, I'll give you the recipes and you can make them yourself."

Surprising Angie, Nadine jumped out of her chair and wrapped her arms around her sister. "Thanks, sis." She placed a kiss on the side of her sister's face.

Angie brushed her off with a laugh. "Okay, calm down. Stay in your lane. Or at least get back in your chair."

# CHAPTER FORTY-FOUR

A brand-new sign had been put up, a wooden sign engraved with the words *Lavender Bay Inn*, hanging off a wrought-iron fixture attached to the porch post.

Nadine was spending her days going over the final details and making sure she was ready. The fire inspector was due later that afternoon for one final walk-through. She had illuminated exit signs, smoke alarms, carbon monoxide detectors, framed floor plans, and fire extinguishers placed throughout the house.

The official grand opening was in a week. Emma, who currently was taking her final exams, would be coming home and spending the summer with her. Her relationship with her father remained strained, but Nadine had encouraged her to go out and visit him while she was home.

Her thoughts of her checklist were interrupted by the doorbell. Through the glass pane in the door, she spied an older man, sixtyish. He stood sideways on her porch, casting a glance up and down the street.

Opening the door, she asked, "Can I help you?"

He was tall, and thin to the point of being gaunt. His white hair was cropped short, and his white beard and mustache were neatly trimmed. She thought the tweed jacket he wore was a little heavy for May, but to each his own.

"Yes, I'm wondering if you have any vacancies."

"Come in," she said, hardly able to contain her excitement. A real live body for one of the rooms. Possibly.

Herman waited, wagging his tail. When he spotted the dog, the man hesitated.

Nadine was quick to explain. "This is a dog-friendly inn."

"That's fine," the man said. "But I don't have a dog."

"That's also fine." She extended her hand. "Nadine Eberhardt. I'm the proprietor."

He shook it. His thin hand was cool, but his grip was firm. "Carlton Brady. May I call you Nadine?" His voice was sharp and crisp, reminding her of a bright, sunny, but cold winter's day.

"Yes. Do you go by Carl?"

He scowled. "Of course not. I go by my name, Carlton."

Her cheeks reddened, and she made a mental note to not assign random nicknames to strangers. "Carlton, would you like to see the rooms?" It was a Herculean effort to contain her excitement. This might be her first guest.

"Please. Although I'm sure they're much better than the motel I'm staying at out on the highway."

Nadine almost winced but didn't, knowing which motel he referred to. She took him upstairs and gave him a tour of the brand-new, spruced up bedrooms. They chatted as he followed her from room to room, stepping inside each one, looking out the windows, and inspecting the bathrooms.

"I'm looking for a long-term rental," he said.

"For how long?"

"About three months. I'm here to do research."

Curiosity got the better of her. "May I ask on what?"

"I'm writing a book about the shipwrecks of Lake Erie," he explained.

"Now that sounds interesting."

His features relaxed and he said, "I hope so."

After she showed him all the rooms, he said, "I'll take the large one with the balcony. I'll need the space for writing and research."

His decision made, they returned downstairs. Carlton sat at one of the small dining room tables and filled out the paperwork.

They settled the bill, with Nadine using her brand-new card reader to take a payment for three months, eyes almost popping out of her head over the large lump sum. She had suggested he might be interested in paying week to week or month to month, but he'd refused.

"I'll go check out of the motel and bring my things over."

"Hold on one moment, Carlton. I've got one more inspection to pass this afternoon before I officially open. I couldn't let you take the room until after that."

"Fine. You have my number on the form. Send me a text when the room is available."

As Carlton was exiting the house, Grace Gibson was walking up the steps, hanging on to the handrail with one hand and carrying a canvas shopping bag in the other. She said hello to Carlton as she passed him, and he nodded a greeting as he left.

"Grace, this is a pleasant surprise." Nadine was delighted to see her; she hadn't seen her in a while. "Come in."

As Nadine closed the door behind her, Grace asked of Carlton, "Is that your new beau?"

Nadine laughed. "Nope. He's my first guest."

"Congratulations." Grace looked around the place. "Is it a bad time?"

"Not at all."

"I haven't been in this house in almost ninety years," Grace said.

That affected Nadine. It was a long time. So much had happened and so much had changed.

Grace handed her the bag. "A little gift from me for your new inn."

Nadine peeked inside and let out a squeal. Inside the bag were two Napcoware lady head vases. Carefully, she lifted each one out. One had blond hair with paler blond highlights, bright red lips, and heavily lined eyes, and wore a pearl necklace and earrings. The second one was slightly different, with darker hair and lighter streaks, and wearing a blue dress adorned with a brooch.

"Are these really for me?" she asked.

"Yes, you said you'd admired them. I want you to have them for your home."

"Thank you, I love them!"

"Good, then I know they're in the right hands."

"Would you like a tour of the house?"

Grace eyed the staircase. "I don't think I could manage the stairs. At home I have a stair chair."

"Then how about a tour of the downstairs?"

"That would be nice."

Nadine took her around the main floor, and they ended up in the library, which was behind the parlor and looked out on the lake. Grace stood for a few minutes, admiring the view, commenting, "The view is the same as it was ninety years ago. Remarkable."

"Sit down and we'll have a cup of tea and catch up," Nadine suggested.

The elderly woman didn't stay long, leaving as soon as she finished her tea. She had no sooner gone than the fire inspector showed up.

The house did pass inspection, and Nadine texted Carlton to let him know he could come over anytime.

She did one more final walk-through, making sure every room had guest towels, hospital corners on the beds, the Keurig storage rack fully stocked, and bottled water.

In the top drawer of each dresser was a small first aid kit and a sewing kit. On the shelf in each bathroom were small individual bottles of shampoo, conditioner, and body lotion.

The welcome basket on each of the beds contained one jar of Gibson's grape jelly, maps and places of inter-est, and stamped postcards of the Lavender Bay area. As the guests arrived, she would add one of Angie's loaves. She was pleased, and she hoped her guests would be, too.

She was officially open for business.

# CHAPTER FORTY-FIVE

Aside from Carlton that first week, a couple celebrating their golden anniversary had booked the inn for two nights. Although they lived in Lavender Bay, they wanted to do something special.

Emma was home and a huge help. She assisted Nadine in cleaning the rooms when guests checked out. Nadine was so happy to have her there for the summer. Although she didn't see a lot of her, as her daughter's days were spent at the beach with her cousins. When the inn was full, Emma stayed either with Louise or over at Maureen's house.

Carlton was a busy man. When he wasn't off visiting maritime museums or diving with a charter to explore shipwrecks, he was holed up in his room, writing.

They'd agreed that Nadine would do a weekly clean of his room, focusing on the bathroom and changing the sheets on the bed. After the first week, she stood in the doorway, her mouth hanging open. The room had been overtaken. There were books everywhere, open on the floor, the little desk, along the dresser.

A laptop sat in the center of the desk. Sheets of paper and notebooks with all sorts of scribblings were piled high on every available surface, some teetering on the floor.

All in all, it looked like a disaster zone. She didn't know how he got any work done in that kind of environment.

Carlton was home by late evening, having stopped somewhere along the way to eat. The married couple had gone to the Annacotty Room for their dinner.

"Carlton, can I speak to you about something?"

"Of course," he said.

After seeing the state of his room, she had come up with an idea. "Would you like to use the library for your work? To get out of your room?"

He seemed surprised. "That would be helpful."

"Understand though, that if a guest wants to access the back porch, they'll be walking through it."

"Understood."

"All I ask is that you keep it tidy," she said. She felt funny asking this, but she told herself to man up; she was an innkeeper, and she had to keep the place neat.

So, it was settled. On the odd days that Carlton was there, when he wasn't diving or trawling through museum archives, he set himself up in the library. Sometimes, Herman joined him, falling asleep on the rug in the corner. Carlton didn't mind. And after a while, he started keeping a box of dog biscuits in the bottom drawer of the desk.

Days before the Parallel Parking Championship, Nadine had managed to book out the remainder of the rooms to some parking enthusiasts that had come up for the contest and a woman who'd come to visit her mother in a nursing home. The woman, though friendly, was rarely there, spending the day with her mother, who was failing.

Her first guest was a young man by the name of Hugo Monteforte. He was in his late twenties, worked at a recycling plant, and drove a late-model Honda Accord.

He was tall and lanky with strawberry blond hair that fell into his eyes, causing him always to be sweeping it away with his hand. He had a habit of shrugging until his neck disappeared into his shoulders and sticking his hands in his front pockets.

He arrived two days before the event and quickly made himself at home, hanging out in the communal front parlor when he wasn't out and about practicing his parking in town.

Nadine had a few minutes as she was waiting for the dryer to finish, and she sat down in the parlor. Back in the library, Carlton Brady sat at the desk, books spread out. He never asked for anything or bothered her. He rarely interacted with the other guests, preferring to keep to himself and work on his research.

Hugo made himself comfortable on one of the sofas. Herman stood in the doorway of the parlor, wagging his tail.

"Dude, come on in." Hugo waved the dog in and patted the sofa cushion.

Herman turned around and, looking over his shoulder, backed in. This resulted in Hugo cracking up. He clapped his hands together. "That never gets old."

Herman stood in front of him and whined. Hugo leaned forward and reached out with his long arms, ruffling the dog's hair and fooling with him. "Great dog, Nadine. He's got a great reverse technique, I bet he could learn to parallel park a car."

Nadine laughed. They were soon joined by one of the other couples. They were in their early thirties and they resembled one another in that they were both dark-haired and soft and fleshy. They sat next to each other on the other sofa. The wife, Sarah, pulled out her knitting from her bag and went to work on a baby sweater she was making for her newborn nephew. Her husband, Phil, wore jeans and a black T-shirt with some obscure band on it. When Nadine questioned it, he replied it was a grunge metal band. Nadine, unfamiliar with that kind of music, could only nod.

"Did we miss the dog backing into the room?" Sarah asked, knitting needles clicking away.

"Yeah, you just missed it," Hugo told them.

"Darn, I love it when he does that," Sarah said.

"What's the plan?" Phil asked.

"Well," Hugo answered, "I spent the morning scouting out possible locations for the contest, but it's really a crap shoot. Who knows where it's going to be."

That was one of the things Nadine had learned about the competition. It was a mystery locale, revealed only an hour before the contest began.

"However, I've been driving around the town, practicing my technique."

"Same." This from Phil.

"Have you tried Java Joe's?" Hugo asked. "The paninis are to die for."

"Not yet." Phil threw an amused look at his wife. "I can't get the missus out of Coffee Girl."

"Their desserts are out of this world," Sarah said enthusiastically, her knitting needles picking up speed.

Hugo stretched out his long legs in front of him and glanced back to the library, where Carlton had his head bent, scribbling furiously in a notebook.

"Hey, professor, why don't you join us," Hugo called.

Without lifting his head, Carlton raised his hand in a wave. "I'm good, thanks." And then as he'd said before, "Call me Carlton."

"I can't call him by his first name, my father would knock me into the middle of next week," Hugo said, leaning back against the cushions with his arms folded across his chest.

Nadine hoped he was joking. Out of curiosity, she asked, "How do they judge a winner? What if everyone parallel parks correctly?"

"Ah, a newbie, I love it," Phil said, rubbing his hands together.

Next to him, his wife rolled her eyes and said to Nadine, "You'll be sorry you asked."

Phil launched into formulas and when he mentioned geometry, Nadine had a flashback to tenth-grade math. All these complicated-sounding terms had her head spinning.

Hugo interrupted. "Long story short, it's how long you take to park the car in a twenty-foot space, and the distance between the tires and the curb."

"Thank you."

Sarah stopped knitting and elbowed Phil. "See? Just say that. No need to go into technical mathematical terms."

Phil protested, "But I'm a mathematician."

"Who likes to parallel park." Sarah giggled and returned her attention to her garment.

Phil shrugged with a smile.

She wrapped up her knitting and tucked it into her bag. "Come on, let's go for dinner. I'm hungry." She looked at Hugo. "You want to join us?"

"Sure." He stood and stretched and called out to Carlton, "Hey, professor, wanna join us for dinner?"

"No thank you, Hugo," Carlton said, finally looking up.

# CHAPTER FORTY-SIX

The night before the championship, the parallel parkers finally coaxed Carlton into joining them in the parlor.

Hugo cleared his throat. "So, Carlton," he said in a tone that suggested he might have been nervous about using the older man's first name. As if it went against everything he believed in.

"Yes, Hugo," Carlton said good-naturedly.

"I know you're some kind of professor, but what is it you do, exactly?"

"Actually, I'm an underwater archaeologist who sometimes guest lectures at various colleges and universities throughout the United States and Canada."

"Cool."

"Are you on sabbatical of some sort?" asked Phil.

"I am. I've taken a year off to write a book about Lake Erie's shipwrecks."

Hugo was clearly impressed. "Dude, that's awesome."

Carlton laughed, amused. "I think so, too."

"Does Lake Erie have a lot of shipwrecks?" Sarah asked.

"No one is exactly sure of the correct number because of poor record keeping hundreds of years ago. But the estimate is anywhere from five hundred to two thousand."

Phil let out a low whistle.

"I had no idea," Sarah said, eyes widening.

"Any treasures? Caches?" Hugo asked with a glint in his eye.

"Not as such," Carlton explained. "Not like those Spanish galleons off the southeast coast of the country."

Hugo leaned back, folding his arms behind his head, and stared at the ceiling. "Can you imagine? Goodbye recycling plant."

"Are you looking at specific wrecks, or all of them?" Hugo said.

"Some of them. As much as I would like to catalogue all of them, it's an impossible task."

"Have you done any underwater dives?" Phil asked.

"I have. I'm working my way from Cleveland to Buffalo, stopping along the way to research, write, visit maritime museums, and if possible, dive at local sites."

"That sounds like fun," Hugo said.

"It is and it isn't," Carlton explained. "There's a lot of research involved, and some days are spent in museums going through their archives looking at ship records and reading logbooks to try and piece together what happened and where."

"Can you tell us some shipwreck stories?" Sarah asked.

Unused to being the center of attention outside of lecture halls, Carlton didn't seem uncomfortable with it. He sat in the wing chair, leaned back, and crossed his legs.

"The oldest known shipwreck is the *Lake Serpent*. That went down in 1829 and was only discovered recently. It's important if only to show us what the ships looked like from that time period."

"What caused it to sink?" Phil asked.

Carlton shrugged. "No one knows. Possibly bad weather. It was a cargo ship carrying boulders."

Phil spoke up. "So, a lot of those wrecks are out there, just waiting to be found."

"Correct."

"And is it possible that there may be some shipwrecks you're unaware of?" Nadine asked.

"Possible."

"Why are these shipwrecks so hard to find?" Phil asked. "Lake Erie is the shallowest of the Great Lakes."

"The water is murky. When I started diving in the late seventies, you couldn't see past the end of your arm, the lake was so polluted," Carlton Brady explained to a rapt audience. Even Herman stared at him, his tongue hanging out of his mouth. "It is better now. The field of vision has expanded to roughly fifteen or twenty feet."

"Even that isn't a lot," Nadine said.

"No."

"What's the shipwreck that keeps you up at night?"

With a wistful expression, Carlton leaned back in his chair. "*The Marquette and Bessemer No 2.*"

"Why?"

"Because it's never been found and because of the mystery surrounding its disappearance." The professor paused for effect.

Hugo leaned forward, elbows resting on his knees. "Dude, don't keep us in suspense."

"It was a ferry carrying rail cars full of steel and coal. This was December 8, 1909. It left Ohio but never made its final destination of Port Stanley, Ontario. It disappeared without a trace. Although there were no eyewitnesses to the actual sinking, there are inconsistent, conflicting witness reports of the distress calls and when the ship was last seen. Afterward, a lifeboat was found containing the bodies of the crew. To this day, the ship has never been found."

The mood turned somber as they digested what Carlton had told them. But Hugo seemed contemplative as he said, "It's very interesting, that's for sure. I'm thinking of giving up parallel parking and going on quests for shipwrecks."

# CHAPTER FORTY-SEVEN

At breakfast the following morning, Hugo, Phil, and Sarah convinced Nadine to attend the championship, and they strong-armed Carlton into going, too, not taking no for an answer until he finally, good-naturedly, agreed to go.

An hour before it was set to begin, Hugo and Phil received texts telling them that the competition was taking place in front of the Fine Print over on Oak Street. It wasn't that far from the house, so Nadine clipped the lead onto Herman's collar and walked over. Carlton joined her. It was a beautiful sunny day. She had to admit that curiosity had got the best of her, and she wanted to see what all this hoopla was about. It was all Hugo and Phil could talk about.

They'd left half an hour before the event was due to start, Hugo in his Accord and Phil in his 1972 Chevy Nova. When Hugo had first seen Phil's vintage car, he let out a low whistle and declared, "Sweet."

As Nadine and Carlton walked down Pearl Street, he took in his surroundings. "This is such a charming street. It looks like not much has changed in the past hundred or so years."

"It seems like it."

There were telltale signs of progress, with cars and security alarms and electric garage door openers, but for the most part, Pearl Street had retained its charm. Big, leafy oak trees ran along the edge of the sidewalk, and all the houses on the street were well kept. Colorful flags and banners hung from porch posts.

"There's comfort in that, isn't there?" Carlton asked.

"I like to think so."

They walked all the way to Pine Street, hung a left, and crossed Main, at which point Pine became Oak Street. The two of them engaged in easy conversation the whole way.

Nadine was both surprised and pleased to see a large crowd gathered on the sidewalk in front of Lavender

Bay's only bookstore, the Fine Print. On the sidewalk in front of the store, volunteers manned two folding tables.

As Nadine and Carlton approached, there appeared to be an issue with something. There was a small crowd gathered around Frank Furniss, the organizer of the event. Nadine had never met him, but she knew him to see. Hugo and Phil were right in the thick of it.

As they sidled up to the edge of the crowd, Herman sat down next to Nadine, his tongue hanging out of his mouth.

Phil looked over his shoulder and with a wave, said, "Oh, hey."

Sarah wound her way back to them.

"Is there a problem?" Nadine asked.

The young woman nodded and pointed to a car parked directly in front of the bookstore. "They had an orange cone here, but whoever parked here threw it up on the curb and took the spot."

"What are they going to do?"

"They'll have to either find another spot or cancel or postpone the event."

To cancel would be a shame. Nadine knew how much Hugo and Phil were looking forward to it. But parking spots in town were a premium.

"Hopefully whoever the car belongs to will show up soon," Carlton said.

"Fingers crossed."

Out of the corner of her eye, Nadine spotted Edna Knickerbocker coming down the opposite side of the street, her arms laden with canvas bags. As the crowd around Frank continued to offer all sorts of suggestions and complaints, Edna crossed the street and walked over to the offending car. She unlocked the door.

The crowd silenced and parted and Frank Furniss, wearing a visor and holding a clipboard, said in a clipped tone, "Mrs. Knickerbocker, didn't you see the orange cone in the spot there?"

Edna loaded her bags into the back seat. "I sure did. But I moved it because I needed a place to park my car."

They all stared at her, speechless. Nadine covered her mouth with her hand to stifle a laugh.

Edna eventually got in, started her engine, and slowly pulled out and drove away. As she did, they all clapped, and she tooted her horn in response.

"Let's get this show on the road," Frank said. He blew the whistle that hung around his neck. "You've all got your numbers, so let's go. Who's number one?"

Number one was someone Nadine did not know. She didn't think they were from the area. She and Carlton hung back. Frank had a stopwatch and yelled "go," and the first car went into action. As soon as the driver completed his parallel park, Frank stopped the watch and noted the time down on his clipboard. As the driver was getting out, Frank whipped out a tape measure and measured the distance between the back tire and the curb, recording that number as well.

"They take this rather seriously," Carlton whispered.

"I can see that," Nadine answered. "They're not playing."

Hugo was number eleven, which he claimed was lucky as he was born on the eleventh day of the eleventh month. As he pulled up his car for his turn, he opened the passenger door and called out, "C'mon, Herman, let's go."

And before Nadine could do anything, Herman trotted off, his lead trailing behind him, and jumped into the passenger seat of Hugo's car. Someone standing nearby closed the passenger side door after him.

"Thanks, dude," Hugo said.

There was a protest over the dog being in the car, and as Nadine walked over to retrieve Herman, Frank Furniss flipped furiously through the pages on his clipboard. He held up his hand and announced, "There is no rule about passengers—canine or human—in the car during the competition."

That settled that. Herman, sitting in the front seat, looked out the window at them, and Hugo gave a thumbs-up.

They all watched as Hugo pulled forward, lining his car up to the one in front of it and, palming the steering wheel with one hand, looked over his shoulder and reversed into the spot.

All the while, Herman looked straight ahead, never moving.

When Hugo jumped out of the car, all smiles, he held the door for Herman to get out, and the dog trotted over to Nadine, who said to him, "Well, that's a first, Herman, your first parallel parking contest."

Frank Furniss stood, snapping his tape measure closed. "Number eleven, you are the score to beat!"

Hugo threw his arms up in the air like a referee indicating a touchdown and shouted, "Yes!"

He joined Nadine, Carlton, and Herman, all smiles. "You're a lucky charm, dude," he said to the dog.

Even though Phil was number thirty-seven, they decided to wait and cheer him on, too. When Phil's time came, he called over to Carlton, "Hey, professor, you want to be my second?"

"Why do I feel I'm being equated with Herman?" Carlton asked. Despite this, he headed over and got into the passenger side of Phil's Nova.

They stepped close to the curb and watched as Phil revved his engine and then parallel parked his car. As he backed in, he tapped the curb slightly, and Nadine held her breath.

Frank shouted, "Disqualified!"

Phil turned the car off and jumped out, arms flailing. "What are you talking about? How am I disqualified?"

"You hit the curb."

"No way."

Phil went around the back of his car and saw what they all saw: his tire parked right up against the curb. He let out a groan.

Sarah was at his side. "It's all right, hon. We'll come back next year and win it."

Despite staying out late to celebrate Hugo's win as the champion parallel parker of Lavender Bay, all three of them were up early the following day, planning to leave right after breakfast.

"We'll see you next year, Nadine!" Hugo said as he heaved his backpack over his shoulder and rubbed the top of Herman's head. He'd already belted his large trophy into the passenger seat.

"I'll look forward to it!"

He poked his head around the corner of the parlor and called back to Carlton. "Goodbye, professor! Can't wait to read your book when it comes out. Thanks for your email address."

"All the best, Hugo," Carlton called back.

Phil shook Nadine's hand and thanked her for everything. And Sarah hugged her goodbye.

For the next few hours, Nadine cleaned the now-vacant rooms. There were beds to be made and rooms to be cleaned and restocked. The washing machine and dryer were going all afternoon. Check-in was at four o'clock and by the time that rolled around, the rooms were ready for the next round of guests.

# Chapter Forty-Eight

Edna Knickerbocker was on her way over. She'd called after dinner and said she had something to give to Nadine and would be over right after the six o'clock news. Nadine had been tempted to ask what it was, in case it wasn't something she needed and could kindly decline, but the older woman was acting mysteriously, and ended the call before Nadine could ask anything.

Edna pulled up by seven, and Nadine went out to meet her.

"Do you think you could give me a hand with this box?" Edna asked, standing next to the trunk of her car. "I've got a tricky back." To add emphasis, she placed her hand on the small of her back.

Herman followed Nadine around the side of the car to the open trunk. Bending her knees to mind her own back, Nadine carefully lifted the cardboard box from the trunk and hefted it out, carrying it quickly to the porch as it was heavy.

She invited Edna in, wanting to show her all the renovations. She set the box down in the front hall. The house was quiet.

The Silvermans and the Jensens were out in their hot air balloons. They were avid enthusiasts and showed up every year for the festival. They'd tried to talk Nadine into accompanying them. They were going offshore and returning later, landing in some farmer's field. Nadine begged off, confessing she was terrified of heights. But they were able to convince Carlton to join them, and Nadine was glad he was getting out and experiencing some of the wonderful things Lavender Bay had to offer.

Edna walked slowly around the front hall, the parlor, the dining room, the library, and the kitchen. Nadine was proud of the renovations that had been done. The hardwood floors gleamed with refinishing, and there was expensive wallpaper from a stockist in London covering the walls in the parlor and dining room. New furniture had been purchased to offer her guests comfort. The library shelves were filled with books, and there was a vintage partners desk in great shape that had been sourced by Aunt Gail. As ever, the large back window offered the view of Lake Erie. The kitchen had undergone a complete overhaul to get it up to code, and it was now state of the art.

Edna stood in the middle of the parlor, whose double-wide entrance looked out onto the front hall, the dining room on the other side, and the grand staircase. She threw her hands to her cheeks and whispered, "Nadine, you've done some wonderful things here."

This pleased her, because Edna had been in and out of this house growing up and would remember how it used to be. The goal had always been to preserve the house's wonderful features while bringing it into the twenty-first century.

"How I wish Aunt Lenore could see this," Edna said, her gaze wandering around the rooms. "She would have loved what you did to the place."

"I'm glad you think so," Nadine said.

"You know, when my grandparents died, Aunt Lenore and my mother received a significant inheritance, and

Aunt Lenore used hers to upgrade the house. That's when all the bedrooms had their own bathrooms added." Edna smacked her forehead, and Nadine's eyes widened in alarm.

"The box!" Edna said. "I forgot about the box." She took off for the front hall. The woman had to be in her mid-eighties, but she was pretty spry. She bent over and opened the box and began to pull things out.

"I thought you might like some of these old things from the house." With her hands full, she straightened up and said, "And now that I've seen what you've done with the place, I know I've made the right decision to hand this stuff over to you."

Edna handed Lenore a framed black-and-white photograph and with a gnarled finger, pointed at the people in the image, gathered on the front porch steps. "On the top step is Aunt Lenore and Johnny. He must have been about five there. Sitting next to them is Hilda. She'd been with my grandparents and then came to Lenore after her husband died. On the step beneath them is Harriet and Alistair Young. They were boarders here, met, fell in love, and got married. Their family still live here in Lavender Bay."

"How romantic!" Nadine studied the photo, loving to see the people of the past, especially Lenore Hadley. She studied each of their faces.

"That was before the war, because Alistair came home missing a leg," Edna said matter-of-factly.

"How awful!" Nadine studied Alistair, who was so young-looking in the photo.

"He did all right. He and Harriet went on to have a pile of children," Edna said with a wink. She picked up a stack of loose photos. "These are more photos of the Hadleys and their boarders and of the house itself. Maybe you'd like to display them."

"I most certainly would," Nadine said, thinking she'd buy picture frames and hang the photos around various parts of the house. There was a photo of a large gathering around the dining room table. On the white border beneath the image, *Christmas 1950* had been written in black ink. This would be perfect for the dining room.

"And look what Johnny saved." Edna showed her a large wooden plaque, stained and glossy and engraved in black script. *Mrs. Hadley's Boarding House.*

"This is wonderful!" Nadine imagined it hanging in a place of honor in the front hall. She looked at the older woman, her heart full of gratitude for her generosity. "I can't thank you enough, Edna. These items are wonderful."

"I'm relieved you think so," Edna replied. "A lot of people don't care for the old stuff, and they end up throwing it in the garbage can."

Nadine shook her head. "No, Edna, rest assured, I will home all of these things."

"Wonderful. Now, there are more photos you can go through on your own time, as well as all the ledgers my aunt used for her bookkeeping."

Nadine looked forward to going through those things in the evenings when things settled down.

Edna left the box on the floor.

"Would you like a glass of homemade iced tea or lemonade?" Nadine asked. She made sure to keep plenty on hand for her guests.

"I wouldn't mind a glass of iced tea," Edna said. "But no lemonade for me. Love the stuff but it makes me belch."

"All right."

Nadine invited Edna out onto the back porch. Nadine carried two glasses of iced tea with her, and Edna closed the door behind them, but not before Herman backed out to join them.

"That's one strange dog you got there," Edna said, shaking her head.

"I know, but he is very loveable."

"He'd have to be with that kind of behavior."

They made themselves comfortable in the new wicker furniture Nadine had recently purchased. The cushions were thick and plump. She knew the professor liked to sit out from time to time when he wasn't using the library.

They looked at the lake and marveled at the colorful hot air balloons dotting the golden-hued sky. In the distance she spotted the Silvermans' balloon in repeating geometric patterns of turquoise, yellow, and orange. But they were too far away for her to make out their faces. She'd be curious to see what Carlton thought of it, considering this was the opposite of what he was used to, spending most of his time underwater, looking for shipwrecks, instead of above it.

They spoke of general things, of news around the bay and upcoming events. Edna appeared to know just about everything going on around town. Soon the conversation turned back to the Hadleys.

"So Johnny Hadley never had any interest in living in Lavender Bay?" Nadine asked.

"Initially, we all thought he'd return, including Aunt Lenore. But you know how it is. Some people move away with the intention of returning someday, but then they get settled in their new community and they start building a life. I think that was true of Johnny. He loved his career, and he loved Chicago. The fact that his father was originally from there might have played into it as well. But he never returned and at the end of her life, Aunt Lenore went to Chicago to live with him."

"She must have been heartbroken to leave the house and Lavender Bay."

"She was and she wasn't. Having been widowed so young, Johnny was her life. It was like her heart was walking around outside her body."

Nadine could certainly relate to that. It was how she felt about Emma.

"Although she cried when she left, I know she was happy living with Johnny. They were always very close."

"I'm surprised you were made the executor of Johnny Hadley's will and not Edith."

It was dangerous territory that Nadine was stepping into, and she knew it. Edith Bermingham, or Mrs. B as she was known in Lavender Bay, was Edna's only sibling. They hadn't spoken a word to each other in years. *Decades.* Their estrangement was as accepted as the fact that the winters could be bleak on the beaches of Lavender Bay. Nadine was nosing around, trying to see if there had been any rapprochement on their parts. At their age, it might be time to bury the hatchet.

Edna let out a bark of laughter. "I'm not surprised at all! Edith is too much like my mother." She beamed and said proudly, "I always took after Dad."

So, there had been no reconciliation. How sad. Old wounds festered for a long time, Nadine supposed. She changed the subject and inquired after Edna's health, which was the older woman's favorite subject, and Edna was off like a flash, diving into a litany of medical complaints. Nadine got comfortable and smiled, continuing to watch the vibrant colored balloons floating across the sky.

As Edna continued with her list of complaints and Nadine asked appropriate questions, she thought the decision to move back to Lavender Bay, though impulsive, had proved to be the correct one.

Because she was happy, and at peace.

***

To stay up to date with news and to receive exclusive bonus material, sign up for my newsletter at www.michelebrouder.com.

# ACKNOWLEDGEMENTS

When researching for a book, it's easy to go down a rabbit hole. With this book, I loved going in that direction because I learned so much! There are many people who provided assistance.

Raymond H. Jordan from the Cattaraugus County Health Department who answered all my questions graciously and who provided me with a lot of information about opening an inn. I'm grateful.

Joseph Rennie who knows all things about Buffalo maritime history. He, too, was gracious with his time and emails. I learned about shipwrecks I'd never heard of before.

Jack Messmer of the Buffalo Harbor Museum. This was a fascinating phone conversation about Lake Erie, why some shipwrecks remain lost, and of course, the shipwrecks themselves.

I'm indebted to all. Any mistakes or misrepresentations are solely mine.

# ALSO BY MICHELE BROUDER

**The Lavender Bay Chronicles**

*The Inn at Lavender Bay*

*Lost and Found in Lavender Bay*

*Second Chances in Lavender Bay*

*New Beginnings in Lavender Bay (coming in January 2025)*

**Hideaway Bay**

*Coming Home to Hideaway Bay*

*Meet Me at Sunrise*

*Moonlight and Promises*

*When We Were Young*

*One Last Thing Before I Go*

*The Chocolatier of Hideaway Bay*

*Now and Forever*

**Escape to Ireland**

*A Match Made in Ireland*
*Her Fake Irish Husband*
*Her Irish Inheritance*
*A Match for the Matchmaker*
*Home, Sweet Irish Home*
*An Irish Christmas*
**The Happy Holidays**
*A Whyte Christmas*
*This Christmas*
*A Wish for Christmas*
*One Kiss for Christmas*
*A Wedding for Christmas*
**Audiobooks**
*Coming Home to Hideaway Bay*
***All books available in ebook, paperback, and large print paperback. Audiobooks coming soon.***